THE
LIMITLESS
SKY

THE
LIMITLESS
SKY

Christina Kilbourne

DUNDURN
PRESS

Publisher: Scott Fraser | Acquiring editor: Kathryn Lane | Editor: Robyn So
Cover designer: Laura Boyle
Cover image: Capitol building: istock.com/smartboy10; landscape: shutterstock.com/
  Tithi Luadthong

Library and Archives Canada Cataloguing in Publication

Title: The limitless sky / Christina Kilbourne.
Names: Kilbourne, Christina, 1967- author.
Identifiers: Canadiana (print) 20210368896 | Canadiana (ebook) 2021036890X |
  ISBN 9781459748873 (softcover) | ISBN 9781459748880 (PDF) | ISBN
  9781459748897 (EPUB)
Classification: LCC PS8571.I476 L56 2022 | DDC C813/.6—dc23

We acknowledge the support of the Canada Council for the Arts and the Ontario Arts Council for our publishing program. We also acknowledge the financial support of the Government of Ontario, through the Ontario Book Publishing Tax Credit and Ontario Creates, and the Government of Canada.

Dundurn Press
1382 Queen Street East
Toronto, Ontario, Canada M4L 1C9
dundurn.com, @dundurnpress 𝕏 f ⊚

For Callie, Bella, and Leo, for believing in ArHK from the start.

ROOK

From down the street, I can see the Fixers set up outside our door, repairing the sky.

"It's about time," I complain.

"Are they finally replacing the piece that hit Sparrow?" Ruby asks.

I nod and we stop at her corner to watch the figures working in the distance. One of them is at the top of the scaffolding with a trowel. Two others are on the ground bent over buckets, mixing plasterflex and paint.

"When was that? Two weeks ago and they still haven't fixed it?" I hear the outrage in Ruby's voice.

"The Fixers didn't even contact us to apologize for almost killing a child. You should have seen the bruise on her back."

"It's inexcusable, Rook! They shouldn't have let it get to that point of disrepair. What if other pieces started falling off? Your mam should submit a formal complaint. That's the only way to get things done."

Her face is flushed with indignation, and I can tell by the way she's twirling the strap of her personal messenger that she's ready for a fight. She loves rules and to make sure people follow them. She'll be a perfect Governor one day.

I shrug but don't commit either way. Even though Ruby has been my best friend since before I can remember, I'm more of a live-and-let-live kind of girl. Sure, they should have noticed the crack in the sky before it became dangerous. But I know the Fixers are busy. They have a lot of repairs to keep up with and complaining just makes everyone miserable. Ruby says my complacency drives her mad, but I call it patience.

Before she heads home she straightens her vest and pats down her hair. Hers is a very proper family — they have to be as Governors — and perfectionists to boot.

"Message me later?"

"Of course," I say. "With so much excitement in the Keeper household, I'll be bursting to tell someone."

Ruby ignores my sarcasm and bounces off down her street. Even though it can be hard to take sometimes,

I admire her energy. It was no accident that she was a three-time recipient of the ArHK Apprentice School Spirit Award.

When I get to our pod, I pause. The Fixers have spread a drop cloth in front of our door.

"Uh, is it okay if I go inside?" I ask, and point at the 78 on the arch above our pod.

"Sure thing," one of the Fixers says. "The cloth's still clean. You won't track any mess inside."

Although I know Mam and Sparrow must be home, the pod is quiet when I step inside; that is, until I close the door and the latch clicks into place. Then Sparrow rushes from the kitchen and just about knocks me off my feet.

"Rook! Rook! Can you take me outside to watch the Fixers?"

She's jumping up and down and clapping her hands, as if she needs to release some of the excitement stored in her wiry little body.

"Why don't you watch out the window?"

"I tried that but I can't see past that scaffold stuff."

"I just got home."

Sparrow stops jumping and crosses her arms. She lowers her head and scowls at me from behind a veil of dark hair.

Beyond the noise of the Fixers, I can hear Mam chopping vegetables. The tap is running, and the radio is playing a new release by the Entertainers.

"Mam! Sparrow wants to go outside and watch the Fixers," I call out.

"I know, but I'm in the middle of making dinner, and I don't want her to go out alone. She'll get in the way," Mam defends herself from the kitchen. I have to admit that Mam has a point. Sparrow is very curious.

"What about Da? Can't he take her?"

"He's still at the Archives. Finishing a report for Governor Hawk."

Sparrow crinkles her nose at the mention of Governor Hawk, and I shiver in response. Neither of us are fans. He has a way of lurking around corners and appearing out of thin air. I've always imagined he's hollow inside, like if he ever took off his robes you'd find out he's just a head hanging on a long hook. One time, when Ruby and I were Sparrow's age, we set up a pretend school outside with our dolls. He stood across the street and watched for so long we ended up going back inside. When I complained to Da and Mam, they said he didn't have a family of his own and was just lonely, that he enjoyed watching us play. But it felt like he was waiting to catch us breaking a rule so he could tell Ruby's parents that I was a bad influence. He's never liked me for some reason, or my family come to think of it. It's nothing I can put my finger on, but it's like there's some weird history there.

"Please, please, *please* will you take me out? Just for ten minutes?" Sparrow pleads. "I'll do whatever you say."

I smile down at Sparrow. I knew the minute I walked inside that I'd take her out to see the Fixers at work. After all, it's not every day they repair the part of the sky that almost killed you.

"Okay, come on. I'll stand out there with you for a few minutes if you promise not to touch anything and not to ask the Fixers any questions."

Sparrow squirms with excitement and slips on her walking shoes. I take her hand and we ease ourselves through the front door. Then we join the growing crowd on the opposite side of the street to watch the Fixers repair the sky.

Sparrow manages to stay in one spot, but she doesn't stop talking.

"Mam told me there was a time when people lived in a limitless world. It was before she was born though. It was before her grandmam was born. Even before her grandmam's *grandmam* was born. The sky went on forever, she says, and it was blue, just like our sky, but it didn't stop. Mam says back then you could throw a ball as high as you wanted and it didn't bounce back."

I know exactly what Mam has been telling Sparrow. She told me the same Creationist stories at bedtime when I was little. I used to believe Mam's stories, but now I know they are exactly that — stories, like the fairy tales our ancestors brought with them to ArHK.

"Mam says the outer edges went on forever too. I don't know how that could be, though. Nothing goes on forever," Sparrow muses as she watches the Fixers smearing blue plasterflex over the hole in the sky, hiding the dull grey subsurface.

"What about time?" I suggest. "Time goes on forever."

Sparrow thinks for a moment, then says brightly, "I guess you're right!"

"Did Da ever tell you how water used to fall from the sky, back when it used to be limitless? The Outsiders called it rain. And sometimes frozen water fell that they called snow," I say.

"Would it hurt when the rain fell from the sky? The way it hurt when the sky fell on me? Did the Fixers have to come and repair the sky after the rain fell?" Sparrow asks.

"I don't know. You'll have to ask Da when he gets home."

"We sure are lucky to live in ArHK, aren't we, Rook? We're lucky to be descendants of the Chosen Ones."

Sparrow smiles up at me, and I squeeze her hand. "We're very lucky," I say, even though I'm not as convinced as I used to be.

When I was little, like Sparrow, I thought everything was an adventure. I loved going to Central Park to play on the grass and throw stones in the ponds. I loved going on the Thrill Rides and running along the paths through the trees. Mostly these days, though, I feel restless. I want to see something new or go somewhere new or discover one new thing. But there's never anything new in ArHK. I'm ashamed to feel this way when I know I should be grateful, but Mam and Da tell me not to worry. They say it's a normal phase for someone my age and that they both went through the same thing.

"Da! Look! They're fixing the sky finally," Sparrow calls out when she sees him round the corner and head toward us.

I cringe when she says *finally*; the Fixers might think we're ungrateful.

"Well, look at that!" Da says when he joins us on the far side of the street. "They *are* fixing the sky."

He leans down to give Sparrow a kiss. He doesn't lean forward to give me a kiss, but I'm sure he would if I let him. Instead, I step back and he takes the hint. He turns to watch the Fixers.

"Da? In the Outside, after the rain fell, did the Fixers have to repair the sky?" Sparrow asks.

"I don't think so. I think back then the sky repaired itself." Da gives me a questioning look and I shrug, as if to say, *Who knows what this kid will say next?*

"Maybe Rook can do some research at the Archives and report back to us," he suggests.

"Sure thing," I say with as much enthusiasm as I can muster. "I'll get right on that."

I love my da, but I don't share his enthusiasm for the Archives. He says I'm the luckiest girl in all of ArHK because one day I will be the Head Keeper, and being Keeper of the Archives means I have a new world to discover every day for the rest of my life. He's delusional, if you ask me. I mean, I've spent my whole childhood exploring the Archives and there's nothing interesting. NOTHING. That's why people rarely visit the Archives unless it's for a school project or a Governor Report. The Archives are filled with details about life in ArHK: birthdates, marriage records, death notices, notable illnesses and injuries, engineer repairs, sports scores, Governor Reports. I couldn't read through a hundredth of the files if I lived a thousand lifetimes. The thought of spending my whole life recording details of life in ArHK and reading about times in ArHK from years gone by sounds like a complete drag to me. Sometimes, I imagine what it would be like to be an apprentice Grower instead, or a Teacher, or a Healer, or an Entertainer, or even a Recycler.

"Da?" I say.

"Yes, Rook?" he says absently, while he grips Sparrow's narrow shoulders to keep her from moving any closer to the Fixers.

"Can we go to the Growing Sector soon?"

He pauses. "Why do you want to go to the Growing Sector?"

"I just like it there. That's all."

Da looks over the top of his glasses.

"You're not a Grower, Rook. You're a Keeper."

"I know," I say reluctantly. "But it's still nice to visit. I hear a batch of feijoas is almost ripe. You know how Sparrow loves feijoas."

My favourite place in all of ArHK is the Growing Sector. I remember visiting with Grandmam Ivy when I was a little girl. I loved it because it smelled sweet and moist and was overflowing with yellow light and green plants, all at different stages of growth. If you ask me, the Growing Sector is the only place in ArHK where something new happens, except for maybe the Health Sector because that's where the babies are born. Plus, the families in the Growing Sector get the first pick of every crop, whereas we have to wait a week or more for our shares to arrive.

Da has turned his attention back to the Fixers. To him, the conversation is over. But to me, it's only just begun. I already know I will talk to Mam tonight after dinner, once Sparrow is in bed. Mam is more like me than Da is. She likes going to the Growing Sector and exploring different parts of ArHK. If I approach her just right, I know I can convince her to take me and Sparrow down for a visit soon, even if Da doesn't want to come.

Before long the Fixers climb down from the scaffolding. They pack up their trowels and buckets and fold up the drop cloths. Then they erect caution barriers so that people can walk around safely. They've left a small entryway into our pod.

One of the Fixers looks at Da. "We'll be back tomorrow to remove our equipment. Hope it's not too much of an inconvenience?"

"Not at all," Da says, still holding onto Sparrow's squirming shoulders.

But Sparrow's attention is no longer on the Fixers. She's watching the next-door neighbour and his two children return home for the evening. Like Sparrow, the kids are hyped up because the Fixers are almost directly in front of their own pod. I can hear them chattering at their father, asking questions about the scaffolding and the barriers. They point up at the sky and comment on the darker blue patch of plasterflex that hasn't had a chance to dry.

Da ushers Sparrow into our pod and holds the door open for me, but I shake my head.

"I'll be right in," I say.

Then I look around our neighbourhood. Most people have returned home for dinner, so the street is almost empty. Back toward the Avenue, one of the widest streets in ArHK that ends in the centre of the Knowledge Level and which ramps down in an enormous spiral to the other three levels of ArHK, a few people scurry home. Only a Clothier is still working, delivering a stack of folded garments to Pod 62. But for the most part, the evening has dropped like a hush over ArHK.

All the pods lining the street are the same, with two arched windows and bold black numbers carved above the doors. Other than the pod numbers, the only difference is the colour of the doors. Ours is blue like the sky. Our neighbour's is yellow like they said the sun was on the Outside.

I remember the first time I went into a pod of a schoolmate. It was on a different level of ArHK, and I was surprised to see that in their pod, the living area and kitchen were a single room at the back and the bedrooms were at the front, by the entrance. They also had a deep square bathtub, whereas we only have a shower. Later, I asked Mam why they had a bathtub.

"We have the public baths just down the street!" she said brightly.

"Don't they have public baths in the Sorting Sector?"

"Yes, but sorting is dirty work. They need their own bathtubs."

That was the first time I realized there were differences in ArHK, that what you did, the purpose and role you were assigned, impacted all aspects of your life.

GAGE

age rolls over in his sleep, then is suddenly wide awake. His eyelids fly open without him even willing them to and his dream falls away, leaving only fragments of images.

He rubs his eyes and peers out through the door flap, where he sees the sky lightening in the east. The edges of the sky, just above the horizon, are pink and orange but fade to ever-changing shades of blue where the sky domes. Rays of the sun reflect yellow on the undersides of the frothy clouds. Gage loves this time of day, when his family is still asleep and the warmth of his quilt lays heavy over his shoulders, the smell of last night's meal has faded, and the sting of crisp air seeps in from outside and chills his face.

Beyond the cluster of yurts that forms the heart of the scouts' base camp, Gage hears the goats bleating in their pens, their bells jangling in anticipation of breakfast.

During birthing season, Gage makes a point of waking before dawn so he can be the first one to see the newborn goats, still shaky on their legs but quick to find confidence and bounce. He likes the way the nanny goats hover over their young, their ears hanging down at the sides of their faces like the braids the schoolgirls wear during the windy season. He likes the half smiles that greet him when he pitches hay into the nursery pen.

But birthing season is still a few weeks away, and Gage has no plans to sneak off to the goat pens today. He rolls over quietly, prolonging his moment of privacy, even though he knows he's not the only one awake in the yurt. Scruff is always awake first; it's almost as if she never really sleeps. Gage can hear her tail thumping gently against the ground, waiting for him to drop his hand down and scratch her belly.

"Mornin', Scruff," Gage whispers over the edge of his cot as he buries his hand in the dog's warm fur.

Scruff whines in response and thumps her tail a little faster.

Gage hears his parents move in their cot on the other side of the wood stove and his younger sister, Brindle, shift beside him in hers. It won't be but five minutes, and they'll all be up and about, taking over the quiet of the morning, he thinks.

Gage reaches to the bottom of his cot and finds his woollen socks. He pulls them over his feet. Then he drags a sweater out from under his head and pulls that on as well. One deep breath and he throws back the covers.

"I'll start the fire," he announces and looks over at Brindle, smiling at him from behind a curtain of tangled brown hair. Her fingers hold her quilt tight around her neck, trapping in the warmth.

"Thanks, Gage," his father murmurs.

Gage sees his father's breath on the air, the stillness of his mother's body under the mound of quilts.

Gage collects a handful of kindling from the woodbox and places it on the dying embers of the fire. He adds a few scraps of bark and then leans over to blow gently into the stove. The fire catches, and he feeds larger and larger sticks into the opening until there's enough flame to warm his hands.

"Is everyone ready for the big day?" his father asks.

"I am!" Brindle calls out from her cot.

"Do you think the scouts'll leave today?" Gage asks.

"If not today, then tomorrow. At least the early scouts will be sent out."

"Are you gonna be a scout again, Daddy?" Brindle asks.

The yurt is suddenly filled with silence. Even from

under the quilts, Gage sees his mother's back stiffen. "We'll see," his father says. "If they need me to be a scout, then perhaps."

"Axle, no!" Their mother rolls over and protests.

"But if they ask, I can't say no."

"Yes, you can. But you won't. You can't help yourself." Their mother scowls, as if their excitement is a personal affront.

Their father slips his feet out from under his quilt and stands up. When he stretches, his hands almost reach the top of the yurt. He scratches at his beard and ties his hair back into a ponytail.

"You know you like it when I get to scout. It makes you proud," he teases lightly.

"It makes me worried, that's what it makes me."

"She's right, Daddy. She worries when you scout. She worries you'll get hurt in a cave-in. Or there'll be Lurkers," Brindle pipes up.

"Lurkers! There haven't been Lurkers for a hundred years."

"That doesn't mean they don't still exist, somewhere," their mother points out.

"What if you did see a Lurker, Daddy? What would you do then?"

"I'd put him in a headlock and make him cry for mercy," their father says, then reaches down to tickle Brindle until she squeals with laughter. Scruff barks with excitement and dances at Gage's feet.

"Someone put Scruff out before she has an accident," their mother says. "I don't want it smelling like dog pee in here."

Gage opens the flap of the yurt and Scruff rushes outside, then stops abruptly.

"Not on the side of the yurt!" their mother shouts. "Gage! Take her away from the yurt!"

But it's too late. They can hear the sound of Scruff peeing against the canvas wall.

"Somebody needs to teach that dog some manners," their mother grumbles. "I have no idea why we even let that mangy stray sleep inside with us."

"Because she's part of the family!" Brindle says defensively.

When Scruff returns, all wagging tail and squirming body, Brindle pulls the dog in for a tight hug.

"Don't worry about Mom," she whispers into the dog's ear. "She's always grouchy before Dad leaves to scout."

Scruff wiggles her way onto Brindle's cot and licks the girl's face before the two settle into blissful stillness.

Their mother shakes her head and mutters to herself, "I just washed that bedding."

Then she sits up with a sigh and pulls on her socks and gloves. She pulls a woollen hat over her head and wipes her hair behind her ears so that it hangs down like cords of hemp rope. Finally, she stands up and moves over to the stove.

"Who's hungry?" she asks as she fills the pot with cornmeal, even though she doesn't expect an answer.

"Do you really think it's Washington?" Gage asks his father.

"The map readers said they're positive. They checked the distances and angles from the river, and they figure it can't be any place else."

"So we might finally find a clue about the Ship of Knowledge," Gage says dreamily. "We'll be legends."

The yurt falls quiet while they think about what it will mean if they really do discover Washington. Their father has spent most of his life trying to reach Washington, as did his father's people before that, back when the Scholars first organized scouting parties, and families left their homeland in the Middle to search for the ancient cities. In the thoughtful silence, they can hear the other scouting families getting up, making breakfast, washing, and dressing. They can hear snippets of conversation from the nearby yurts and, beyond, a general buzz of voices, like a swarm of bees.

"It could be weeks before we know for sure. You know these things take time to explore proper. And even if it's not Washington, there'll no doubt be something of value to learn," their mother says, shattering the moment of quiet optimism.

"Dontcha just love being an explorer, Mommy? Aren't you glad we get to be on the frontier line insteada being back in the Middle?" Brindle asks.

"Yeah, Journey. Dontcha just love being on the frontier line?" their father teases. "Insteada being back in the fields stacking hay and hoeing weeds?"

"I dunno," their mother says nostalgically. "I sorta miss spending my days in the fields."

Gage laughs. "Then you never shoulda fallen in love with Dad and agreed to sign on as the camp's headmaster."

Their mother snorts. "Like I had a choice?"

She ladles water into the teakettle from a bucket on the ground then puts it on the stove beside the pot of porridge. "It's not like anyone asked me, exactly, if I wanted to join a scouting camp. I liked living in the Middle. We were happy there."

Their father clears his throat before speaking. "Aww, Journey, you know I couldn't take living in the Middle another year. I tried. But Scouting's in my blood and it's important work. If everyone stayed in the Middle, how'd we expand our knowledge?"

He busies himself at the washing-up basin, splashing water over his face, then scrubbing his teeth. Their mother scowls and stirs the porridge. She drops the metal pot lid with a clang, then sets up the foldaway table next to Gage's cot.

"No matter what you say, living in the Middle was easier. We didn't have to pack up and move camp every couple months. We didn't have to sleep on cots and use camp tables."

Their mother moves briskly. She takes a heavy knife and slices shavings off a thick block of goat butter, then scoops four helpings of porridge into four wooden bowls. Wanting to be useful, Gage pulls Brindle's cot close to the other side of the table. Neither Brindle nor Scruff move, and both eye him warily from their cozy nest.

"It was safer too," their mother says with a bit less energy because she knows nobody really wants to hear more on the matter.

Their mother pours goat milk over the mounds of porridge and tops them with the butter shavings. Then she hands a bowl to Gage, who takes it to the table and sits on his cot to eat. Brindle finally climbs out of her cot, dislodging Scruff to the floor, and takes a bowl of porridge from her mother as well. Soon all four of them are sitting at the foldaway table, eating their hot porridge and waiting for the kettle to boil.

When Gage is finished, he sets his bowl on the ground for Scruff to lick clean and, instead of protesting, his mother sighs quietly. She stirs her porridge and takes a slow, half-hearted mouthful.

"I'll do the dishes," Gage offers, cheerfully. He moves to the stove and fills the kitchen basin with a splash of steaming water from the kettle.

His mother looks up and smiles, but it's a weak smile, like a cup of tea after the third brew with the same leaves. When he reaches over to collect the dirty bowls and utensils from the table, he puts his hand on her shoulder and she reaches back to squeeze it. The mood in the yurt warms then, and their movements slip back to calm routine. Their father relaxes into the cot, and Scruff lays down on the ground at Brindle's feet.

The morning horn blares, three long blasts from the centre of camp. It's Chief Coil's way of letting everyone know the day has officially begun and it's time to get a move on.

ROOK

"**A**re you ready to start?" Da asks.

I put as much enthusiasm as I can into a nod and a smile. "Should I research the Outside sky, like you promised Sparrow?"

"Not today. I have an assignment for you."

I try not to let my shoulders slump. If there's one thing I hate more than exploratory days in the Archives, it's assignment days. On exploratory days I can put my face in front of a file and dream. On assignment days I have to read. And absorb. And repeat what I've learned. And to make matters worse, Da and Mam will want to talk about my assignment over dinner, and Sparrow will ask a million questions about what I learned and how I found the information. That will lead to her talking about where she wants to apprentice when she's old enough, which changes about every three days. Last week she wanted to be a Teacher at the Instructional School, and the week before that she was convinced she had to apprentice with the Entertainers so she could write ArHK Novels.

As usual, I've lost track of the conversation, but Da is still talking. "First, tell me, what year is it in Outside Time?"

I protest. "Who cares? I mean, we haven't been in contact with the Outside for, what, like, over two hundred OT years?"

"That's right. At least that's what's on the official record. But, of course, we can't know for sure." Da pauses thoughtfully before continuing. "That's exactly why we follow protocol. It's our responsibility to keep track of the past, and to do that properly you need to be fluent in Outside Time as well as ArHK Time."

I turn away and roll my eyes. I've been hearing about the importance of being Keepers since I was Sparrow's age. My whole life has revolved around Da's responsibility to run the Archives and monitor the Great Hall of Human Knowledge.

"Have you finished your calculation yet?" Da asks. "You only need to go to two decimal points and round up."

"I know, one ArHK year equals 2.28 Outside Time years. Then I have to factor in the year of arrival," I mutter and envision the numbers in my head.

"Twenty-seven sixty-one OT!" I say.

Da smiles proudly. "Wonderful! Now I'd like you to go back to 2412.8 and find out what important decision was made by the Governors that impacted our Day One Celebrations."

"Seriously? You want me to go back to 2412 Outside Time?"

"Do the calculation and take it from there."

I sigh. I wish Da would just use regular ArHK Time and save me having to do the calculations. I find Outside Time confusing. First of all, the months were not measured consistently, and then weeks and months were calculated on different base numbers. ArHK's base-ten time is so much easier: two ten-hour cycles per day, ten days in a week, ten weeks in a month, ten months in one ArHK year. Simple.

I sit down at my terminal and scroll back to the beginning of the filing system.

"Da, this system only goes back to 2450 OT."

"Interesting," he says without taking his eyes off the screen in front of him.

"Do we even have records that go back to 2412, or whatever you said?"

"I said 2412.8. It's in the old system."

"What old system?" I ask.

Da peers at me from over the rims of his glasses. Then, when I'm feeling suitably embarrassed, he points to the back of the Archives.

"That old thing actually works?" I ask.

"Did you think it was a museum piece?" he asks sarcastically.

"Well, actually, yeah. I sort of did," I say before I approach the gangly machine and look for a way to power it up. It takes me a few minutes, but eventually I find a switch on the side, at the bottom, as if anyone in their right mind would think to look there.

I press the switch on and wait for something to happen. But when nothing does, I slouch in my chair. Is the switch broken? Is there another way to start this piece of junk?

My personal messenger beeps. It's Mam. I smile at the screen and wait for her to speak.

"Rook? Are you busy?"

"Just in the Archives," I say. I can see the Refinement Salon in the background, and from the angle of her face, I assume she's sitting in the consultation chair.

"I'm just about to get my hair done. Which style do you prefer?"

Two pictures of my mother with different hairstyles flash across the screen. They look practically the same: one is mid-length with a side part and the other mid-length with uneven strands across her forehead.

"Ummm. I think they both look great," I say.

I don't mean to be dismissive. I know my mother cherishes her turn at the salon, and if she gets a style she doesn't like she has no choice but to live with it for months.

"I can't decide. Bunny says I should definitely go for the side part if I want to grow it out, but I —"

"Bunny's right. Definitely the side part." I wince as I interrupt. Even though it might feel like a life-or-death decision for her, I don't have the patience for a long conversation about something as trivial as a hairstyle that will look exactly the same as it does now when it's up to Mam to style it herself. I move to end our talk but she blocks my request.

"I think you're right. Thanks. Now, I was also thinking about getting my nails capped. Maybe in blue." She holds up the colour caps on her left hand to show me what she's planning. "What do you think?"

"Sounds great, Mam. Anyhow, listen, I've got to go. One of the Governors just came in and Da's on a break."

As soon as the lie passes through my lips, I end our talk and my personal messenger goes blank — just as the screen in front of me eases to life.

GAGE

age picks up the empty water bucket by the door and lifts the flap to the yurt. Before he steps outside, he turns to his mother.

"I'll go fetch the water so you don't have to do it after school," he says kindly. As excited as he is that the scouting party is about to depart, he's concerned for his mother. He understands some of the stress she's under, having to be headmaster to all the kids in base camp while also taking care of him and Brindle, especially when the scouts head out on overnight missions or, worse, week-long missions. His mother looks up from where she's finishing the last braid in Brindle's hair and smiles to let him know she's not hanging on to any hard feelings from the morning.

Gage whistles for Scruff to follow and lets the flap fall back against the wall of the yurt. It's a beautiful, clear day, and he can already see some of the younger kids outside, waiting to head off to school. Chevy, the boy from the next-to yurt, is kicking at stones in the dirt while he waits for his mother to come outside. He crouches down and pries a few stones free, then tucks them deep into his pockets.

The riverbank is busy with people fetching water, and Tansy, the camp's newest mother, is hanging freshly scrubbed diapers over sun-soaked branches to dry. Her baby is fussing in its cradleboard, and Tansy looks ready to burst into tears.

"Let me help," Gage says and stops to finish hanging her laundry.

"Thanks, Gage. I'm having one heck of a morning. This little one just won't settle, and I was up half the night tryin' to keep him from waking the whole camp."

Gage steps around to look at the baby strapped on Tansy's back. He's so young he hasn't even had his naming ceremony yet. His bottom lip is trembling, while at the same time his eyelids are heavy with exhaustion.

"He looks like he's just about to nod off. Maybe if you keep moving he'll stop fussing and let himself fall asleep."

Tansy adds a bounce to her step and puts a finger to her lips as she turns away from Gage. Then she heads along the riverbank, away from the morning activity.

Gage fetches his bucket and steps onto the stony river edge. He reaches out and scoops a bucket of clear, cool water from the deepest pool.

"It was nice of you to help Tansy, but you're gonna be late for school if you don't hurry."

Gage twists around to see Pepper standing behind him with her own bucket hanging at her knees.

"It's okay," he says and smirks. "The headmaster owes me a favour. How 'bout you?"

Pepper's laugh chimes off the surface of the water, as bright and sparkly as the reflected sunshine. Without even meaning to, Gage smiles in response. He can't think of anything quite as satisfying as watching Pepper's face transform when she finds something amusing.

"I'll tell her you was hogging the best place for clean water," Pepper teases.

Gage takes Pepper's bucket, quickly sinks it, then pulls it upright with a jerk.

"Here you go," he says, placing the bucket of water at Pepper's feet. Scruff sniffs the bucket, but Pepper shoos her away.

"There's a whole river to drink from, Scruff. Go git your own water."

Unoffended, Scruff trots off and joins another dog sniffing the bushes under the drying diapers.

When Gage picks up a bucket in each hand and starts back toward the centre of camp, Pepper protests.

"You don't have to do that. I'm perfectly capable of lugging a bucket of water."

"I know. But it's easier with two. Better balance," Gage says while water splatters the legs of his overalls. He straightens his back. His father always says the most important measure of a man is how much he helps others.

Pepper pretends not to notice the knowing looks their mates offer as she follows Gage through camp. They pass the horse ring, the empty horse carts tilted down at the ground, the haystacks, and the outdoor bake oven. Gage breathes in the smell of fresh bread.

"Why do your parents always pick a spot furthest from the river?" Gage asks as he sets the bucket down outside her yurt.

Pepper shrugs. "It's quieter on the edge of camp." She pauses, then says, "Anyhow, we better get a move on. Your mom's gonna ring the school bell any minute." Then she disappears inside.

"See ya in class," Gage says to the swinging yurt flap, before he circles back through the cluster of yurts to his own.

Gage puts the lid on the bucket and leaves it by the stove. The yurt is empty, and he wonders if his father has already headed to the muster. *It won't hurt to go have a look*, he thinks to himself, then heads back outside and toward the meeting circle where the men will be gathering for instructions.

When he approaches the goat pens, he spies his father and ducks behind a feed barrel.

"I know you're there, son," his father says over his shoulder, then turns in time to see Gage dive behind a nearby juniper bush. "And I don't think your mother will be too pleased when she finds you missing."

"Don't worry," Gage says as he appears. He hangs his head, and his shoulders fold forward. "I can get back before the lesson starts. I promise I won't stay long."

"It's not really a place for a boy," his father warns.

"Come on, Dad. I'm not a boy. I turn sixteen this year. You started scouting when you were sixteen."

"I know," his father sighs. "But things were different back then."

"Yeah, it was more dangerous. And Granny still let you go."

"She didn't exactly let me go," his father says and pulls down the brim on his hat so it's shading his eyes from the early morning sun.

"No, you ran off," Gage reminds his father. "At least I'm not sneaking away. I'm just coming to listen to what Chief Coil has to say."

Gage's father motions for him to hurry and starts walking again. When Gage catches up, they walk toward the meeting circle together.

"You know I'll tell you everything later anyhow."

Gage looks up at his father. "I know, but that'll be hours from now. I can't wait that long. This could be a historic moment. I don't wanna miss it daydreaming at school."

"Daydreaming?" His father snorts. "You're supposed to be paying attention to your mother's lesson."

"I can catch up on my school work later."

"You can't expect your mother to teach all day then catch you up at night. She has plenty of other chores to do."

The other men toss questioning glances at Gage when he enters the meeting circle behind his father. To avoid seeing the disapproval on the scouts' faces, Gage looks down at the toes of his boots while the conversations wrap around him.

"Why you looking so tired, Harley?"

"Didn't sleep much."

"Why not?"

"Up chasing a rat out of our food chest. Darn thing chewed right through the side. The wee ones were too afraid to go back to sleep after. Had to let them crawl in our cot."

"I got a trap you can borrow."

"Thanks, Winch. But I set one already."

"Any luck?"

"Nope. Still empty."

The familiarity of the voices comfort Gage, and before long he forgets that he's an intruder. He begins to feel a deep sense of belonging, the way he always feels when there's a gathering in base camp. When the other men start to settle, Gage takes a spot beside his father.

He can feel the cold seep up from the ground through his overalls, but being part of the group makes him blush hot with pride. One day he'll be a scout. He'll be the first to enter the old cities and collect artefacts, uncover lost knowledge.

Chief Coil strides to the centre of the circle and climbs onto the platform. The men settle into silence as he clears his throat and in a loud voice begins to detail the mission ahead of them.

"My map readers are convinced beyond a scrap of doubt that we're at the gateway to the ancient city of Washington. If such is the case, we must take care to explore every corner and crevice. We know from knowledge past that Washington was the centre of human knowing, and we think there's a good chance we might find a clue as to the whereabouts of the great Ship of Knowledge."

A rumble rises up from the circle of men like a gust of dry wind on the grasslands, but the chief raises his hand.

"This exploration will take time and patience. Do you remember how the scouts almost missed the ruins of the Empire State Building in the ancient city of New York? Or how the Statue of Liberty was discovered by accident, ten years after resettlement, by two young girls?"

The crowd murmurs in agreement. Gage looks around at the serious expressions on the faces of the men. Nobody needs to be reminded of how important exploration is to the survival of the human race. Everyone knows that ancient humans were able to cure the very diseases that now ravage their settlements, that humans were once able to generate power by harnessing the forces of nature, that they could calculate unfathomable equations using sophisticated gadgets, and communicate across vast distances using only the air. But so much knowledge was destroyed during the Storm Ages. What was once possible can now only be imagined.

Chief Coil raises his arm and gestures toward the wide, flowing river in the distance. Gage has spent half his life on the banks of this river, inching along it year by year. Its smell and life-giving water have been the backbone of his world.

"We're gonna follow this river to the centre of the city and focus our looking there. It'll be at least a day's walking, maybe two."

Chief Coil closes his hands into fists and pulls them close to his chest. "I feel it in my bones that humankind is about to make a great leap, and I don't want to delay progress a moment longer than necessary."

He pauses to look up at the sky, then back out at the men seated in front of him.

"We leave in the morning. First thing. Bring as many supplies as you can carry. We won't come back to base camp 'til the next full moon. Some of you'll stay behind to hunt and to help the young families, but we need as many of you on this mission as we can spare."

The men exchange glances. Being away for a month is unexpected, but everyone understands it's safer for base camp to be on the outskirts, where there's no risk of cave-ins, no underground caverns waiting to swallow a curious child.

"The map readers are passing out the fate sticks now. One notch, you're staying put. Two notches, you're coming along."

Gage rises up as high as he dares on his haunches to see over the heads of the men seated around him. On the far edge of the gathering, one of the map readers is handing around a roughly woven hemp sack. As it is passed from hand to hand, each man reaches in and pulls out a thin pine stick. Gage can tell by their reactions whether or not they see one notch or two. Those with only one notch hang their heads in disappointment but without complaint. The rest sit up straighter and try not to look as pleased as they feel. The youngest men don't contain their pride as well as they should, and Gage looks away when he sees his friend Boulder get a jab in the side from his father. The process goes quickly and quietly. When the sack comes around, his father reaches in and pulls out a stick. Then he nods at the men around him. Gage is not offered the hemp sack and doesn't even try to reach for it.

When all of the fate sticks have been passed around, Chief Coil begins speaking again.

"We'll need as many Readers as possible to come with us and, if we have to, we'll recruit young students from the school. Anyone know any Readers willing to be gone a month?"

Without planning to, Gage throws up his hand. Chief Coil looks down and sizes him up.

"You're a Reader?"

Gage nods and from the corner of his eye sees his father staring at him, hard. Gage shifts uneasily on the ground.

"Yes, sir. Top of my class. My mother's also a Reader."

Chief Coil considers Gage then glances at his father. "Your mother's camp headmaster?"

"Yes," Gage says proudly, straightening his spine.

"We're lucky to have your family in camp so more of our young folks can learn to be Readers. How old're you?"

"Almost sixteen, sir."

"And you've got your parents' permission to scout?"

Gage takes a deep breath and sits as tall as he can.

"I do," he says before his father can protest.

ROOK

Once the old computer finally comes to life, I start to have some fun. The operating system is like a child's toy, and the touch screen makes me laugh. I can't believe they used to input all the words by hand. Da says I should learn how to do something called *keyboarding*, that it used to be an important skill, and if I ever had to survive on an old system, that I'd navigate way faster using the keys. But I don't think I'd ever be able to learn keyboarding. I mean, seriously, if you ever saw their keyboards you'd have more proof that our ancestors had no idea what they were doing. The letters aren't in order but placed in rows randomly. Even voice activation was better than touch screen keyboards, and voice activation was pretty tedious compared to the Rapid Eye Movement Detection system we use now. Kids younger than Sparrow can operate REM Detection systems.

Da walks to the front counter, and I look up when I hear him greet someone with a friendly, "How can I help you today?"

It's not very often someone comes to the Archives besides us Keepers or Governor Hawk. Most people save themselves the walk and submit their files electronically.

Da greets the Head Clerk warmly. Even though he lives on the same street as us in the Records Sector, and only five pods down, we rarely see him. Mam says he's a bit of a hermit and that she feels sorry for his family because they rarely go out. She said his kids don't even go on school field trips, not even to the newborn nursery in the Health Sector, where every kid goes in year three to foster empathy. Field trips are an important part of everyone's education, and it's important to get to know the different sectors of ArHK. How else can you expect to learn appreciation for everyone's purpose and role and how we all need each other to make society run smoothly? I remember being surprised when kids at school talked about what happened in their sectors, and it always sounded like more fun than what was happening on our streets. Apparently the Growers are big into music and have impromptu street dances, and the

Recyclers have an annual robotics competition for actual prizes.

"Are you having trouble submitting yesterday's council report?" Da asks the Head Clerk.

I tune them out. Only government protocol bores me more than reading old files. I don't care who voted, or who seconded an amendment to some ArHK bylaw, or who passed a motion, or who wants something struck from the official record. The whole thing numbs me clear through to my central nervous system.

Not surprisingly, Ruby enjoys the long, structured meetings. She takes detailed notes, then edits them the next day just to be sure they're accurate. Her goal is to be the youngest apprentice Governor in ArHK history to be written into the Official Record, so she's always coming up with ideas for motions and proposals. At least twice a week she's pestering me to find out if something's been put forward before: a seniors' ArHKball league, tighter restrictions on the Growing Sector, a new policy for dropping items at the Recycling Sector. The problem with Ruby, though, is that she's so concerned about procedures and rules that she sometimes forgets to have fun. Last week when we went to Central Park together, she spent the whole time fuming about what people were doing that they shouldn't be doing.

"Everyone knows it's against ArHK bylaw to pick the foliage! Why isn't Pixie doing something? Her son is destroying the flower bed!"

She was so upset her voice trembled and her neck flushed red. She was about to rush over to confront Pixie, but I grabbed her shirt to keep her at my side.

"Chill, Ruby. He's like two years old. He just wants to pick a flower for his mother."

"But if everyone picked a flower, there wouldn't be any flowers left to admire. Oh dear, look over there!"

She was so distraught she hid her face in my shoulder. I glanced over to see one of Sparrow's school friends ripping up the grass with her hands and throwing it in the air like confetti. Sparrow has done it a hundred times, and I used to pull up the grass when I was that age too. Even Ruby probably picked the odd piece of grass or leaf at *some* point in her life. Seriously, she's so uptight I sometimes wonder how we manage to stay friends. But you don't just throw away a lifetime of being best friends over a few awkward moments, and I can't help but admire her passion. Sometimes I even wish I cared as much as she does. There must be comfort in being so committed.

It takes me awhile, but eventually I find the files for the year 2412.8 OT. I figure it makes sense to look at the entire month first to see what reports were filed, before going through each week and day. Sometimes decisions are made one day but not submitted until another. From the file names, I see there were two Fixer reports filed that month, one death notice, one birth notice, no marriages. There were two reports from the Governors filed too: *Day One Celebration Decision* and *Proposal to Restrict Access to Museum Artefacts*. I open the report about the Day One Celebration first and skim it until I read "after a heated debate in the Council Chamber, Governors Hailstorm and Oak passed the motion to initiate live re-enactments using schoolchildren to depict the arrival of the Chosen Ones in ArHK."

The phrase "arrival of the Chosen Ones" has been hyperlinked, and clicking on it opens a file named *Arrival Footage of the Chosen Ones*.

Curious. There's actual footage of the Chosen Ones arriving in ArHK?

I mean, I'm not the only person in ArHK who stopped believing the Creationist stories. Only fanatical historians, preschoolers, and old people actually believe that we are descendants of the Chosen Ones. I stopped believing when I was about Sparrow's age. Now I know ArHK is it: capital *I*, capital *T*. It may sound cynical, but I don't believe there's such a place as the Outside. I mean, has anyone ever seen the Outside? Has anyone ever been there and come back to talk about it? Where exactly would the Outside be? I don't even believe there was a time of great winds, floods, and fires or that poisonous air killed off the human race. I think these are myths created by early humans to explain our existence, to explain ArHK.

I hear Da say goodbye to the Head Clerk and return to his terminal. I scroll quickly through the file, looking for any reference to where the video footage is stored, and suddenly I stumble upon a link that opens a new screen. Images roll in front of my eyes. Images of people standing in a part of ArHK I've never seen, wearing clothes that look so bulky I can't imagine how they got things done.

Coats! I think to myself.

I remember learning in history class about how humans in the Outside had to wear coats to keep warm because the temperature changed from hour to hour. They harvested the hair from animals and turned that into fabric to keep them warm. It's hard to connect the lesson with the reality of what my eyes are seeing. Somehow the teacher made the Outside, the Chosen Ones, seem quaint and charming. But what I see looks weird and awkward.

I try to imagine what wearing a coat might have been like and where someone would have kept it during the day as they went about their business. Did they have to carry their coats for when the temperature changed? Did mams have to carry coats for their kids everywhere?

The image shifts to people climbing down a steep set of stairs from the side of a huge metallic-looking machine. The Creationists say the five hundred Chosen Families arrived on five flying machines called jet planes over a period of five days. The people are holding hands and carrying babies or gripping tightly onto bags with straps. Now, the people are smiling and looking around, pointing to things off-screen and talking excitedly. A small boy breaks free from his mother's grip. He runs to the stairs and starts to climb back up into the jet plane until his father retrieves him and carries him, kicking and screaming, to his mother. Another group of people step in from the edge of the screen to greet the newcomers. Everyone is shaking hands, embracing one another, and mingling the same way people do on our festival days.

By the time the footage ends, my skin is covered in a layer of rough bumps. I feel chilled, like when I had tonsillitis and got a fever. I desperately want to know if Da meant for me to find that footage or if he'd be upset to know I saw it.

"I can't very well ask him, though, can I?" I say out loud.

"You can't ask me what?" Da is standing so close behind me, I can feel the heat of his breath on my neck. I gasp and turn around.

"Steady there, Rook. Are you okay? You look like you've seen a ghost."

He puts his hand on my shoulder and raises his eyebrows with concern.

"Um, yeah, I'm just feeling a little dizzy. Maybe I need to go back to the pod and lie down."

"Did you find the answer to your assignment?" he asks, as I stand up and steady myself.

"I think so. They decided to have the little kids put on plays at the Day One Celebrations to show the arrival of the Chosen Ones in ArHK."

"Excellent work, Rook," Da says and kisses my forehead. "You deserve a break and maybe later a trip to the market square for some ice treats and a walk in Central Park."

I smile weakly and nod. "That sounds good."

My head is swirling and I feel weak, but I walk to the front of the Archives. I look up at the darkening dome above me and wonder for the first time if there's something on the other side.

"Rook?" Da calls when I'm about to open the front door and step onto the busy Avenue.

I turn.

"Do you agree now that there *are* new things to discover in the Archives?"

GAGE

age is leaning over his cot, rolling his spare blanket into a bundle, when his mother storms into the yurt. Her brown eyes are full of terror. Gage knew that someone would have rushed to the school to tell her the news, but this was even faster than he expected.

"Whaddaya think you're doin'?" she demands, out of breath and flushed.

She yanks off her woollen hat, releasing a mane of hair.

"I'm sorry, Mom," Gage says as he turns to face her.

At first, Gage is afraid of the intensity of her expression. But then, like storm clouds racing across the summer sky, her face changes. She looks down and wipes the corner of each eye with the sleeve of her blouse. This is a good sign, he thinks hopefully — she's resigned to him going.

"They need Readers, Mom! You don't want the mission to fail just because they don't have enough Readers, do you?"

His mother sinks onto Brindle's cot. "We're not the only Readers, Gage. That's why I joined this scouting camp as headmaster. So I could teach more people to read."

Gage sees her shoulders slump, and he sits beside her. His excitement gives way to sadness. He's never been away from his mother, not even for a day.

"A whole month?" she whispers, then begins to cry.

"There'll be messengers every few days. So you'll know we're safe. Besides, I'll be with Dad. He'll watch out for me." Gage feels the back of his eyes burn.

"No! I don't want you scouting together. It'd be better if you were apart. That way, if something happens, I won't lose you both."

Gage drapes his arm over his mother's shoulder and pulls her close. "I'm gonna be okay. I promise." He presses his forehead against the side of her face and they sit motionless for a moment.

"I know you will," she says finally and wipes her eyes. "I taught you good. I'm just gonna miss you, is all."

"I'm gonna miss you too," Gage whispers so that his voice won't crack.

He startles when she straightens her back and slaps her hands on her knees.

"Right then. We need to have a proper send-off meal tonight. A celebration! My boy's a Reader and going on his first scouting mission!" She turns and takes his face in her hands. "I'm real proud of you, Gage. Don't ever forget that."

Then she moves across the yurt in a flurry and opens the food chest. Gage watches her rummage inside, then pick out a jar of honey. She holds it up to the light coming in through the open door flap.

"Liquid gold," she says, her eyes flashing with mischief. Then she tucks the jar into the pocket of her skirt and heads outside.

. . .

That night they feast on roast goat, fried onions, and turnip mash. Gage takes thirds and then sits back and rubs his tummy, which is so full it's as tight as a rawhide drum.

"There's still a bit left," his mother says. "Can I bring you some more, Gage?"

Gage moans and shakes his head. "I'm so full. I don't think I'll be able to eat for a week."

"I doubt that." Brindle laughs and pokes at his full belly.

"What about me?" his father asks. "You gonna offer me another helping? I'm leaving tomorrow too."

Journey shoots him a sideways glance and sucks her teeth. "You can get up and help yourself."

Their father sets his knife and fork on the side of his plate with a clatter, and Brindle and Gage stop rough-housing. Is it a play fight or serious?

Their mother continues, "Gage is the guest of honour tonight. You been out scouting plenty of times."

She turns her back on him and the message is clear. She's not going to pick a fight, but she's not happy he let Gage volunteer.

"Brindle, can you clear the dishes, please?" she asks politely.

Brindle begins stacking the plates.

"Thanks, Brin," their father says when she takes his plate away. He pats his own tummy. "I'm full too. That was a great meal, Journey. Thanks."

"Yeah, Mom. Thanks for the special meal," Brindle chimes in as she carries the dirty dishes to the washing-up basin and drops them with a splash. "Maybe Gage should go away more often."

Gage begins to protest when their mother turns around with a honey cake in her hands.

Brindle gasps. "You made cake?"

"Not exactly." Their mother laughs. "I traded a jar of honey with Briar for this and the roast. There was enough honey for three cakes, so she made one for us, one for them, and she's gonna trade the last one for an extra bag of flour. She says Little Burl is eating like a horse lately. Apparently, she can't keep enough food in the pantry for that boy."

Their father reaches over to rough up Gage's hair. "I remember those days. When Gage was having a growth spurt he'd eat every last scrap." Then he turns and smiles at Brindle. "Lucky for us, though, he's probably too full for honey cake!"

Brindle squeals at the thought of her brother missing out on cake, but Gage clears his throat. "I'm pretty sure I can manage a slice of cake." Then he stands up and does a few jumping jacks to make room in his stomach.

. . . .

Gage has a hard time falling asleep. He tosses and turns in his cot and listens to Scruff dreaming below him. His father is snoring but his mother is still, and he guesses she's also awake, worrying.

"I just did what I had to do," Gage whispers to himself. "They need Readers." He replays the morning muster in his mind to see if things might have gone differently had he not been so eager to raise his hand. By the time he falls asleep, the entire camp is shrouded in stillness.

As usual, it's early when Gage wakes. The sky outside is barely lightening at the horizon, but he can hear sounds of men getting up in the nearby yurts. He jumps up and looks around. His father is already gone. Gage pulls on his warmest socks and sweater, then wraps his still-warm blanket around the bedroll he prepared the previous day. He's cinching it tight when Brindle leaps from her cot and wraps herself around his waist. He can feel the warmth of her body pressing into his.

"No, Gage! Please don't go and leave me and Mom here alone."

Gage kneels down and puts his hands on Brindle's shoulders. She's shivering in the cold air without her socks and sweater. "You won't be alone. You'll be with all the other families."

"But we'll miss you."

"And I'll miss you. But this is important. Dontcha want us to find Washington?"

Brindle nods and sniffles.

"Then just stay in camp and promise you won't go exploring on your own, like we agreed last night. That's your job," he says sternly.

"I promise," Brindle whispers.

She sniffles again and huddles under a blanket with their mother while Gage finishes packing his things. He doesn't make eye contact with either of them and instead concentrates on what his hands are doing until the air in the yurt feels so thick, he thinks he might choke. He wraps his whole bundle tightly in his greased overcoat and puts a leather hat firmly on his head.

His father pokes his head into the yurt.

"You ready, Gage?"

Gage nods, shoulders his pack, then ducks out the doorway with Brindle and their mother at his heels. He takes a lungful of morning air, but it doesn't calm him the way he hoped. All he can feel is his heart jerking in his chest like a jackrabbit running for its life. Gage gives his mother a long tight hug, then turns to Brindle.

"You keep Scruff inside 'til we're gone. We can't have her following us. Don't forget to scratch her belly for me every morning. Okay?"

Brindle kneels down and hides her face in Scruff's fur until the dog starts whining. Then, with the good-byes as over as they're going to be, Gage falls into step beside his father, and they walk toward the outskirts of base camp to meet up with the other men. Gage glances back to see his mother and Brindle lead Scruff into the yurt. The dog starts to yowl.

"Gage!"

Pepper's voice rings out, and Gage spins around to see her running toward him. Her bare feet kick up small clouds of dust, and her skirt gets tangled between her legs. She holds a rope of hair out of her face with one hand as she approaches.

He stops to wait but his father keeps walking.

"Uncle Winch says you're going scouting!" She pulls to a stop in front of him and lets her arms fall at her sides. Her fingers pick at the hem of her sweater. Her chest rises and falls rapidly, and Gage feels his heart bump in response.

"They need Readers," he says.

She wipes a strand of hair behind her ears, hair the colour of wheat at harvest time.

"It's not fair. I read as good as you. I should be able to come too," she says indignantly.

"But you're only fourteen!"

"Do you think they'll let me, even when I'm old enough?"

"Sure. Why not?" Gage asks.

"Because I'm a girl."

"You're the best archer in camp. Better than all the men. I bet they need Readers that can also drop a wild boar with one shot."

"Maybe," Pepper says reluctantly, but a smile of satisfaction tugs at the corners of her mouth.

"We'll make them bring you next year."

"You better," she says before her smile dissolves.

"Listen, Dad says they have female scouts in other camps, so why not in ours?"

Gage's father calls for him to catch up, and Gage looks at Pepper anxiously.

"Just promise you'll be careful," she says softly.

Gage nods, embarrassed by the tears suddenly filling his eyes.

"I want to hear you say it," Pepper says quietly, then leans forward and kisses his cheek.

"I promise."

This is all Gage manages to say with Pepper's soft grey eyes searching his face. Then he turns and runs hard to catch up to his father.

ROOK

The Avenue is streaming with people going about their daily business. A huddle of women leaves the market square together, each holding onto their black-market goods with one hand and their preschoolers with another. No doubt they spent a long morning bartering refurbished woks for jars of handmade fruit preserves while their children played tag around their feet. Da says the black market has been around as long as ArHK has existed and that even though it's illegal, the Governors don't dare shut it down. Even the Governors have things they want to trade. Ruby's family can't stand chickpeas but can never get enough tomatoes for their favourite salsa. And rumour has it Governor Hawk has such a sweet tooth he's willing to wear his shoes twice the allotted time just to get extra shares of cane sugar.

As I pass a side street, I see Strider and another delivery boy from the Growing Sector pushing their carts of vegetables. Now that we're apprentices and no longer in school, I can't hang out with Strider as much as I used to. He knocks on the door of Pod 22 and waits for it to open. When it does, he hands over a basket overflowing with vegetables. The mam wraps her arms around it with a smile and disappears back inside. When she returns with the empty basket, Strider hands her the Share Tracker and she enters her ID code to verify the delivery.

"The apples look delicious," she says when she hands back the Share Tracker. "Will there be more next week?"

Strider nods. "We still have the outer orchard to pick so we expect there should be one more delivery. And the bananas are coming on fast."

Strider looks up and waves when he sees me. I smile and wave back in response. I miss seeing him every day. When we were still at Instructional School, Strider sometimes brought Ruby and me surprises from the orchard, a soft peach or shiny red apple that he'd pick on his way to school and hide in his pocket.

Strider takes the basket back to his cart and fills it up again. Then knocks on the door of Pod 24. It would be fun to do deliveries for the Growers, I think. Everyone's always happy to see you, and you get to visit all the different levels and sectors.

A street vendor is set up on the side of the Avenue, shaving ice into a huge metal bowl, calling out his flavour of the day, and trying to entice parents to stop and buy treats for their children.

I skulk behind people who are taller than me, hoping to avoid seeing anyone I know, especially Governor Hawk. And I definitely wouldn't want to talk to my annoying cousin, Heath, who one day will join us in the Archives. But I can't face going back to the pod yet either, where Mam and Sparrow will be returning home from school. I can't face anyone at the moment, not with the images of the Chosen Ones in my head and a thousand questions chewing through my brain.

Mostly I am trying to decide one thing — whether the footage is real or is something the Entertainers created? Both possibilities merely lead to more questions. All I know for sure is that I'm perched on the edge of a great hole, a hole as deep and black as the drain in the bottom of our shower.

I arrive in Central Park and walk around the lily pad ponds to my favourite bench by the waterfall. I sit with my back to the path so I can think without being disturbed. The sound of the rushing water drowns out the chatter of people nearby. It soothes me and gives me the illusion of being alone. It reminds me of all the times I've been in Central Park with Mam and Da, and Grandmam Ivy when she was still alive, and then with Sparrow once she was born, just to admire the waterfall and enjoy an ice treat. We're lucky to live so close to Central Park. Some families, like the ones who live on the lower levels of ArHK or out in the Growing Sector, have a long walk to Central Park. Sure, they have smaller parks on their levels and in their sectors but nothing as grand as this.

I lean over and let my fingers trail in the water rushing past. Governor Hawk would blow a gasket if he saw me doing this. He might even put forward a motion to keep people at least three metres back from all water features at all times. Every time someone does something a Governor doesn't like, they introduce a new rule. Two years ago they locked the entrance to the park at night after they found an old man bathing in one of the ponds. He'd gotten out of the Elderly Care Pod and found his way up from the Health Sector to the Knowledge Level and Central Park. I look around to see if anyone is watching, but the truth is I don't care. I love the feel of the water bubbling around my fingertips. I love watching the changing patterns of white as the water runs over the rocks. I don't think there's anything as splendid in all of ArHK.

My mind circles back to the files on the ancient computer and the Governor Reports filed in 2412.8. If there's actual footage of the Chosen Ones arriving in ArHK, why don't they show it at the Day One Celebrations instead of having little kids put on plays? Why did they decide to permanently archive that footage, and does that mean there are other things they decided to hide as well? Then I remember the second report that was filed that same week. What was it about again?

Suddenly I'm overwhelmed with the need to read the second report. Like, if I don't get back there right now, I'll never find the file again, or it will disappear and I'll never know the truth. I jump up from the bench and run through the park, back in the direction of the Archives. People look at me with puzzled expressions as I streak past.

"Slow down, Rook, before you run someone over," a voice calls out.

I don't stop to see who is shouting at me, but I wave my hand above my head and jump over a flower bed. When I get back to the Archives, I burst through the door and sprint past Da.

"Rook?" he asks, taking his eyes off the screen to watch me. "I thought you were going back to the pod to lie down?"

"I feel better now. There's something I want to look up."

Da turns back to his terminal, a smug smile pulling at the corner of his mouth.

I pull a chair close and sit down. My heart is racing, and I drum my fingers on the table while I wait for the computer to boot up. A series of numbers flash across the screen and the machine hums slowly to life. I swear our ancestors must have wasted half their days just waiting for their computers to warm up.

When the operating system is ready, I find my way back to 2412.8 and open the file labelled *Proposal to Restrict Access to Museum Artefacts*.

Normally, this file name wouldn't make me suspicious, but today the hairs on the back of my neck start to dance. It's common knowledge that ArHK contains many specialized areas protected by restricted access locks and highly sophisticated entry codes. Everyone knows, say, that only the Governor-approved Head Grower is allowed into the Seed Vault. Only the Governor-approved Computer Engineers are allowed access to the Information Technology Development Lab. And as Head Keeper, my father is the only person in ArHK who has access to the Great Hall of Human Knowledge. The Great Hall, Da says, contains information and artefacts that go back before the beginning of ArHK.

What isn't common knowledge, however, and what has me acting erratically is my realization that access to these artefacts wasn't always restricted. Why it was restricted starting in 2412 is the question I desperately want to answer.

I'm just starting to read when the ArHK-wide intercom crackles. The birth music begins, and people outside the Archives cheer when Governor Alder welcomes ArHK's newest citizen: Sandpiper Sorter.

The music softens while the credentials are announced: "Sandpiper is the firstborn daughter of Robin and Hemlock Sorter. She was born at 4:22 of the wake cycle and weighs 3629 grams. Sandpiper is the twelfth baby born this year."

Da's cheer echoes through the Archives, but I'm too busy reading to join in. He immediately powers down his terminal and pushes his chair under the desk.

"Rook, it's time to go celebrate," he says. "Whatever you're reading will have to wait until tomorrow."

Celebrating the birth of a new citizen is not optional in ArHK. Even the Head Clerk and his family will be on the Avenue showing their dour faces. But the Recycling Sector will be going all out today, because there hasn't been a firstborn Sorter in seven years.

"Do the files on this computer go back to Day One?" I ask as Da turns off the lights and sets the security lock for the front doors.

"Yes and no. The files from the first one hundred OT years have been restricted."

"How do you access them?"

We're outside, pressed up against the glass wall of the Archives, waiting for a break in the long stream of people who have flooded out of their pods and work-places to celebrate Sandpiper's birth.

"From that computer, but they're protected by a pass code."

"What if someone hacks the pass code?"

"Then they'll learn a lot of new things about our ancestors, I'm sure. And I'd be in a lot of trouble if the Governors discovered the breach."

"But I'll have access to the restricted files when I'm Head Keeper?"

"Of course, Rook. When you're Head Keeper, you'll have access to everything in the Archives, including the Great Hall of Human Knowledge. Isn't that exciting?"

"It sort of is," I agree. "But that's still a long time from now."

"Time has a funny way of slipping by. One day, before you know it, you'll be the Seventeenth Head Keeper. Do you remember what I taught you about Roman numerals?"

"Of course." I nod. "In ancient times, they used letters to represent numbers. So for instance, X represented ten and V represented five."

"That's correct. So you'll be Head Keeper X-V-I-I. It's very important that you remember. Only Head Keepers learn about Roman numerals."

From down the Avenue I see a group of Governors heading our way. It's the flash of their purple robes that catches my attention. I stand on my tiptoes to see if Ruby is among them, but she's not. It's Governor Hawk and a few of his closest allies. As usual, I shiver when I see the stoop of his shoulders. I look at the ground when he approaches so I don't have to make eye contact. But his hard-soled shoes stop directly in front of Da and me, and I have no choice. I look up the length of his long, thin frame and into his narrow, pinched face.

"Good afternoon, Governor Hawk."

Da's demeanour is polite, but I sense the usual tension between the two and once again wonder what happened in the past that led to the animosity I feel whenever Governor Hawk comes near.

"Hello, Fern," Governor Hawk says without even glancing at Da. Instead he tilts his head in my direction. "Rook, I trust you are keeping out of trouble?"

"Always," I say with a hint of insolence that I can't help.

Governor Hawk narrows his eyes and I feel myself shrink under his glare. "Be sure to keep it that way." Then he snorts and continues along the Avenue with the other Governors at his heels.

Da stares at me a bit too long before speaking. "Is there anything you want to tell me?"

"Not that I can think of," I say.

"Good. Please don't antagonize that man. The last thing we need is more scrutiny from him," Da says and wipes the sweat from his upper lip.

"Why does he hate us so much?"

"He doesn't hate us. Exactly. And it's a long story. For another time." Da sighs.

"It sure feels like he hates us," I mutter as I merge into the moving crowd.

Da has no choice but to follow me.

GAGE

When Gage arrives at the departure point, the men are standing in a circle around Chief Coil and Burl, the camp's deputy chief. Gage and his father squeeze into the circle and wait for the ceremony to begin. Gage has never seen a setting-off ceremony. Not even his mother has seen it. It's only for the scouts. When everyone arrives, the men fall silent and Chief Coil walks a lighted bundle of dried cedar around the circle, letting the smoke drift in ribbons over the men. Some of the men use their hands to wash the smoke over their shoulders before Chief Coil moves on. When he arrives at Gage, Chief Coil touches both of Gage's shoulders with the top of his walking stick, then makes two passes with the smouldering cedar bundle. Gage drinks in the fragrant smoke and silently recites a prayer for safety.

Behind Chief Coil, Burl carries a talisman dangling on a thin strand of hemp rope. He puts this around Gage's neck, then offers a blessing for good luck, good speed, and, above all, a safe return. Gage looks down at the amulet lying against his shirt, a small bone disk with a symbol carved on each side: a stylized yurt to ensure a safe return and four loops joined in the centre to call forth luck. He reaches up and rubs the amulet between his thumb and forefinger, then tucks it inside his shirt to keep it safe, the way his father does with his own.

His father steps out of the circle, then returns with a brand new walking stick, freshly carved, still shiny and clean. Before he hands it to Gage, he takes his pocket knife and carves a circular notch around the top. Gage takes the walking stick and swallows the lump in his throat. Then, while he's fighting back tears, the scouts begin whooping and whistling, stomping their feet, and clapping their hands. Gage doesn't join in but feels the energy travel up from the ground through his feet.

The journey begins and the men fall in behind Chief Coil, their walking sticks moving in rhythm above their heads like an ancient synchronized machine. Gage and his father walk side by side at the back of the group and when they have taken a few hundred steps up a slight incline, Gage stops to look back at base camp and at Burl standing at the departure point, waving them off. He looks at the twenty-eight yurts clustered around the centre of camp like a patch of mushrooms, the goat pen on the near side of the camp, and the horse ring on the far side. He sees buckets and baskets strewn outside yurts and registers the random pattern of paths worn in the grass, criss-crossing the camp, leading down to the river, stretching into the forest. The day is still young so base camp is quiet. Other than the deputy chief who is now in charge of camp, only the milkmaids are up and at the pen readying the nanny goats for milking. Gage wonders how many kids will be born while he's away.

It isn't until the camp slips out of sight that Gage's father begins to talk. He and his father walk a few paces behind the pack and keep their voices low. The other scouts are quiet and keep watch in all directions as they move along the bank of the river.

"I guess I better let you know what scouting's all about," Gage's father says. "I wasn't expecting to have to say all this for awhile yet. But I don't have a choice now."

"Whaddya mean?" Gage asks.

"Scouting's dangerous work. It's not just about making discoveries."

"I know that," Gage says.

"There are three main dangers to being a scout, and you really need to understand them all," Gage's father says. "First, there's cave-ins."

"Everyone knows about cave-ins, Dad. Even Brindle."

"No. You might think you know. But hearing something and experiencing it are very different. It's like reading. Your mother can explain to me *how* she reads. But that doesn't mean I know how to read words when I see them myself."

"I guess," Gage says.

"Much of the land we're walking on was once covered with homesteads, villages, and cities. The ancient people lived in permanent structures built over caverns dug into the ground. Caverns are the biggest danger for us scouts. If you take one wrong step, you can kiss your backside goodbye. Sometimes these caverns are only ten feet deep or thereabouts, which means you get yourself scratched up pretty good on the way down and maybe break a leg or two, but you still come out alive. Sometimes, though, these caverns stretch deeper than you can imagine. If you fall through one of the deep ones, you're a goner. Never seen again. Then, sometimes, the ground around these caverns is so unsteady, just one step causes a cave-in and you get buried alive at the bottom. It's a terrible way to go."

"Why would anyone want to live in anything other than a yurt? With yurts you can move whenever you need to."

"They just did things different back then is all," his father says. "They stayed put more than we do."

"But even in the Middle, people still live in yurts. And people have been living there for hundreds of years."

"I dunno, son. They had more advanced technology, so they could build things we can't."

"Why'd they build caverns in the first place?" Gage asks.

"The Scholars think the caverns were safer in those days. They think the people used them to store goods, like food and such. Others think the ancient people dug caverns to protect themselves, like a defence against enemies or invaders. But nobody really knows."

"Did you ever fall into a cavern?"

"Yep. A few times. Luckily only the shallow ones. Scared the bananas out of me. I thought I was a goner until I landed and could still see the sky, still move my limbs. That's why you need to beware of where you're stepping. See that lump over there? Where the trees are spread apart?"

Gage's father points his walking stick to a spot beyond the riverbank where Gage can, in fact, see a small clearing and a lump in the undergrowth.

"That was once some sorta structure. If there's no others nearby, it mighta been a single dwelling, which means the cavern would be shallow. But when there's a lot of other lumps in the same area and signs of other structures, there's a good chance you risk stumbling into a series of underground caverns," his father explains.

Gage scans the riverbank for signs of other structures, but all he can see are trees towering at the edge of
the forest and the undergrowth spreading down toward
the river.

"When you approach an ancient structure, you have
to step careful and carry your walking stick across your
body, like this, at your waist. Hold it tight with both
hands. That way, if you do step through, the stick'll
keep you from falling all the way down."

His father demonstrates by grasping his stick from
the top, with his fingers curled toward the ground.
His father's walking stick is worn and dark with age,
notched with a series of circles to track how many
scouting missions he's been on. Gage takes his own
walking stick and practises the hold. A few of the
scouts look back and nod in recognition. When his
father tries to pull the stick from his grasp, Gage holds
tight.

"Scouts always explore in pairs and never any
closer than ten feet apart. That way if one of you does
fall through, the other'll be able to help you back up or
know where to begin searching. Too many scouts are
lost because they get off on their own and disappear."

Gage remembers what his mother said earlier that
morning.

"Mom doesn't want us scouting together, in case …"

"I know, son. Your mother's right. You'll be paired
with someone else once we start exploring."

They walk in silence while Gage practises with his walking stick.

"The walking stick is the scout's most important tool," his father continues in a voice as steady as his stride. "It'll not just save your life if you fall through a cavern, but you can also use it to test the ground before you start stepping someplace new. If you reach out with your stick and tap the ground, you can listen for hollow sounds, like an echo. Sometimes the stick'll even break through the ground and save you a fright. I've seen a mouthy old raven land on a hillock and break through a cavern. It sure doesn't take much weight sometimes."

"What's inside the caverns?"

"Well, now, that's a good question. Sometimes they're fulla muck, and I tell ya, you'll stink out the camp faster than an angry skunk if you end up in one of those. But sometimes they're full of artefacts. All just depends on the cavern. That's the tricky part. We want to explore the caverns but we don't wanna kill ourselves first." His father chuckles, but Gage doesn't understand the joke.

"Have you ever found any artefacts?" Gage asks.

He more or less knows the answer, has heard his father's stories when he returned to camp. But asking feels respectful and listening to the familiarity of his father's deep voice comforts him, eases some of the uncertainty he's feeling about leaving camp.

"I've found old jars and metal tools. Even pieces of furniture. Once I found a whole shelf of books."

"Books," Gage says dreamily.

"Imagine me staring down a bunch of books? That's where you come in. We find lotsa things we need Readers for. Sometimes the buildings have words on 'em. Or we find old road signs that help us find our way."

"I hope I get to find a book."

His is one of the few families he knows who owns ancient books. His mother's grandfather had a small collection that was passed down through the generations before such artefacts were taken and stored for the collective good. Most scouts won't see a single book in their lifetimes, not to mention feel the smoothness of paper on their fingertips. Important artefacts, like books, are carefully packaged and sent to the Middle for the Scholars to study and keep safe.

Gage sees a flicker from the corner of his eye and turns quickly. He squints into the forest.

"A deer," he hisses as he watches the animal pick its way through the trees.

His father turns in time to see the deer flash its white tail, then disappear from sight. Next comes a crash, a thump, a grunt, and then a high-pitched squeal. Gage glances at the group of men who have continued to walk, then at his father who has motioned for him to be still.

"Wait here. I'm going to investigate. Keep your eyes on me. Just in case."

Gage panics. "But you can't go off on your own. Mom said —"

Again his father raises his hand for silence. Then he grasps his walking stick tightly at his waist and walks toward the clearing.

"Dad! The caverns!"

His father doesn't respond but continues walking. When he gets to the clearing, he uses his walking stick to poke at the lumps and hillocks. Eventually he stops and stares at the ground, then motions for Gage to approach.

Gage wants to remind him about his mother's orders, but he's too curious to stop. He follows his father's path and grips his walking stick so tightly his fingers turn white. When he gets to where his father is standing, he sees a deep, dark hole in the ground. The grass and dirt have crumbled away, and down in the darkness Gage can just barely make out the white flash of the deer's tail and the glow of its eyes in the sunlight. It grunts and pants, thrashes and scrabbles in its narrow prison.

"And that's how fast it can happen," his father says. "But this time, it's lucky for us."

His father yells to the group of scouts while Gage watches the deer struggle below, trapped and afraid of what will happen next. It's not that Gage is against hunting or eating animals — it's what humans need to survive — but right now he knows a little too much how that deer is feeling.

ROOK

The next morning, I'm awake before Da and waiting by the front door of the pod when he's ready to walk to the Archives.

"You're up early," he says when he finds me sitting in the window seat looking out at the street. I'm watching the Cleaners sweep up the debris from the previous night's birth celebration.

"I guess," I say and stand up to leave with him.

"You even have on your uniform?"

"I just want to make you proud," I say with a hint of sarcasm.

Although I was awake early, I'm not at all rested. I spent most of my sleep hours staring at the ceiling above my bunk, listening to Sparrow breathing beside me and Mam and Da snoring down the hall. I've stared at that ceiling for hours upon hours and never thought twice about that flat white square above me. Last night, though, I couldn't help but wonder what's on the other side, if there really is someplace called the Outside. I mean, I know what's on the other side of the wall beside my bunk — the kitchen with its long flat counters and double-stacked cupboards. And I know what's on the other side of the wall beside Sparrow's bunk — Mam and Da's bedroom. I know what's below our pod, more or less. Below the Knowledge Level, the Developers live and work on the second level of ArHK. They're responsible for developing new technologies that make life in ArHK more efficient. Like every other year they upgrade the personal messengers we hang around our necks, the life-links that monitor our health and location and allow us to keep track of ourselves and others. And below the Development Level is the Manufacturing Level and below that, Waste Management, which is circled by the vast fields and orchards of the Growing Sector. But what's above our pod, above the Archives, above the Knowledge Level of ArHK? That's something I don't know.

"Do you believe in the Outside?" I ask Da as I wait for him to deactivate the security system to the Archives.

A sweaty jogger passes by with a wave and I nod in response.

"Yes, I do," Da says. "I believe the Creationist stories are real."

"You believe in the five hundred Chosen Families and in the winds, floods, and fires?"

"Yes."

"You believe in the poisonous air?"

"I do. I know it's hard to believe in something nobody has ever seen, but you have to have faith."

As usual, the temperature in the Archives is a steady twenty-one degrees, and the dark dome is lightening as the wake hours progress. Because the Archives are considered a public space, the ceiling changes hue depending on the time of day. Like the sky high above the parks and avenues, side streets, and public markets on each level, the dome inside the Archives changes from dark grey at the beginning of the wake hours to bright blue midway through, then fades to black by the time the sleep hours arrive. In the living pods, the ceilings are only two and a half metres above the floor and citizens are responsible for decorating, upkeeping, and lighting their own spaces.

"Is today an assignment day?" I ask as Da powers up his terminal.

The first thing we do each day is check for orders from the Governors. Next we check on the Great Hall of Human Knowledge by logging into the monitoring panels. As usual, there are no problems with the heat or humidity levels.

"No, I think today should be an exploratory day. You're free to read whatever interests you, but I want a brief summary of your discoveries."

I don't want to appear excited, but inside my heart is colliding with my rib cage. The feeling is exhilarating and startling at the same time. It takes me a moment to decide where to start.

"Do you mind if I go back to the old files?" I ask and motion to where the clunky old computer sits under a bank of lights.

"Go for it. I hope you learn something interesting," Da says. "Oh, and don't forget about the Daily Log this afternoon."

"I won't," I call over my shoulder.

When the computer asks for a pass code to the restricted files, I have to think hard before I have any idea what to try. Then I remember Da's lecture on Roman numerals. I wonder if, at some point, the Educators decided that Roman numerals were no longer essential learning for ArHK citizens.

Da is Head Keeper number sixteen and I will be Head Keeper number seventeen. Because Mam married into the Keeper family, she trained to be an Assistant Keeper when she moved in with Da. On the other hand, my firstborn will be Head Keeper number eighteen. Head positions are always passed down from parent to firstborn child. Luckily for Sparrow, second- and third-born children in ArHK have more freedom. These days she wants to be an Entertainer, and I think it would break her spirit if she couldn't dream about her future. Although she will have more choices and may get to learn a new job or move to a new sector, she will never be Head of anything.

Until yesterday I wished I was born second. I didn't want to live in the same pod my whole life. I didn't want to care for my parents, like all firstborns are required to do. I didn't want to spend all my days in the Archives and train my own firstborn child or other apprentices, like my cousin, Heath, who actually wants to apprentice in the Archives.

Yesterday, the thought of spending the rest of my life in the Archives made me feel like a thousand pounds of metal was riding on my shoulders, but today I'm anxious to finish my apprenticeship and become Rook Keeper XVII.

That's it! Rook Keeper XVII.

I input *Rook Keeper XVII* into the computer but am denied access. I try using just *XVII*, but again it comes back as invalid. Then I try *RK* for my initials, followed by the Roman numerals. I almost jump out of my skin when the computer greets me by name: *Welcome Rook Keeper.*

Sometime after I was born, Da must have programmed this pass code into the old computer system, knowing I'd eventually need access to the restricted files.

There are so many folders I don't know where to start, and I can't find a search function. The folders are organized by year, according to Outside Time. Within each year are folders by month, then folders by week, then folders by day. It isn't until I get down to the daily folders that I start to see file names. Not a very efficient system for exploring, so I decide to start at the beginning — at the very first file of the very first day of the very first year — the day the Chosen Ones arrived in ArHK.

I open the Daily Log of year one, week one, day one and am amazed to find that the format has changed very little.

Population: 2123
Deaths: 0
Births: 0
Marriages: 0
Structural Enhancements: 0
Structural Repairs: 0
Temperature: 21°C
Food Production: Not yet productive.
Narrative Highlights: The full complement of citizens is now inhabiting ArHK. All five passenger jets arrived without incident and citizens were settled into their assigned pods.

For the first few weeks, the Daily Log changes very little, and there are no linked terms. But in the third week, I see a new folder: Citizen Communications. Inside are folders numbered from 1 to 500. These historic folders, I realize, track families by their arrival number.

I belong to Chosen Family 78. In fact, it still says 78 above the entrance to our pod. So I assume the original Keeper family, my ancestors from the Chosen Ones, were also Family 78.

I take a deep breath and open the folder numbered 78. Inside is an electronic letter addressed to Isobel 78 from Jule Richardson (New York) and a letter from Isobel 78 to Jule Richardson (New York).

Hi Isobel!

How is life in ArHK? I can't believe you have been gone three weeks already. We miss you all terribly and not knowing when we will see you again is making it difficult to know what to write. I guess the main thing is that we are all fine on the home front and I thank God every day that you are safe and I don't have to worry about you or William or the kids.

Not much has changed here. There was a terrible storm last week. It took out the power again, or I would have written sooner.

Write when you can to tell me all about life in ArHK. Everyone here is so curious to find out! There hasn't been much on the news except that

you all arrived safe and sound. They transmitted
some footage of your group arriving off the air-
plane, but I couldn't find your face in the crowd.

Love, your sister, Jule.

"Rook?" Da calls out from the front of the Archives. "I'm going to the market to see if there are any soup vendors today. Would you like a soup?"

"Isn't it a little early for soup?" I call back.

"Perhaps, but I'm afraid if I wait too long I'll be out of luck. Mam's helping out at the school today, so we're on our own for lunch."

"Soup would be great, thanks. Anything but mush-room," I say.

"I'll be back in ten minutes. Let me know if any files arrive from the Governors," he says and leaves.

I open the next letter and read quickly.

Hello Jule,

It was great to get your letter but it made me miss you too! I wish we could livechat so I could see your face. But the Governors say it takes too much bandwidth and monitoring our systems and secur-ity is more important.

How are the twins? Were they terribly scared during the last storm? Did you go down into the storm shelter? You can never tell how strong the winds are going to be from the newscasts. The weather forecasters just don't have a clue anymore.

Have the water levels risen more since we left? I wonder how the Bronx is making out. I think often of our old neighborhood and wonder if any of it still exists.

Anyhow, enough doom and gloom. We are all enjoying our time here in ArHK. It was hard saying goodbye but once the airplane got in the air, the kids settled down and enjoyed the flight. Wesley enjoyed it the most. The trip was very calm, luckily, and we arrived in about six hours. I'm curious to know where we are exactly, somewhere we could have flown in six hours. Have you heard anything? I know they intend to keep our location a secret for our own safety and to protect our purpose here, but I expect there will be a leak eventually.

William has been busy cataloguing the books for the Great Hall of Human Knowledge, as well as working with the IT experts to set up a system to record our daily operations. Most positions have several families assigned to them, but the Archives, which is a grand facility like the New York Public Library and stretches the equivalent of four segments along the street, is a one-family job for now. Still, even though the Archives is big, it is nothing compared to the Growing Sector, the biggest sector *by far in ArHK. A lot of resources are diverted there.*

The levels and sectors of ArHK are purposely designed so that people live near their places of work. We live on the top level of ArHK. Our pod is very comfortable. We have three bedrooms, a small kitchen, a living room, and an eating area. We also have a bathroom but there is no tub, we have to go to the public baths for that. The food so far is good. We are still eating from the stores that came on the airplanes before us. They say it will be at least six months or more before we will be able to eat fresh fruit and vegetables grown here, and the meat labs should be going within a year.

ArHK is well built and there are very many beautiful features. As promised, they created parks and public areas that feel just like being outside. Even the sky is blue and changes colour throughout the day to imitate the sun going down. But there is no wind to feel on our faces or sunshine to warm our skin. Still, I can't complain. I know we are lucky to be here and I do not take it for granted.

Write soon and often so I know you are all safe and well.

Love, Isobel

When Da returns from the market, he brings a steaming jar of soup to the back of the hall. I turn off the screen before he can see what I'm reading. It was one thing to watch the arrival footage since it wasn't pass code–protected, but hacking into restricted files is not something I think he'll be happy to know I'm doing.

"I got you a tomato soup," he says and puts the jar on the desk beside me.

"Smells good," I say. "What did you get?"

"Split pea and I don't care that it's still early. I'm going to have it now. I'm starving."

Da unscrews the lid and sips his soup. When I see him wince, I decide to let mine cool.

"I read a curious term this morning. Maybe you've run across it. Or maybe Mam has. Have you ever heard the word *God*?"

Da chokes on his soup and looks quickly over his shoulder as if he expects Governor Hawk to be standing there.

"What exactly have you been reading?" he whispers.

GAGE

The scouts stop for the first night in a small clearing on the riverbank. Although they have materials to make lean-tos, Chief Coil points to the clear skies and everyone decides to sleep rough.

Gage and the other boys go out in pairs to find dry branches and fallen trees for the fires, one for cooking and two others that will be kept burning throughout the night for warmth and protection. Two of the boys have axes. The rest have large machetes. Gage is paired with Jett, who is two years older but not a Reader. Jett was born into a scouting camp and never lived in the Middle like Gage did when he was young. Jett never had a chance to go to school. By the time Gage's family joined the camp, Jett's family decided it was too late for Jett to start school learning.

Jett has been scouting for a year, but in that time they haven't reached an ancient city, only a few small villages and two large towns.

"Do you think it's gonna be Washington?" Gage asks as they head into the forest. The question is on everyone's minds.

"My dad says not to get my hopes up, but I can't help myself. I can't wait to get to the centre of the old city. Just to see for myself. I can't wait to see one of them statue things."

"Remind me, what's a statue again?" Gage asks.

"They're hunks of rock or metal fashioned to look like things, like people and horses. But they're really big. Much bigger'n real life. That's what's so interesting. My dad saw one once. It was a man standing on an outlook. Probably ten times the size of a real man."

They walk carefully with their walking sticks in their hands and machetes strapped around their waists. Gage tries to imagine a statue, but he can't really bring the idea into focus. Instead, his mind drifts back to the deer and the cavern that swallowed it whole.

"Hey, Jett? Did you ever fall into a cavern?"

"No. But I saw someone go through once. Just a shallow one. He came up covered in black oily stink." He pauses and sighs. "And I had an uncle fall through once. They never found his body."

Both boys fall into silence and fish their talismans from their shirts. It's tradition to honour a lost scout with a minute of reflection and a silent prayer, no matter when he's mentioned or remembered. After they share a quiet moment, they take out their machetes and begin to hack at the dead branches on the ground. They cut the branches in five-foot lengths and throw them in a pile.

Gage swings his machete at a branch lying on the ground and slices it in two. He steps farther along and swings again. This time his machete stops with a thud and sends a vibration up the length of his arm. He yelps and drops the machete.

"You okay?" Jett asks.

"I hit something there in the ground."

"Was it a rock?"

"Dunno."

The boys kneel down to clear away the dead leaves and dirt. What they discover is a thick, heavy rusted circle of some sort. They pull it free and heave it up on its edge. It stands as tall as Gage's waist.

"What is it?" Gage asks.

Jett nods. "Dunno really. I mean, looks like a wheel. From some old machine. Maybe a farming machine. I seen one of them before, with the wheels still attached."

"Should we tell the others?"

"Nah, these things are everywhere. It ain't special."

They kick around in the undergrowth to see if there are more machine parts, but when they don't find anything they abandon their search and cut more firewood.

By the time they return to camp with their load, the cooking fire is roaring and the camp is bustling. Some of the men are butchering the deer, which is hanging by its back legs from a nearby tree. They shave thin strips of meat from the carcass. Other men are sharpening long green branches to fine points, and others are skewering the slices of meat onto the branches, which they stick into the ground around the fire. Gage feels his stomach growl.

Gage's father comes up from the river with buckets of water. Then he lays out their bedrolls. With the night's firewood collected, the boys stop to rest. Gage sits down beside his father on their blankets. It feels good to get off his feet and feel the heat of the fire warm his face.

"We found an old wheel in the forest," Gage tells his father. "Buried in the leaves and dirt."

"Did you find anything else?"

"Nope. But it was a big one."

"You never know what you're gonna find. Even when it feels like you're in the middle of nothing, you're usually near some ancient site."

"I wonder if people ever camped right here? On the bank of this river?" Gage muses.

"I suspect there were dwellings all along this river. This was a highly inhabited part of the world, and big cities were always surrounded by villages."

"It's hard to imagine there being so many people back then," Gage says. "They musta been tripping over each other."

In the dimming light, Gage watches the men tend to the skewers of meat, rotating them every few minutes to ensure the meat cooks evenly. Drips of grease land in the fire and sizzle, sending the aroma of roasting deer into the air.

Chief Coil and the map readers are on the far side of the fire, examining a map so old it's soft like Scruff's ears and as wrinkled as the elders' faces. Gage aches to have a look too but watches the fire instead and wonders what Brindle and his mother are doing. He remembers how empty the yurt felt whenever his father went on scouting missions.

"Hey! You never told me about the second and third dangers for scouts," he says to his father.

"Didn't I? Let's see. The second biggest danger is in the cities where pieces of structures are still standing. Walls made of bricks or blocks are worst. They look solid, but they're not always stable and can collapse any time, especially if a nearby cavern falls in."

"How many walls will still be standing, do you reckon?"

"Who knows? Hundreds. Wait 'til you see. Sometimes whole buildings will be more or less intact."

"I can't imagine what it's like to be in the middle of an ancient city with walls all around."

"It's quite the sight, I tell ya. And I'm sure you'll get a peek tomorrow."

"Really?"

"We expect to reach the outskirts tomorrow. That's where we'll start to see a few ruins. We'll have to be extra careful. There'll be thousands of caverns to watch for. These cities used to be crammed with houses, rows and rows of them. Even the roads had caverns below. You'll need to be alert at all times."

Gage stares at the fire. The flames lick at the logs, and sparks dance into the night sky, up toward the thickening darkness and speckling of stars overhead.

"What's the third danger?"

"Oh," his father shrugs. "Lurkers, and wild animals like wolves and cougars. But Lurkers aren't really a danger these days. People couldn't make it on their own. Those who tried died off a hundred years ago."

"What about wild animals?"

His father shrugs again. "Even the dangerous animals generally stay clear of humans, but if you ever get cornered, use your stick. Make lots of noise. Look as threatening as you can. And holler for help."

When the deer skewers are ready, the men pull the sticks from the ground and pass them around. Gage doesn't wait for the meat to cool. He tears off bits with his teeth and swallows as fast as the temperature allows.

"You were right about one thing," he says between mouthfuls. "It WAS lucky that deer fell into the cavern."

His father smiles and softens his tone. "It's nice to have you along, Gage. I enjoy being with the other scouts and camping rough, but I always miss you all so much when I'm away."

When Gage is full of roasted deer he stretches out on his bedroll with his head toward the fire. His eyes falter as he watches the men light the other two fires. He can barely stay awake while everyone finds a place to lie down within the triangle of heat.

Gage's father has been assigned first watch and sits on his bedroll whittling a willow stick with his hunting knife.

"What're you making?" Gage asks. He's so tired, his tongue feels slow in his mouth.

"A whistle to give to Brindle when we get home." His father turns the stick over in his hand.

"She'll like that," Gage manages to say before he falls asleep.

When Gage opens his eyes, the sky above is black and sparkling with stars. He shivers and rolls onto his side, then drifts quickly toward sleep again, feeling satisfied when he remembers he's on his first scouting mission. But when he hears the yelp of what sounds like a dog, his breath catches in his chest. His brain wakes up fully but he doesn't dare move, doesn't even blink his eyes. In the stillness he can hear the soft padding of feet in the undergrowth, the crinkling of dry leaves, the movement of bodies brushing past branches. His heart pounds. He squints into the darkness and sees the wolves moving beyond the dying firelight, some hungrily lapping at the patch of deer blood where the carcass had been suspended.

When he hears a deep, low growl, close and threatening, Gage reaches for his walking stick and jumps up from his bedroll. He looks quickly around, only to see the night guards slumped over and snoring. Beyond all the sleeping scouts, wolves circle, inching their way closer with each slow step. A shiver runs up Gage's spine and he spins around to find himself face to face with what he assumes is the leader of the pack — a large black snarling wolf.

ROOK

While Da chokes on his soup, I work at holding my face steady to make my lie seem credible.

"I haven't been reading anything in particular. Just skimming through files, looking for something you might not have discovered."

Da wipes his face with a napkin and then dabs at the front of his shirt where he spluttered the pea soup. I can tell he's considering whether or not to tell me something. Finally, he clears his throat.

"Much of what we know as Keepers we have to keep to ourselves. You do realize that?"

I hadn't thought of it in so many words, but I nod.

"Sometimes we discover things that are hard to keep secret. But we can't tell anyone. Not even our best friends," he warns.

"I get it."

"We can't even tell members of our family if they aren't Keepers. There are things I can't ever tell Mam. Or you. Not yet at least."

"Okay."

"If you did, you could put your own life at risk and the survival of everyone in ArHK. You could put the entire purpose of ArHK at risk."

His tone is freaking me out, not to mention the whole putting-the-purpose-of-ArHK-at-risk thing. My heart races so fast it feels like my blood is over-oxygenating and I might faint.

He sighs deeply. "Do you understand the term *religion*?"

"Sure, it was a system of beliefs held by a group of people in the Outside."

He nods again, and I can tell by the way he's staring off in the distance that he's choosing his words carefully.

"Mam discovered the term *God*, actually. When she first came to the Archives, before you were born. God was the figurehead of an early Outside religion known as Christianity. *Christ* was another word for God, said to be the creator of all things. You probably learned in school that there were many religions in the Outside. When the Chosen Ones first came to ArHK, they still practised the religions they brought with them. Eventually, this became problematic, and the Governors elected to ban all religions."

"The Governors can do that? They can stop people from believing in things?"

Da shifts in his seat and looks even more uncomfortable, if that's possible.

"They can try," he says quietly. "But I suspect there are still remnants of some religions kicking around ArHK, even today."

"Did our ancestors believe in God? Was Chosen Family 78 part of the Christianity religion?"

"I'm not sure, Rook. They most likely believed in some higher being. Most Outsiders did." His voice is still hushed, and the way he's glancing around the Archives makes me wonder if we're committing some sort of offence just by talking about religion.

"Why did religions become such a problem?" I whisper.

"I'm still trying to piece that together myself."

When I don't ask another question right away, Da picks up his soup jar and looks like he's ready to leave. But before he can move, my big fat mouth blurts out another question.

"Did anyone from the Outside ever figure out where ArHK is?"

Da considers me for a moment, then he clears his throat.

"I'm not sure what you mean." He pauses briefly but not long enough for me to speak. "And I think we've wasted enough time for one day." He stands up and his tone changes again, back to the one brimming with authority. "It's time to submit the Daily Log. Why don't you come do that now? Give this old computer a rest."

I'm reluctant to go, but I turn off the computer and follow him with my jar of tomato soup. As I walk, I wonder exactly how much trouble we'd be in if Governor Hawk found out what I was reading — and thinking.

I sit at a terminal across from Da and prepare to submit the Daily Log. It's hard to switch my mind from past to present. All I really want to do is read more letters between Jule and Isobel, but I'm sure it's going to be awhile before Da lets me back on the old system.

"Don't forget to cross-reference the reports from yesterday afternoon. I know there's a Repair Report from Manufacturing. Oh, and don't forget about Sandpiper," Da reminds as I pull up the screen.

"I won't forget. There's a death notice too. The Growing Sector submitted one for Hawthorn Miller. Did you know him?"

"Of course! He used to deliver our flour shares when I was apprenticing with Grandmam Ivy. He always had a smile on his face. I'm sorry to hear he's left us."

I begin to fill in the fields for the Daily Log and link the reports.

Population: 5028
Deaths: 1 (<u>Hawthorn Miller</u>**)**
Births: 1 (<u>Sandpiper Sorter</u>**)**
Marriages: 0
Structural Enhancements: 0
Structural Repairs: 1 (<u>Manufacturing Level: Weaving Sector: Ceiling repair by Pod 398.</u>**)**
Permit Requests for Structural Expansion: 0

I think the Daily Log is a waste of time, but Da says it's a good way to track what's happening in ArHK. He says the Governors rely on the statistics to make important decisions, like which sectors are going to need more human resources in the future. It also helps them plan for the secondborn and thirdborn children. Da says it's easier to run comparative queries, too, when information is presented in a consistent format. He always stresses the importance of projecting population growth so the other sectors can keep pace. Apparently, sometime around 120 AT, the Head Keeper miscalculated, and there was a six-month shortage of beans. It was such a crisis nobody has ever forgotten, especially Da.

He can say what he wants about the importance of the Daily Log. But I think he's fanatical about it because he still believes the Outsiders are monitoring our progress, even though he would never admit it.

When the front doors of the Archives open, I can't help but look up. I smile when I see Sparrow running full tilt down the aisle toward me. Her little shoes pound against the floor and her hair streams down her back.

"Rook! Rook! We got out of school early today!" she squeals, doing a little hop when she stops in front of me.

"You did?" I ask, even though I know the afternoon is a school holiday. I swivel in my chair and pull her close so that our noses are almost touching.

"There's a new cartoon. It's about fairies who live in the pumpkin patch and steal from the Growers."

Sparrow's eyes are glowing. She loves when the Entertainers release a new cartoon. She grabs my hand and pulls me from my chair, digging in with her feet until her cheeks turn pink.

"Mam says you can have the afternoon off to watch with me while she works with Da."

I look up at Mam who has arrived behind Sparrow and is nodding, then over at Da who is shooing us toward the front doors.

"By all means," he says. "You don't want to miss the new cartoon."

"Come on. Come on!" Sparrow says as she pulls me to move faster. "We still have to make snacks, and it starts in fifteen minutes."

Although I feel a tug to sneak back into the restricted files, I'm also happy about having an afternoon off with Sparrow. I'm too old to be excited about new cartoons, but we don't often get the pod to ourselves, and I can almost taste the warm popcorn and cold apple cider I know Mam has been saving for this occasion.

When we get back to our pod, Sparrow and I settle in front of the wall screen with our snacks. Sparrow is so excited she can't sit still for longer than two minutes. She squirms on the couch and munches the popcorn so quickly I wonder if she thinks it's the last bowl of popcorn in all of ArHK.

"Slow down there, Sparrow. Save some for the actual cartoon."

She swallows and sits on her hands, then leans over and sips cider through a plexstic straw.

When my personal messenger beeps she rolls her eyes.

"Can't you turn that off, just for the cartoon?"

I glance down and see Ruby's eyebrows narrowed with concern.

"Just let me answer this one," I say. "I'll be quick."

"Rook! What are you doing?" Ruby blurts out.

"Getting ready to watch the new cartoon with Sparrow."

"You and all the other little kids in ArHK!" Ruby laughs.

Sparrow leans over to see Ruby's face. Sparrow waves and Ruby waves back.

"You're in your pod?" Ruby asks.

"Yeah, why?"

"No reason. Just that there was an odd agenda item at council today. We talked about assigning a Governor to review the monitoring practices of the Archives."

"Why?"

"I don't know. Has anything different been happening in the Archives?"

"Not in the past two hundred years," I say as calmly as I can manage. But my heart is churning worse than my stomach, and the tomato soup feels like it might reappear.

"It's that mean old Governor Hawk," Sparrow interrupts. "He just likes to cause trouble, especially for us."

I pull my personal messenger away so Ruby can't see Sparrow. She knows better than to say anything bad about the Governors in front of Ruby. Saying things in the privacy of our pod is one thing, but saying them to others is dangerous.

"Sorry about Sparrow." I laugh outwardly but wince inside. "She's out of sorts because of the cartoon."

The title of the cartoon appears, and Sparrow stands up. She jumps in place, clapping her hands and twisting her hips in time to the soundtrack.

"Rook!" she says. "Get off that thing and watch!"

"You better go," Ruby laughs. She knows what a handful Sparrow can be and, as usual, I appreciate her understanding, especially since she doesn't have younger siblings of her own to deal with. "I figured nothing unusual was going on, but I wanted to check. Unofficially, of course."

"Thanks for having my back."

"Of course. Always. That's what friends are for."

"Hey. So let me guess. Was it Governor Hawk's motion?"

"How did you know?"

I shrug. How can I explain to Ruby that Governor Hawk has it out for my family and always has; that he treats us like we're breaking rules even when we aren't?

"I'm sure it's just something they do whenever a new Keeper comes on," I say.

I try to sound casual, like I'm not at all worried. But nothing could be further from the truth.

GAGE

Gage looks around desperately, willing someone else to wake up. He knows if one wolf moves to attack they all will, and it will mean disaster for the scouting party. He wants to shout and wave his hands, he wants to look threatening so the wolf will think twice about messing with him. But Gage can't muster a single sound. His arms are like dead weights at his side.

The wolf steps one paw forward tentatively, then crouches low. The sound of its growl mixes with the fear vibrating in Gage's brain. Then, without warning, the wolf lunges through the air. Gage raises an arm for protection, and the spell is broken. His legs move and he stumbles, tripping over his father's legs. He lands on the hard ground face down and feels pain shoot through his skull, yet he still can't make a sound. But when he feels the hot weight of the wolf on his legs, he screams his throat raw.

• • •

Some of the men are already awake and ready to move by the time Gage stirs the next morning. As soon as he opens his eyes, he recalls the face of the large black wolf. He thought he was going to die, far from his mother and sister and friends, without ever seeing an ancient city.

"G'morning," his father says. "If you didn't wake up soon I was gonna start shaking you." It's a good-humoured comment and puts Gage at ease.

"Sorry," Gage says as he climbs out of his bedroll. The chill of the early morning air sends a different kind of shiver through his body, and he blows warmth into his hands.

His father leans forward to inspect Gage's nose.

"At least it's not broken."

Gage looks around the camp and sees Chief Coil in the distance, skinning the wolf. If it wasn't for the chief's strong arm and accurate aim with that hunting knife, Gage isn't sure what might have happened. He shakes the thought loose from his mind. Like his father always says, there's no point wasting time and energy on what-ifs.

Some of the scouts, like his father, cinch their bedding into rolls while others sit atop their already tight bundles, chewing skewers of cold meat. Gage is relieved he isn't the last one in bed. Most of the young scouts are just stirring in the near darkness: stretching, yawning, and opening their eyes to the breaking dawn.

"I swear I was awake every ten minutes to make sure the guards didn't nod off again," Jett's father says. "If Gage didn't scream when he did, sure as shootin' one of us wouldn't be here today."

Gage clears his throat and feels the raw patch. "Did I really scream?" he whispers to his father.

His father nods but smiles kindly. "It's a good thing too."

The night guards who fell asleep avoid looking at anyone and concentrate on chewing cold venison. They tear at the meat violently and stare at the ground beyond their feet.

Gage's father heads to the edge of the river. A faint mist hovers over the glassy surface, and in the distance a raven blasts a raucous cry across the sky as it takes flight. Gage crouches beside his father, and together they splash their faces with the clear, cool water.

"Do you think the whole pack would've attacked if everyone was asleep?"

"They mighta. It's pretty unusual for them to approach like they did. But the main thing is, everyone's safe and sound."

"I can't believe the guards fell asleep."

"Don't be too hard on them. They're feeling plenty bad. Things is, any one of us coulda fell asleep. Plenty of us have before and plenty will again."

His father stands up and wipes his face with the tail of his shirt, then tucks it into his pants and cinches his belt. "You ready to get scouting?"

Gage stands up and smiles. "Sure am."

The sky is dark in the west, but a band of light thickens along the edge of the eastern horizon. A few stars hang loosely above but fade quickly. The fires are piles of ash with a few meagre orange embers glowing at the centre, and only a few scraps of bark and twigs are left on the ground. Gage pulls on his overcoat and hoists his pack. He'll get too warm when he's walking, but for the time being the heavy coat keeps him from shivering. He walks the ache out of his legs and straightens his back. It's going to take a few days to get used to carrying the load.

When the men are ready, Chief Coil and his map readers lead the scouts along the river. The men follow in single file, watching the footfalls of those in front. There's a gentle slope down to the water, but in other places the banks are high and steep, and they have to make their way up the embankment through thickets of undergrowth. As they walk, the distance to the far bank narrows and the water quickens. Gage carries his walking stick in the ready position, even though he knows he's safe walking at the back of the pack. On the far side of the river, three turkey vultures circle and float on the updraft, and Gage wonders what carcass lies below. He shivers, not from the cold but from the previous night's memory, grateful none of the scouts were dragged away for the wolves to feed on for breakfast.

Gage's father scans the ground constantly. The farther they walk, the more overgrown humps and lumps they see among the trees, and Gage knows these are old dwellings or meeting structures. He feels his pulse race in anticipation of arriving at the city centre and tries to imagine what he'll see. They emerge from a thick stand of trees and head toward the water's edge for a break, when his father puts his arm across Gage's chest.

"Look," his father says and points downriver.

Gage squints into the sun. He sees what his father is pointing at but his brain can't understand. In the distance is a long arched structure spanning the river. It reaches from one bank to the other, like a giant snake slithering through the air.

Gage can tell by the excited voices he's not the only one who's never seen such a thing before. "What is it?" he whispers to his father.

"It's a bridge," his father says. "It was part of the road system their machines used to travel. Ancient societies had bridges everywhere, over rivers, over other bridges, over ravines. Not just one here or there, sometimes many in a row, Lord knows why. Depending on the river, some bridges were long and high, but others were flat and short. Many broke down and crumbled centuries ago. But some of them are still standing."

Gage stares with his hands above his eyes to block the sun. He wishes he could tell Brindle and his mother all about it, and Pepper too. It's so high above the water he can't imagine what it would be like to walk across. What would happen if someone fell off? How did the machines keep from plunging into the water below?

"Ancient humans musta been awful clever back then. To build something like that."

"It sure is something to see," his father agrees. "But never in all my days have I seen one high as that."

The men continue slowly along the edge of the river toward the bridge. Gage wants to watch it loom bigger but has to watch his footing. There are too many loose rocks to be reckless. But he stops every few steps to sneak a look. The closer they get, the sweatier Gage's hands feel, until he is wiping the slickness down the legs of his overalls. Because he's at the back of the line, he's one of the last to arrive where the others have stopped. From the base of the bridge, he has to tilt his head to keep it in his vision. Its shadow stretches far out into the water.

"We'll rest here 'til the advisers determine if it's safe to cross," Chief Coil calls out.

Gage looks at his father, alarmed.

"He doesn't mean we're gonna walk over it, does he?"

His father sits down in a patch of sun on the bank of the river and leans back with his hands behind his neck. The sun hits his face, and he closes his eyes.

"I think that's exactly what he means."

"But what if it collapses?" Gage gazes toward the top of the bridge. "We'd never survive."

"That's why the advisers are gonna check it out carefully before we walk across."

Gage isn't comforted. He can't help worry about something happening to the whole group. Nobody would ever know what happened. Their families would wait month after month for news or for their return. Gage paces in front of his father's outstretched body. How can he be so relaxed?

"Why do we have to cross it anyway?"

"It must lead to wherever we wanna go," his father says. "Don't worry. Chief Coil won't let us cross if it isn't safe."

"If we don't cross, then what?"

"We could swim," his father says and chuckles, his eyelids still closed to the sun.

Gage doesn't like the thought of swimming across the river either. Even though the air has been warmed by the morning sun, he knows the water is cold. Just washing his face was enough of a feel for this early in spring. Most of the trees don't even have their leaves yet.

"I wish I could look at the map," Gage mutters, then takes his walking stick to explore the bank of the river.

"Don't go too far alone," his father calls out after him.

"I won't," he says and scans his surroundings to be sure there're no wolves peering from the depths of the forest.

"Stay where I can see you."

"I will."

Gage pokes his walking stick at the ground before he takes a step. He taps and listens for hollow sounds. When he hears none, he moves forward. He steps closer to the river, where the trees have grown up along the steep bank. He looks upriver toward the bridge, then downriver where he can see a wide, flat island. When he's ready to take another step, he pokes his stick into the ground. But his stick stops dead. He's hit something solid.

Maybe another wheel? he thinks as he leans over and begins to scrape away the layers of dead leaves and dirt. It takes him a few minutes to uncover the entire length and width of the flat, wide object. He digs around it until he can slide his walking stick under, then he pries it upward.

Gage's heart pounds when he flips over the thin rectangular object, and it falls flat on the ground. He can see faint white letters on a dark background. Is it a sign? Something to help the map readers navigate? He wipes the dirt from the surface so he can make out the words.

"Gee-o-r-ge." He traces his hand under each let-ter the way his mother taught and sounds out the first word.

"Wa-she-ing-t-on."

He pauses and repeats the sounds faster.

"Wash-ing-ton.

"Washington!" he shouts out when the sounds blend together in his brain.

Then, without bothering to read the rest of the words, he runs back to where his father is lying in the sun. His father sits up when he hears the excitement in Gage's voice.

"Dad! There's a sign. Just like you said. With words on it to help us navigate. We found it! We're here! We're in Washington!"

ROOK

Even though it's an exploratory day, Da says he'd like me to work up front on a modern terminal. He doesn't say why, but I suspect he's nervous about my looking at old files. I wonder if he knows what else I might find, or if he's just nervous about what I already found. Or did he find out about the Governor's motion to review the monitoring practices of the Archives?

The first thing I ask the search assistant is: *Where is ArHK?*

Thousands of records come up, and I scan through the first twenty or so before I realize I'm not going to find what I'm looking for. The search function has turned up anything that includes the words *Where* and *ArHK*, but nothing that hints at its actual location.

I try another search: *Where is ArHK located?*

Another list appears on the screen, and I start to sift through them one by one. Quite a few records deal with the locations of resources in ArHK; others make mention of the location of people and functions within ArHK. There are Governor Reports about changing the location of people from one sector to another. But nothing that hints at the location of ArHK.

I lean back in my chair, frustrated, and stare up at the dome above. The sky is quickly turning from pale to bright blue, so I know the lunch hour is fast approaching, and my stomach rumbles in response.

I try as many possible ways as I can to ask about the location of ArHK, although I don't really know what I'm asking or what I even hope to find.

Where is ArHK in relation to the Outside?

How do you get to ArHK?

Where is the Outside?

How do you get to the Outside?

Is the Outside real?

Is ArHK part of the Outside?

Nothing seems to work, and I think back to the letters between Jule and Isobel to remember exactly how they worded their comments about the location of ArHK. Finally, as a last search attempt, I try *secret location of ArHK.*

Three results appear. Two Governor Reports dated 2410 0T, listed in the restricted files, and a file that appears to be an obsolete part of the ancient history curriculum: *USA Presidential Script for ArHK Media Recruitment Campaign from 2251*. Although I understand the document was created in 2251 OT, I'm not familiar with the words *USA, presidential,* or *media*. I open the file and begin to read.

> *Dear citizens, I do not need to tell you that we live in uncertain times, but as President of the United States of America I am here to remind you that such drastic times as these require drastic measures. I thank everyone in this great nation for doing their part. If you are a scholar, I thank you for your innovative thinking. If you are a scientist, I thank you for the rapid and creative solutions you have developed to problems we couldn't fathom twenty years ago. If you are a politician, I thank you for your strong and steady leadership. No matter who you are or what role you fill in society, I thank you for your continued faith, loyalty, and personal sacrifice. The resiliency and brilliance of our human race is truly inspirational.*

I stop reading to absorb the meaning of the words. I suppose the reference to drastic times must mean the era of winds, fires, and floods when, according to the Creationist Stories, the poisonous air made millions of people fall sick and die. I wonder, however, what *drastic measures* refers to.

> Today I am proud to announce the launch of the ArHK Preservation Experiment. For the past twenty years, the United Nations has been working to ensure the survival of humankind, no matter what catastrophes lay ahead. With the co-operation of each and every country on this planet, we have created a facility built to house our collective human intellectual resources.

Although I read through the script quickly, it takes me awhile to piece together the meaning of what is in front of me. Again, there are several words I've never seen before: *country*, *United Nations*, and *Preservation Experiment*. But I'm too impatient to research every word I don't understand.

> The Archives of Human Knowledge has been constructed in a remote, secure, and highly classified location — in short, a secret location. The leaders of the nations around the globe do not know the location of this facility. The pilots who have flown the many materials and supplies great distances do not know the location of this facility. Even the engineers who built this facility with their very own hands do not know where it is located. Secrecy is of the utmost importance. It will guarantee the survival of the information

*kept there, as well as the survival of the people chosen
to protect humankind's most precious resources,
come what may. We hope the location of ArHK will remain a secret for many generations to come.*

Is this for real? Or was the script invented by the
Educators to make history more interesting? And if it's
real, why is it no longer part of the curriculum? Could
it really be that ArHK is a *facility*? If I understand the
word properly, the way people use it now, it sounds like
we're living in some sort of development lab. I skip back
to the top of the document and ponder the phrase *ArHK
Preservation Experiment*, then I shiver. This whole
document makes it sound like we're in some sort of sci-
entific research laboratory.

*This remarkable facility is completely self-sufficient. It
produces its own food, power, and water. It manages
its own waste. It is the first completely sustainable facility in the entire world. And it will be indestructible:
safe from floods, fires, tornadoes, earthquakes, and
explosives. The people chosen to inhabit it will be safe
from natural disasters, disease, starvation, and death.
They will escape the destructive forces of nature that
are levelling our great cities and societies. The people
who live there will be fed, clothed, and housed in the
most technologically advanced facility ever conceived
by humans.*

My personal messenger beeps, and I see Ruby on the other end.

"Do you want to go for lunch?" she asks.

She's in her Governor robe and has her hair carefully pinned back according to regulation.

"Where?"

"We can meet at my pod or go to the market square. My parents are in meetings all day. No apprentices allowed. So we'll have the pod to ourselves."

"Either will do. You choose," I say.

The truth is I'd rather stay and keep exploring the Archives. But Da will insist I take my lunch break.

"Market square. I'm craving a cherry ice."

"Cherry ice for lunch?" I ask.

"No, for dessert. I'll get a lentil pocket for lunch. Meet you out front of the Archives in thirty minutes."

"Sounds good," I say and end the chat.

I immediately turn my attention back to the president's speech.

Now that it is complete, the ArHK Preservation Experiment needs the leading thinkers and scientists from around the world. We need agricultural engineers, electrical engineers, structural engineers, computer science engineers, doctors, surgeons, medical researchers, teachers, political leaders, and everyday labourers. As of today, the facility has the capacity to house 2500 citizens and construction will continue. Applicants will be screened based on skill, expertise, health, cultural heritage, and racial background to ensure a well-rounded and self-sufficient population. There will be psychological evaluations, physical and endurance tests, medical screenings, and criminal checks. Immediate family units will be sent together, based on their most qualified member. We cannot accurately project the length of time the lucky few will be living in this facility, but in six months the transfers will be complete. I encourage you to apply today.

Suddenly the concept of the Chosen Ones takes on a whole new meaning. I'd always imagined the Chosen Ones were, well, actually chosen. Like some fairy princess flew over the population with a magic wand, selecting people at random, instead of being selected from a long list of potential applicants that included every living human being in existence.

I am busy pondering the different meanings of the word *chosen* when my personal messenger beeps impatiently.

"Ruby!" I say out loud and stand so quickly my chair crashes to the floor. I pick it up and rush out of the Archives.

• • •

Ruby and I walk side by side down the Avenue toward the market square, weaving between and through other groups of people also out on their lunch breaks. She starts talking about a proposal she wants to put forward at the next council meeting, but I change the topic.

"How do you even know they have cherry ice today?"

"I don't really know," Ruby admits. "But didn't the ancient philosophers say we create reality with our thoughts?"

I shrug and flatten myself against a vendor stall to make room for a group of boys rushing back to school.

"Well, I've been thinking of nothing BUT cherry ice all morning, so I'm confident I won't be disappointed." Ruby smiles and leads me over to the vendor selling lentil pockets.

"Lettuce and tomato," she tells the vendor, then turns to me. "What are you having?"

"Falafel," I say. "Tahini and sweet onions."

We take our lunches and find a bench in the park.

"How're things in the Archives?" she asks before she takes a bite.

"Good," I say a little too enthusiastically, then cover with, "How's life in the Council Chamber?"

She chews and nods. We sit quietly for a moment and watch people walking past.

"There was a new motion this week about changing the program for the Day One Celebration," she shares finally.

"What kind of change?"

"Putting the Creationist Prayer at the end instead of the beginning. Governor Star thinks it'll flow better that way."

"Do you believe the Creationist stories?" I ask suddenly. "Do you believe in the five hundred Chosen Families and all that? Do you believe in the Outside?"

Ruby doesn't miss a beat or a bite.

"Sure," she says, around a mouthful of food. "Don't you?"

"Yeah, I guess," I admit. "But do you ever wonder where the Outside is? I mean, like in relation to ArHK?"

"It's all around us, I think," Ruby says thoughtfully. "Just like the air we breathe."

"But do you think it's a place you can go to? A physical place?"

"No, I think it's probably just another dimension within ArHK. How could it be someplace else?"

I'm thinking about the Outside and chewing on my falafel when a scratchy voice chills the air. The sound sends a shiver across my shoulder blades and up my neck, but I try to mask my physical reaction by sitting up taller.

"Good afternoon, girls."

"Good afternoon, Governor Hawk. How are you?" Ruby says politely, wiping her mouth again to be sure she isn't committing some Governor offence that could shame her family.

I glance up and swallow hard when I see him staring right at me. I try to hide the sneer that plays at my lips and smile instead. It might look more like a grimace to someone who knows me well.

"I'm fine, thank you for asking. I trust you are enjoying your lunches?"

"Yes, sir," we say in unison.

He continues to drill into my skull with his eyes.

"And you, Rook. You are enjoying your apprenticeship? Keeping your mind on your assignments?"

I nod and hope he can't hear the thrumming of my pulse. In my own ears it's so loud I can barely hear what he says next.

He narrows his eyes and his thin lips press into an even thinner line of disapproval. "I wouldn't want you to get on the wrong path. You never know where you might end up."

The falafel in my mouth feels like sandpaper, and I'm afraid I might choke before I can swallow it. Ruby stops chewing and looks at me too. The sweat starts to pool in my armpits, but I resist the urge to peel off my vest.

"Just pay attention to what your father tells you. He's an excellent Keeper," Governor Hawk says before turning and walking away, the hard soles of his shoes punctuating the sound of happy voices around us.

Ruby finally swallows. "What was *that* all about?" she asks.

I shake my head and force the falafel down my throat.

"I have no idea."

Ruby carefully folds her napkin and tucks it into her back pocket. It's a measured effort, which signals to me that she's making a hard decision.

"Well, I'll tell you one thing if you swear to never repeat it."

I nod and she leans close to my ear.

"You do not want to get on the bad side of Governor Hawk. Even my parents say he has a nasty streak, and they never have a bad thing to say about anyone."

GAGE

Gage is reluctant to step onto the bridge. He kicks at it with the toe of his boot. The surface is hard, like a rock, and worn down like the dirt inside a yurt in the Middle after years of being on the same patch of ground. Metal numbers — 2159 — are inset at the base and around these, pockets of dried weeds and grass struggle to grow now that spring has arrived. A fuzzy brown caterpillar inches along the desolate surface. Its chances of survival are slim, and Gage resists an urge to reach down and tuck it into his pocket for safekeeping.

"C'mon. The bridge isn't gonna bite you," his father teases from a few steps ahead. "We need to catch up to the others."

"I just don't like it," Gage says.

He stops to watch the scouts moving away and above him, as if they are climbing a hill. Their steps are tentative, but when they turn and look around Gage sees their faces full of curiosity. Only Gage seems to be afraid of the structure, and he wonders if he should have waited until he was sixteen, or even seventeen, to come on a mission.

"Doesn't feel safe," he mutters, then, like a mule, takes one stubborn step forward.

"Hurry, Gage! You have to see this," Jett yells from the middle of the expanse. He's dropped his load at his feet and is pointing at something in the distance.

Gage takes a deep breath and one last, long look at his father, who nods with encouragement.

"You best go ahead. Mom doesn't want us to be together."

His father turns and leans into the incline, strides up the narrow hill.

To start, Gage stares down at his feet, afraid to look beyond the edge of the bridge. A breeze ruffles the hair around his neck, and he takes off his hat so the wind can't lift it into the air and send it into the water below. The sun burns hot on the crown of his head, and sweat beads along his hairline. Again he glances up at the other young scouts who have dared to walk closer to the edge where, he can now see, there's a barrier to keep them from slipping off. They grab the barrier with both hands and lean over, their necks bent at a sharp angle, their faces mesmerized by what they see below. As Gage looks up, something catches his eye, and he turns his head. Then he stops dead in his tracks.

"Oh my Lord!" he whispers, but the wind gusts suddenly and whips his words away.

Beyond the river, the ancient city spreads out before him. There are hundreds, maybe even thousands, of old dwellings in the distance, silhouetted against the horizon like a vast forest. It goes on forever, walls upon walls, stretching as far as he can see. Some walls are joined together into squares, others stand alone. It reminds him of standing on top of a high hill about a year after they joined the scouting party. They'd hiked to the top of an incline and stared out at a valley below, the greens of the leaves and the brown-greys of the tree trunks blending into a beautiful mosaic.

"It could take us years to explore all that," he whispers.

"Yep, it very well might," his father replies quietly from his side. "The other scouting parties are still exploring parts of New York."

Wide-eyed, Gage turns to see his father smiling down at him, his eyes sparkling and a dimple denting his cheek.

"It's quite the sight, isn't it, son?"

"I had no idea." Gage breathes the words, and they float as soft and light as milkweed floss on a gentle fall day. His emotions catch in his chest and, trapped, fill him with thanksgiving. "I had no idea it'd be this remarkable."

They stand for what seems like hours staring at the ancient city, at the river winding through the tangled geometry of walls and forest, at seagulls soaring overhead, at squares and sparkles of sunlight glinting off flat structures and the surface of the water. It's a jumbled mass of overgrown structures so complex Gage has a hard time comprehending what's before him. He looks greedily, trying to take it all in, trying to commit every remarkable detail to his memory so he can recall it all later during a moment of quiet. But it's impossible to know which parts to study first, so his eyes scan back and forth randomly.

"See the old road pattern?" His father points in the distance at the lines between the brick and stone structures, where the trees haven't grown as tall or as thick.

"And more bridges, I think." Gage points at a structure similar to what they're standing on, even though it doesn't cross a river.

"Sure looks like a bridge. The Scholars say that in New York City the ancient people had those things everywhere, three deep in places. Apparently, they needed them to keep the machines from piling up like logjams. That's how many machines they had back then, all moving and scuttling around like an ant colony."

Jett's eyes are gleaming when he trots back toward Gage.

"Isn't it something?" he asks. "Did you ever imagine such a sight?"

Gage is at a loss for words and shakes his head.

"I tell you, I've seen towns before. But nothing compares to this. It's unbelievable! Wedge spent the past two days bragging about all the ancient buildings he's seen, but by the way his jaw's hanging, I know he's never seen this many!"

Jett's excitement has transformed him. His limbs twitch, and he rubs the back of his head repeatedly as if he's trying to keep the image of the expansive city from spilling out of his mind.

"C'mon. It's even a better view at the top," Jett says, then sprints back toward his father.

Gage and his father are left alone, and Gage welcomes the space to explore his own feelings and thoughts as they tumble around inside him. Is it really possible there's nobody, not a single human, in all that space?

Gage wishes he could stay and admire the view longer, but Chief Coil and the map readers move on and begin descending toward the far side of the river. His father follows, but Gage is reluctant to move. He's no longer worried about falling off the edge or about the structure collapsing; he's eager to keep admiring the view. But instead, he tucks his thumbs into the straps pressing against his shoulders, hoists the pack farther up his back, and follows the others.

The map readers flank Chief Coil, and together they trace a route on the map as they walk into the depths of the city. From the top of the bridge, Gage had no idea how tall the structures stood, but as he walks among them he's amazed. Some cast shadows farther than the tallest tree he's ever seen. When he tilts his head back and looks up so he can see past the brim of his hat, it feels like his heart is up there among the open walls, floating high and free.

"I didn't know they'd be so tall," Gage says to his father, who stays close as they walk along an overgrown road.

"Some woulda been government buildings, where leaders spent their days making laws and running things. Kinda like our Scholars. Others would be factories, where they made things like furniture and clothes. Even their machines were built in these huge structures. And some structures housed many families, hundreds of them. Every family woulda had their own private compartment inside the tallest buildings, stacked on top of each other like a pile of firewood."

Gage points to a structure with rows upon rows of window openings.

"Maybe that was a compartment building where many families lived? But how on earth did they get to the top?"

"Stairs. Lots and lots of stairs," his father says. "They musta had strong legs from so much climbing."

"Did the ancient cities have boreholes for water, like they do in the Middle? So everyone didn't have to walk down to the river every day with buckets and water bladders?"

His father considers this question. "I don't really know. It might be a question for Chief Coil or the Scholars."

"Where did they wash and hang their clothes on laundry day?"

Gage's father shakes his head and shrugs, but by then Gage has more questions swimming in his brain.

"How did the hunters find enough game to keep their cities fed? And where were all the gardens and crops grown?"

"You're just full of questions, aren't you?" his father asks, but in a good-humoured way.

"There's so much I don't understand," Gage says wistfully. "I want to know more."

"We all do," his father agrees.

Everywhere Gage looks there are crumbling walls, lumps of grass and leaves, piles of broken brick tangled with weeds, and thickets of underbrush. They carry their walking sticks carefully at their waists and watch the men in front, careful to take the same path.

It takes his brain a moment to separate the endless sprawl into individual dwellings, but eventually he begins to see patterns. With two identical hollows at the top of a squat square structure, and a large gaping hole in the centre by the ground, he sees a hungry face waiting to swallow him whole, beckoning him to come close with a rolled out tongue. Gage shivers and moves quickly to catch up to his father.

It takes a moment of looking at the bright blue sky to settle himself, to remind himself that the world is still the same one he's always known; it just looks different. And before long, he settles into the rhythm of moving steadily through the ruined city and follows the other scouts in an absorbed trance. So his heart leaps hard when a commotion at the front of the pack shatters the sunny afternoon. Two scouts break rank and run into a thicket of trees surrounded by a crumbling wall. They move so quickly Gage isn't even sure who's disappeared. Chief Coil raises his hand and everyone stops, holding their walking sticks still and their breath even stiller.

"What're they doin'?" Gage whispers to his father. "What 'bout caverns?"

His father places a single finger against his lips, and Gage turns his head slowly toward the space where the scouts disappeared. Every scout stands motionless, their eyes trained in the same direction and narrowed against the sunlight.

Suddenly, shouts and moans, grunts and squeals come from behind the crumbling walls. It sounds like one of the scouts is being slit from the top of his throat clear through to the bottom of his belly. Gage's heart slams up against the inside of his chest, and his mouth feels as dry as kindling.

What if it's another pack of wolves? Or worse, what if his father was wrong and Lurkers do exist? Gage scans his eyes from side to side, chastising himself for letting his guard down. He looks into the shadows of the trees and deteriorating structures to see if there's any movement, the shine of eyes staring back. What if they're surrounded?

The shrill screams and grunts continue from beyond the broken building, followed by the sound of bones being smashed. *Why doesn't Chief Coil send backups?* Gages wonders. Gage glances at Jett, a few paces away, and sees the tension high in his shoulders, the fear set tight in his jaw. In fact, he sees tension and fear in the faces of all the scouts. He wonders what he should do if they're attacked? Run or stand his ground? Death by cavern or death by Lurker? He wishes he'd asked his father more questions when they were talking about the dangers of scouting, like what made him think there were no more Lurkers? But he's too afraid to make a sound and he has no feeling in his legs. He's completely numb with fear.

ROOK

parrow is watching a cartoon on the wall screen. She and Mam are just back from the public baths, so Sparrow's wet hair is still clinging darkly to her head, and her cheeks are red from soaking in the hot pools. Da is in his armchair reading a book from the old times, the sort made out of paper with hard covers. It comes from the Great Hall of Human Knowledge, and he isn't supposed to bring it to the pod, where the temperature and humidity aren't monitored. In fact, he isn't even supposed to enter the Great Hall except at designated times. Whenever I ask him if he's breaking a rule though, he avoids answering the question and says he figures the Governors would be happy if they knew he was bringing his work home with him.

But we're sworn to secrecy whenever he has a book in the pod and when someone taps at the front door, he hides it in the drawer beside his chair before we can answer the door.

"Sparrow, sweetie, time for bed," Mam calls out from the kitchen.

Sparrow looks to Da to see if she has a chance of begging for a few more minutes, but Da takes off his reading gloves and pats his lap. Sparrow stands up reluctantly and joins him on the armchair for a quick cuddle.

"Mam's right. It's time for bed, and we have the ArHKball quarter-final in the morning."

Sparrow brightens at the mention of ArHKball.

"The Sorters are going to win!" she announces. "Baby Sandpiper will bring them luck."

"I bet you're right," Da says. "Now, if you go to bed right this minute, there's time for a story."

Sparrow nods eagerly.

"Then say good night to Rook."

"Good night, Rook," Sparrow says quietly as Da helps her onto his back for a ride.

"Sleep well, Sparrow," I say, then wave my hand the way Governor Hawk does during the Day One parades. Sparrow laughs. She always laughs when I make fun of Governor Hawk, even though we both know it makes Da nervous.

When Da and Sparrow are out of sight, I sneak over to the armchair and pick up the book. I'm not supposed to touch it without reading gloves because of the oils on my fingers, but I have pretty clean hands, and besides, I figure one day I'll have access to it anyway. The book is called *Religions of the New Millennium: 2000–2200.* I laugh when I think about 2000 OT being the *new* millennium.

I can hear Da in the bedroom reading to Sparrow and Mam in the kitchen cleaning the dinner dishes, so I flip through the book. It's split into various sections: Christianity, Islam, Judaism, Buddhism, Hinduism, Sikhism, Rastafarianism, Scientology. I'm surprised there were so many religions back then, and I wonder why they needed them. What exactly was so important about religions? Did people collect them the way Grandmam Ivy collected plants or the way Sparrow collects all the little cartoon action figures? I also wonder if Da decided to read up on religions after our conversation about God and ... what was that religion he told me about? Christianity?

When I hear Da saying good night to Sparrow, I replace the book and scurry into the kitchen. Mam is stacking the dinner dishes into the cupboard. Like Sparrow, her face is still glowing from the public baths, and her wet hair is combed back off her face.

"Ruby and I are going to the Thrill Park for a little while. We won't be long."

She looks up and smiles softly. She's always relaxed when she returns from the public baths. "Have fun. Don't forget tomorrow's a sports day."

"I won't," I say and kiss her on the cheek. She smells of her favourite lavender soap, and I suddenly hate that I lied to her.

I hope Ruby doesn't come by the pod and blow my cover. I'd warn her to stay away, but because she's so strict about keeping rules, I'm not sure how she'd react about being my alibi, especially if she knew what I was really doing.

On my walk to the Archives, I plan my approach. Da often stays late or goes back after dinner to finish a report, but I've never gone in alone after hours. I wonder how many tries on the security system before an alarm goes off?

I've watched Da lock and unlock the Archives hundreds of times, so I clear my mind and try to picture the pattern he makes when he sets the security system. If my security code is RKXVII, I reason, there's a good chance his is FKXVI.

When I get to the front doors of the Archives I try to look casual. I nod politely at the ice vendor who is passing by with his empty cart, heading back to the Growing Sector for the night, then punch my best guess into the security pad. The door clicks and I slip inside.

The dome inside the Archives is dark, but there's enough light shining in from the Avenue that I can see my way to the back of the hall. I sit down at the old computer and turn it on. When the system is ready to go, I find my way to 2412 and open each month and week to find the Citizen Communication files. It's cumbersome having to go month by month, week by week. It would have been much easier if all the citizen communications were kept in one folder and I could search by date. But then again, back then they probably weren't expecting someone like me to be nosing around their files hundreds of years later.

Even though it doesn't do me much good at the moment, I'm grateful the Records Management Engineers updated the filing systems. It could take me weeks to search out and read what I imagine are hundreds of letters, and I'll be lucky to steal an hour now and then.

My fingers get used to the touch screen keyboard, and before long I'm flying through the filing system, opening, scanning, and closing files. I wish I could download the files onto my personal messenger and read them in bed. But I know restricted files can't be copied. When I was a young girl, Governor Marsh tried to download a restricted file. The security alarms went off and Da had to ask him to leave. I never saw Governor Marsh after that. I wonder what happened to him? I wonder what he was reading?

For the first few years, letters for Chosen Family 78 arrived and were sent in a predictable pattern. Every week one arrived from the Outside and a return was sent back within a day. After that there were fewer letters and longer gaps between. I decide the best thing is to jump ahead in five-year increments. Then if I find nothing, I can start looking back. As near as I can figure, I have about an hour before I need to log off, lock up, and get back home before my parents get suspicious and beep me or, worse, think to launch the tracking system on my personal messenger. I have a fakescript ready if I need to override the system, a video I shot weeks ago of Ruby and I in Central Park, but that's a risky move best saved for an absolute emergency.

I skip forward five years, then ten, fifteen, twenty. The last letter I can find from Jule is dated fifteen OT years after ArHK was first inhabited by the Chosen Ones. I don't have time to keep searching, so I open it and read.

My Dearest Isobel,

I apologize it has taken me so many months to write back. I realize you must be worried sick. Glen and the twins and I are fine, but I have not been in touch with Joel or Elisa for months. It's a very long story but the country is in chaos. Most of New York City has been evacuated because of severe flooding. It happened in June and almost overnight. We had no choice but to flee and have ended up in old Kentucky. We didn't get a choice where to go. The government sent refugees like us to various states based on our zip codes. We think Joel might be in old Tennessee but we have no way of knowing for sure.

Gas and electricity are scarce so travel is out of the question. Food is also scarce. We are living in a camp southeast of Lexington. We have run into a few people from our neighborhood, which is nice, but for the most part we feel very isolated. The government provides rations and has given us a three-bedroom trailer to live in, but conditions are crowded. There are two families per trailer and with more and more people arriving from the coastal areas each day, we never know when another family will be assigned to live with us.

I don't want you to worry about us, but I don't want you to think we have forgotten about you either. Power everywhere is unpredictable and there are very few computers in camp, which have to be shared by everyone.

I know there was talk last year of giving the people in ArHK the chance to come home, but I beg you to stay put. Tell everyone to stay put. Things are not good anywhere. I only pray that you are still safe and protected, wherever you are.

No matter what happens, I love you and I am thankful you are safe. I hope the weather settles soon so we can build new lives, even if it means moving to the Midwest and putting up with tornadoes.

My time on the computer is up and the line is long, so I have to sign off now.

Your loving sister, Jule

The next file in the folder is the return letter from Isobel, dated the same day. I glance at the clock and estimate I have five minutes before I need to be back on the Avenue. If I'm out too late, Da will definitely check the location of my personal messenger. If he sees that I'm on the Avenue, I'm safe. If he sees me in the Archives, I'm in more trouble than I can imagine.

Dear Jule,

You have no idea how distressing it was to get your news. Many people in ArHK are getting similar reports from their families, and the mood here is very sombre. Even as I write, the Governors are having an emergency council session to decide how to deal with the situation.

There are rumblings of a revolt here, headed up by those in the Growing Sector who have formed a sort of counter government. The opposition leader is demanding we be allowed to return home to support our families. A group from the

Health Sector already petitioned the Governors to let every Chosen Family bring displaced family members to ArHK. They estimated we could house and support at least three times our current population. But this motion was struck down immediately due to projected fuel shortages. Apparently there is only enough fuel to move every member of ArHK one way.

I have to say, even though you have told us to stay put, if I had a choice, I would come home no matter what I would find. Fifteen years is a long time not to see the sun or feel the rain or wind. Maybe I have romanticized life on the outside, but the longing is more than I can bear some days. What is the point of living when all of your family and friends are suffering? I suppose in the face of your challenges, ours seem trivial, and I apologize.

We no longer get news from the outside. The Governors banned all news broadcasts as they were bad for morale. Some people say our letters are being monitored — both in and out — and some swear they are being tampered with. I don't believe it though, as I cannot imagine how much worse your news could be. I suppose I will never know if you receive what I have written, altered or not. I pray to God you get this because I want you to know I think about you every day and we pray every night for your safety.

It pains me to sign off, but I am hoping this gets to you while you are still at whatever computer you have found to use and while there is still enough power to receive this message.

With much love, Isobel

I close the file and make a mental note to start my next exploratory day searching for any Governor Reports that mention banned news broadcasts from the Outside. The more I find out about life in early ArHK, the more I'm uncertain about everything I've ever been taught. I lean back in my chair to think. Did Da and Mam experience this much uncertainty when they were apprentice Keepers?

I'm still trying to understand the implications of what I've just read when my personal messenger beeps. Panic rises in the back of my throat and I swallow the taste of bile.

"Please let it be Ruby," I whisper.

But it's my father trying to contact me, and I'm definitely not on the Avenue. My armpits are suddenly damp with sweat, and my mind kicks into overdrive with a mix of panic and self-doubt. I consider running the fakescript for Central Park, but then my brain reminds me that telling a lie and showing a lie are very different things. What if Da sees Ruby tomorrow and asks if we had a good time together? What if Ruby's parents come into the Archives later this week, and Da mentions how much time we are spending at Central Park lately? Then I'd be in trouble with both Ruby *and* Dad, and I'd have to come up with an even better lie.

Instead, I take the safer option. I turn off the computer terminal and rush to the front of the Archives. I peek out the front window and sigh with relief when I see the Avenue is empty. There isn't a single Cleaner or Night Guard in sight, and the street lights are already dimming in preparation for the sleep hours. *How long have I been buried in those files?* I wonder, as I slip out the door. I glance up and down the Avenue to be sure nobody has seen me, then scurry home as quickly as I can.

GAGE

When the two scouts finally emerge from behind the crumbling wall, they're covered in blood. Even their faces are smeared brown and red. The taller scout is limping. But they're both smiling and dragging a wild boar behind them. A collection of whoops rises above the scouts like a flock of birds. Nothing bolsters the mood of camp more than knowing that, after a long day of walking, they have a good dinner ahead of them. Gage joins in the celebratory cheer and forgets about the fear that just moments ago radiated from the pit of his chest.

When the wild boar is quartered and packed, the scouts continue along the old roadway toward the centre of the ancient city of Washington. Gage can feel his excitement mount as they walk past more and more ruins. At first they pass mostly small structures that his father explains are thought to have belonged to single families, although Gage can't imagine what a single family would do with so much space. Even the smallest dwellings look to be the size of at least five yurts.

But the closer they get to the centre, the larger the structures loom and the more unusual the shapes. Every scout in the group knows there are a thousand important discoveries waiting to be made beyond the crumbling walls, and he can barely focus knowing he could be within shouting distance of the Ship of Knowledge.

He can't help but let his imagination run wild as he thinks about what life in the ancient world might have been like with machines galloping by, people crowding the streets, and buildings shining with the lights of a thousand tiny fires. How different were those ancient people? Were there young men his own age who walked along the roads? Where did they go every day? What did they do to help their communities survive?

The scouts at the front of the pack stop to examine something in the middle of the overgrown road, and Gage hurries forward.

"C'mon, Dad," he calls back when his father keeps a steady pace.

"You go ahead. I'll be there'n a minute. Careful where you step."

When he approaches, Gage sees a long brown structure lined with a row of window openings. It's anchored in the middle of the forest by trees and bushes that have grown in and around it.

"If the summer leaves were out, we'd never have seen it," Chief Coil says and pokes the side with his walking stick. Chunks of rusted metal crumble to the ground.

When the scouts at the front of the group move, Gage sees the structure has wheels front and back on each side, like the one he and Jett found in the forest.

"What sorta machine is it?" Jett asks.

"It was called a bus," Chief Coil says. "These machines held fifty or more people at once."

One of the scouts tries to climb inside, but the floor is so decayed there's nowhere to step.

"I read about buses in one of Mom's books," Gage tells Jett, who is standing nearby.

"What happened in the book?" Jett asks. "Like with the bus?"

Gage turns back his memory to a time he and his mother were alone together in the yurt. It was evening in early winter, so the Middle was already tucked up in darkness, and the fire in the stove was burning warm and bright but not hot enough to keep the drafts completely at bay. Brindle hadn't been born yet and his father hadn't returned home from hunting, so his mother draped a quilt around Gage's shoulders and made him sit at the table. She told him not to squirm and warned that if he knocked over the candle it would burn the book to ashes. That was the first time Gage saw a book. When she laid it out on the table and opened the bright red cover, it felt like she was gifting him the world. He remembers how hard it was to keep his hands to himself. He so badly wanted to stroke the smoothness of the paper, trace the letters with his fingers. He had just mastered the alphabet so was eager to point out the letters he knew. But that day his mother made him sit on his hands and listen. Then she showed him how the letters huddled together with their friends to form words. She pointed out the smallest words first: *is*, *it*, *the*, and *me*. One of the words in that first book had been *bus*, and Gage remembers thinking it looked like a goat, its long neck stretching up from its flat back.

He turns his face toward Jett and watches his friend studying the bus.

"A sister and a brother took the bus to school. It was yellow. And the steps up into it were hard for the little sister to climb. The two kids sat together and waved goodbye to their mother. They held their lunch boxes on their knees."

"Lunch boxes?" Jett laughs. "They did such strange things back then. Why would you want to carry your lunch in a box when you can just carry it in your pocket?"

With that, Jett pulls a strip of venison meat from his pocket, unwraps it from a square of waxed cloth, and tears off a piece with his teeth.

"You're sure lucky to have a book like that and to get to learn how to read," Jett says while he chews.

Gage thinks about the collection of books tucked away in his mother's private trunk. They're wrapped in layers of waterproofed deer hide and packed between wool blankets. They only take the books out on special occasions, and never for long. But it doesn't matter that they don't see the books often. His mother knows them by heart.

Gage's father finally catches up and walks around the entire machine.

"We saw a row of these farther inland once. There musta been twenty or thirty, all lined up nose to tail. We were in a city called Pittsburgh, I think. I thought we'd see more of this sorta thing by now. Normally the ancient cities are full of them."

"Why do you think it's here?" Gage asks.

"They say people abandoned their machines when they ran out of energy. Or there mighta been a flood or fire, and the people had to run away quick on foot. Who knows?"

Eventually the scouts lose interest in the bus and continue along their way. But Gage is still trying to imagine the last day the bus moved and why it stopped in the middle of the road. He thinks about the people, like the brother and sister in his mother's book, who would have been abandoned and had to find another way home. He's heard the stories from the times of the Storm Ages, about how families got separated in the chaos of fires, floods, and tornadoes; how sometimes they never found one another. Parents took pity on orphaned children and raised them as their own, and kids had to seek out new families when their own parents stopped coming home with food. Gage shivers at the thought of Brindle wandering around the Middle, lost, alone, and hungry.

When the trees thin out, Gage catches sight of more ruins. One structure has a long set of stairs in front, and one, he sees when he walks close enough, isn't square at all, but curved like a yurt.

He looks everywhere and tries to take in as much as he can. At one point the ancient road dips into a dark cavern. They see the silhouettes of machines inside but don't investigate. Instead, they climb an embankment and get back to where they can use the river to keep their bearing. The ancient roads are completely overgrown in places. They're not easy to follow but, still, the scouts find enough of a path through the trees to keep them going in the right direction.

After walking for some time through a thick forest, Gage begins to wonder if the map readers have made a mistake and led them to the other side of the city. Then, without warning, they come upon a square white building flanked by a row of thick, tree-trunk-like structures without branches.

"What're those tall things lined up across the front?" Gage leans over and asks his father.

"Haven't a clue," his father says. "I've never seen anything like that. But they must mean the structure had some sorta special purpose. People did that back then. Used design features to let others know it was an important place."

The map readers lay two maps side by side on an animal hide on the ground and look back and forth from one to the other. They send a scout through the forest, back toward the river to determine how far away it is. When the scout returns, Chief Coil leads everyone around the structure, where they see every side is protected by the same tall, round white tree trunks.

"It could be this place here. The one called the Lincoln Mem-or-ial," one of the map readers says to Chief Coil and points at one of the maps.

The news travels through the group like wildfire after a drought.

Chief Coil leads the group through the underbrush and around the structure. On the far side, they find a wide set of stairs. There are more than twenty stairs, maybe more than thirty, and everyone climbs them tentatively until it's clear the steps are solid, and then they climb a little faster. Gage looks up at the white tree trunks as he steps closer. He's near the front of the group when he gazes up the height of the structure and feels suddenly small and insignificant. He knows how much work it takes to construct a single yurt and can't imagine how many years it must have taken to build something so large and solid.

When the scouts reach the top of the staircase, there's a collective gasp. Inside the building is an alcove where the figure of a man sits on a throne. He's enormous, more than twenty times the size of any man Gage has ever seen, and this, he knows, is the most astonishing statue *any* of the scouts have ever seen. Even Chief Coil is speechless.

"There are words!" Gage shouts as he approaches the statue. "Above the man!"

The words are faded and some have disappeared behind centuries of dirt, but Gage can make out a few. He starts to sound them out.

"Tem-ple. Hearts. Peo-ple. Saved. Un-i-on. Mem-o-ry." Gage pauses.

"Memory of ... Linc-lon ... En-shrined For. Ever," one of the other young Readers adds.

Chief Coil smiles at the group before him.

"This *must* be the Lincoln Memorial. Bravo to our map readers! We're at the centre of the ancient city at last," he says. "We made it!"

The scouts send up an enormous cheer, and the forest echoes with the noise. Gage is the only scout who stays silent and looks down at the ground. He doesn't know what to do with the emotions inside him. They take up so much space it feels like his eyes might start leaking again.

The scouts set up camp during the late afternoon in a place that was once called West Potomac Park. It's a heavily forested area just beyond the Lincoln Memorial, surrounded by remnants of roads on three sides and the river on the fourth. Inside the park the trees are tall and broad, and the undergrowth is dense. There are no structures nearby, and Gage hopes that means there are no caverns either. There are also pools of water within the forest. Chief Coil says they could be remnants of other ancient monuments. He says the map shows that the forest they are camping in was once full of monuments: monuments to wars, monuments to people, even a monument to the ancient city itself.

Gage and his father set up a lean-to to protect them from the cold and rain; then they go with the other men to collect firewood. Chief Coil has given strict instructions to stay within the boundaries of the forest for safety and not to cross the ancient roads until an exploration plan is in place.

From the edge of the forest overlooking the river, Gage and his father see another bridge in the distance, but this one has collapsed in the middle.

"They had so many bridges, so many buildings. I can't for the life of me figure how they built so many structures," Gage says.

"There were lots more people back then. The Storm Ages wiped out billions, they say. And they had mighty powerful machines."

"Do you think we'll ever be as great as they were back then? Do you think humans can rebuild all this?" Gage motions at the crumbling city.

"I dunno. Maybe we aren't meant to rebuild."

When they return to their lean-to, Gage unrolls his bedding. Then he stretches out with his hands behind his head.

"I can't wait to get exploring. I wonder who I'll be paired with?"

"We're all anxious to get going, but we have to be patient. It's gonna take months and months, even years, to explore and collect what's here. I'm sure the messengers will bring back other scouting parties eventually. But I wish we could get started now too." Gage's father stretches out beside him, and they stare up at the deer hide above them.

"What would it hurt if we just had a little look around? Maybe walked between the buildings but didn't go inside?"

"It's sure a temptation, isn't it? But it has to be done right and safely. We can't afford to lose any men. And if something happened this early in the search, people'd think it was a bad omen. It'd throw off the whole exploration."

They rest together in silence until they hear Chief Coil calling everyone together.

"Let's go," Gage's father says. "He must have something important to announce."

Chief Coil is standing by a blazing fire, and when the scouts arrive they sit on the ground around him.

"We're gonna begin our exploration in the morning. At daybreak, two scouts will return to base camp to give our families the news. Any volunteers?"

Gage doesn't dare raise his hand or his head. He has no intention of missing out on his first real scouting mission when he's so close. Finally, whether they volunteer or are chosen, Chief Coil selects Jett and his father to return to base camp and send messengers by horseback to the Middle with the news that Washington has been discovered.

"When you come back, bring a pair of scouts. That way they can return to base camp and escort the new scouting party from the Middle while you stay and join the search missions," Chief Coil instructs.

Gage sees the disappointment on Jett's face and feels bad. While he wouldn't mind seeing his mother and Brindle, or getting a chance to tell Pepper all that he's seen, there's nothing that could stop him from his first day of exploring.

"Every scouting party will be assigned a structure chosen by the Scholars. You'll need to be thorough. Don't leave any corner unexplored. Any artefacts you find will be collected and marked on the maps so we can record the location for the Scholars."

Like the other young scouts, Gage listens intently.

"Now, I need all the Readers to come up so I can put you into scouting parties."

At first Gage doesn't move. It isn't until his father nudges him that Gage finds his feet and steps tentatively toward Chief Coil.

"Ah yes, our newest Reader. Are you looking forward to tomorrow?" Chief Coil asks Gage.

"Yes, sir. I don't know if I'll get any sleep tonight."

There are eleven Readers, including Gage. The remaining scouts are divided into groups so there are three scouts to each party. Some men are selected to stay in camp to act as guards, messengers, and artefact recorders. They will also construct crates to transport the artefacts back to the Middle. And, of course, Chief Coil will also stay at camp to make sure the exploration runs smoothly.

Like his father predicted, Gage is paired with two experienced scouts. The first, Harley, is a father with two young daughters back at base camp. Gage doesn't know the girls well, only that the youngest is Brindle's age. Harley is tall and thin like a walking stick. The second is Pepper's uncle, Winch, who is as broad and strong as a bison.

When Uncle Winch steps up to join his party, he puts his meaty hand on Gage's shoulder. Gage is so nervous he can't even look into his face.

"So, I hear you've taken a shining to my niece, huh?"

Gage looks up at the man and swallows in response. Suddenly he's not quite as sure as he had been about setting out to scout in the morning.

ROOK

The next morning is a sports holiday, so we're not expected to go to the Archives until after lunch. It's funny how fast things can change. A week ago I would have been happy with a morning away from the Archives, and now it seems like a punishment.

I've never been much into sports. It's hard to get excited when our teams lose in the first round every time. We don't have a very athletic population in the Knowledge Level. The strongest teams always come from the Manufacturing and Waste Management Levels, or from out in the Growing Sector. But despite my reluctance, I get ready for the last game of the quarter-finals: the Propagators against the Sorters.

Mam has packed us a lunch to eat while we watch the game. I'm thankful there will be at least one distraction. I'm also thankful Da hasn't questioned me about where I was the previous night. I know there's a chance he didn't check my location before he beeped me, but I'm still nervous.

While I avoid Da, Mam double-checks that everything is by the door, and Sparrow hops around the living room on one leg. She has her whistle gripped between her teeth so she can cheer for her favourite team, which this time is the Sorters because they have a brand new baby. Mam and Da and I always side with whatever team Sparrow chooses since none of us really cares who wins.

"I feel bad for the essential services workers. They never get to watch the games," Sparrow says.

"I'm sure they take turns. It doesn't take everyone in the Utility Sector to monitor the power and ventilation systems," I point out.

"Did you remember the lemon drinks?" Mam asks as Da pulls open the front door. "I put them in the chilly bin to keep them cold."

"Yes, I remembered. Now we better get moving or we won't get a good spot."

His tone is tense, I think. Or am I imagining it?

Mam picks up the picnic pack and I grab the blanket roll. Da hoists the chilly bin onto his back, and we all file out the door. The street is already busy with people headed for the stadium, and when I look toward the Avenue I can see it's shoulder to shoulder.

"Hurry or we're going to be late," Sparrow says as she skips ahead.

The whistle around her neck swings back and forth. I can already feel a headache starting.

We're approaching the stadium when Da stops walking and looks uneasy. He plasters a phony smile across his face.

"Governor Hawk, sir. Good to see you. Really looking forward to the game," Da says nervously. I swear whenever that man gets near us Da starts to sweat.

Governor Hawk dips his head quickly in greeting and Mam forces a smile in response. He makes a point of looking directly at me with his beady, creepy black eyes and holds my gaze for a moment. Then he melts into the crowd. Da looks at me with a question on his face, and Mam shivers but tries to hide her discomfort.

"That guy gives me the creeps," I say, because something needs to be said.

"He has a crooked nose," Sparrow chimes in and I want to hug her.

"That's enough, girls," Da says sternly and looks around to be sure nobody has heard us criticizing a Governor. It makes me wonder if Governor Hawk has super-sensitive hearing or if Da's been caught bad-mouthing him before. Whatever the reason for the obvious tension, we drop the subject. Normally we could go on for hours talking about all the things we dislike about Governor Hawk, but today I'm happy to let Da cut us off.

By the time we get inside the stadium it's obvious we're never going to get seats. It even takes us a while to find an opening on the spectator hill, and then it's only because Heath's family makes room for us to spread out our blanket.

The ice treat vendors and popcorn sellers are making their rounds through the crowds. Sparrow's eyes light up, but Da tells her to wait until after lunch. I sit down and try to get comfortable on the slope. I know it's going to be a long morning. Heath shifts down to sit beside me.

"Hi, Rook," he says.

"Hi," I say back.

He doesn't say anything for a long time after that and I'm grateful. I watch the opening ceremonies and look around the crowd to see if any friends are nearby. All I see, though, are a few kids I used to go to Instructional School with, before we graduated into our apprenticeship years.

"Did you hear I'm compressing Curriculum Seven and Eight? We applied to the Head Educator and he approved it. My teacher says I might as well get on with my apprenticeship instead of sitting through another term of school. I've completed the whole curriculum already," Heath says.

In my opinion, even though Heath is clever academically, he's slow socially. He doesn't pick up on facial expressions or non-verbal clues the way most people do. Even Sparrow understands about personal space and body language. Like, for instance, Heath is sitting so close to me he is almost touching my leg with his, and I can smell his minty breath. Even though I'm staring off in the distance and nodding numbly while he talks, he doesn't understand that I wish he would stop, shift back up the slope, and annoy his parents instead of me.

"Are you looking forward to me coming to apprentice?" he asks.

I turn and look at Heath suddenly. I wonder what he knows about the Outside and life in early ArHK. He's looking at me expectantly with his bright-blue eyes. His eyes startle me every time. Blue eyes are rare in ArHK. It astounds me that we're related, even though he's my cousin once removed, or maybe it's twice. At any rate, our grandmams were sisters.

"Well?" he prompts.

"Well what?" I ask.

"Are you looking forward to me coming to apprentice?"

"Oh, sure. Yeah. It'll be great," I mutter.

The starting horn sounds and the two teams run toward the ball, which is suspended from the sky. Each team launches their smallest player into the air to get possession of the play. I cringe as they sail close to one another. There is entirely too much blood involved in ArHKball, if you ask me.

"I don't care much for sports," Heath says.

He itches his ear and keeps staring at me. I keep my face angled toward the playing field to avoid prolonging the conversation.

When my personal messenger beeps, I'm so relieved I almost cheer. I look to see Ruby's smiling face.

"Who are you cheering for?" she asks.

"Sorters."

"Did you let Sparrow pick again?"

I nod. "She's very opinionated."

"Well, we're all cheering for the Propagators so prepare to lose." Ruby whoops it up. She's beaming from ear to ear. That girl has too much energy, but I can't help feel a rush of affection.

"Where are you?" I ask.

"Section D. Row five."

"What time did you get here?" I ask, amazed. I think I've only been in the seated section four times in my entire life.

"Two hours before the horn," she says. "We ended up in row twenty last time, so Mam got us up an hour earlier today."

I groan. I don't think anyone in our pod was even conscious two hours before the horn.

The crowd erupts into a loud cheer. The Propagators scored.

"Go Propagators!" Ruby shouts over my personal messenger.

Sparrow blows her whistle in protest until my ears burn. I clap to be polite, but Heath doesn't move. He wasn't exaggerating when he said he doesn't care for sports.

"Where are you guys?" Ruby asks when play resumes.

"On the hill. About two-thirds up from the bottom. Near exit five."

"At least you'll get out quickly when the game ends," Ruby says brightly.

"Yeah, at least," I say.

"Want to see our view?"

"Sure." I nod.

Ruby scans her personal messenger across the stadium. I'm amazed to see how close the playing field is. She can actually see the players' faces, not just the names on the back of their shirts. They look sweaty and intense, and one of the Sorters has a bloody nose. I cringe.

"Pretty cool, huh?" she asks when her face appears back on the screen.

"Yeah, pretty neat."

"So do you want to do something after dinner tonight?" Ruby yells over the noisy crowd around her.

"Sure. Beep me later."

The game drags on. Sparrow jumps and shouts and trills her whistle whenever the Sorters score and boos and hisses and blares her whistle whenever the Propagators score. Heath sits beside me and stares at me for long periods of time until I want to pull his eyelids over his eyes and scream. Mam and Da talk politely to Heath's parents even though I can tell they'd rather be daydreaming the game away. We eat our lunches and suck back the ice-cold lemon drinks. In the end, the Propagators win, and Sparrow looks so sullen that Da buys her a large feijoa ice treat. She slurps it on the walk back and gets so sticky Mam has to stop at a fountain to clean her hands before we drop her off at school. I look around nervously, hoping one of the Governors doesn't see.

"Have a good afternoon," Mam instructs as we leave Sparrow at the front of the school pod. "I'll be here to pick you up when the bell goes."

Mam and Da and I make our way through the crowds to the Archives. Da tells me my first task is to complete the Daily Log and I don't complain. But as usual, I'm so bored by the idea I start to yawn.

I pull up the Daily Log screen and input the population (5028), the births (0), and the deaths (0). I record the certificate that finally came through on the only marriage that took place in ArHK all month. I link files to the structural enhancements and Governor Reports. I think for the five thousandth time that the Daily Log is a complete waste of energy.

"Da, in the old days, did anyone from the Outside ever respond to the Daily Log? I mean, we learned in school that we lost contact with the Outside about two hundred OT years ago. But have you ever seen anything in the files, any Governor Reports to prove that?"

Da and Mam are sitting at their terminals working. Mam is reviewing requests for access to various Governor Reports, and Da is plotting out my assignments for the next couple of weeks. He likes to make sure I have a good balance between assignment and exploratory days.

"I don't think I've seen anything like that, Rook. Willow, how about you? Have you seen any specific date reference to our last recorded contact with the Outside?"

Mam shakes her head but doesn't look up. "Why do you ask?"

"Because I'm beginning to think the Governors control a lot more than we realize. I'm not sure anyone even knows the truth anymore."

Mam and Da look up at me in unison. They exchange concerned looks but try to act casual, as if I'm not smart enough to pick up on the sudden tension.

"These are very serious accusations. I hope you haven't voiced your concerns to anyone else, especially not to Ruby," Da says.

"I haven't said a word to anyone. But I'm beginning to think ArHK is *part* of the Outside and the Governors don't want us to know."

Mam looks around the Archives uncomfortably, and Da pulls his chair close to mine. I know they wish I'd stop talking and thinking, but I can't.

"I think we should try and find a way to get back to the Outside," I say quietly.

Da leans so close his lips are almost touching my cheek. "Do you hear yourself, Rook? I don't think I've heard anything as ridiculous in all my life. There's no way back to the Outside until you die. The only way in is being born and the only way out is to die."

I look at Mam to gauge her reaction. Her expression makes me think she agrees with Da, but she doesn't say anything.

"You don't believe in the Outside?" I ask.

"I do believe in the Outside. I just don't believe in your version," Da says.

"Mam, what about you?" I ask.

She is slow to answer and picks her words as carefully as Sparrow picks mushrooms out of her dinner.

"I believe in the Outside too, but I don't believe we can choose to go there whenever we want. It's not like walking to Central Park or to the public baths. You have to earn your place in the Outside."

"Like, how? By dying?"

Mam nods.

"So you think the Outside is more of a metaphor, not a real place where you can go?"

"That's right," Mam says. "Some of the files I've read make it seem like an actual place, but I think our ancestors were writing allegorically when they portrayed it that way."

"But there must be a place. The Chosen Ones came here from somewhere. Why can't we go back to wherever that is?" I press.

Da sighs and I know it's a bad sign.

"I'm worried about you, Rook. You're going to be a Head Keeper one day, yet you're beginning to sound like the early revolutionaries."

"The who what?"

Mam flashes a warning look at Da and then turns her face away.

"Oh dear, did I just say that out loud?" he says and rubs his temples.

"Let me go on the old system again. Please? I think there's a lot of stuff hidden in old files that we've lost track of. It's our duty to keep the knowledge alive, remember? I think the people of ArHK deserve to know the truth."

"I can't let you do that, Rook. Not while you're so obsessed with the Outside and talking about *truth*. It will come to no good. You have so much to learn. An apprenticeship requires timing with regards to the acquisition of knowledge. There's a system to what you learn and when. You can't go rushing ahead."

"How do you know it will come to no good?"

"Because you aren't the first person to start questioning things in ArHK," Da blurts out.

My pulse quickens.

"Who else questioned things?"

He sighs so deeply I'm afraid he's going to deflate.

"Your Grandmam Ivy always questioned things. Every little thing she read, every bylaw the Governors passed. She wrote papers full of outrageous ideas and put them forward as proposals. The Governors wasted hours refuting and documenting all these things. She caused so much trouble that she not only got banned from the Archives, she also got sent to the Growing Sector until she was too old to keep up with the other Growers."

I stop to sift through this new information. Is that why Grandmam Ivy was always growing plants in our pod when I was a little girl? Is that why she took so much pleasure in taking me to the Growing Sector on weekends and holidays? Is that why the people in the Growing Sector were always happy to see her?

"Grandmam Ivy lived in the Growing Sector?"

"Yes, and she was only let back to the Records Sector because she could no longer work a full day and couldn't take care of herself."

"She wasn't always Head Keeper? She didn't always live in our pod?"

Da shakes his head sadly.

"So who was Head Keeper when she was banned?"

"I was. But I was overseen by Governor Hawk until I finished my apprenticeship."

"Governor Hawk?" I scowl.

"Yes, Governor Hawk was new at the time, and he was assigned to monitor me. Mentor me. He made my final years as apprentice very unpleasant. He watched every little thing I did, as if he expected me to make trouble like Grandmam Ivy did. I had to be extra careful, do everything perfectly, or he would make me do it again. And then again. Some nights I barely got home in time for the sleep hours."

"Who lived in the pod with you?" I ask, because I know Da's father died when Da was still a boy.

"Your father lived by himself from the time he was a little older than you until we got married," Mam answers sharply.

I can't believe I never knew any of this. For a moment, I'm so stunned I don't know what to say. Mam's and Da's shoulders begin to relax.

"And Grandmam started a revolution?" I ask suddenly.

Mam's face goes bright red, and Da slams his hand down on the desk.

"No, she didn't, and I don't want to talk about it. It was awful. I barely got to see her after that and then only when we were supervised."

"Is that when the Governors restricted the files on the old computer?"

As soon as the words leave my mouth I regret saying them, but maybe not as much as I can tell Da regrets hearing them.

GAGE

G age feels small standing in his scouting party. Harley is at least a foot taller, and Uncle Winch is so broad, Gage feels like a stalk of wheat standing next to him. Somehow, after all the hours imagining his first morning as an actual scout, the moment is not lining up with his expectations. He'd always imagined more formality, or at least for the day to feel different somehow, the way the first day of school felt when he was Brindle's age. He doesn't mean to let it creep into his head, but there's an image of Brindle and his mother heading off to school hand in hand, the other kids streaming between the yurts toward the centre of camp and pushing open the flap of the communal yurt. Who's going to take his usual seat beside Pepper? Who's going to fetch the school's drinking water now that he's gone? Who's going to start a fire in the stove if there are any cold snaps?

All of the scouts are standing in their groups, chatting quietly. They cluster around the dying embers of the night's fire to steal a last few moments of warmth before they head out. It's not just the warmth they are soaking in, it's also the safety and familiarity of being at camp. Through the trees, Gage sees a few rays of sunlight straining to reach above the horizon. It promises to be a clear day when the sun makes its way fully into the sky.

Everyone abandons the firepit to say goodbye to Jett and his father before they start back to base camp. Jett puts on a brave face as everyone watches him hoist his supply pack onto his back. Gage stands next to him.

"You'll be back in no time, few days tops. We won't have explored much by then."

"Just don't go finding anything important 'til we get back," Jett says quietly.

Chief Coil talks to Jett's father, gives last-minute instructions, and reminds him about the landmarks they passed along the way.

"Do you have your walking stick?" Gage asks.

Jett points to the far side of the camp. "Leaning against that tree."

"Maybe you'll find something interesting on the way? Ya never know. Dad says this part of the country was full of old villages and homesteads."

"Yeah, maybe. Ya never know," Jett agrees, but his spirit is so low it's dragging on the ground.

"It's still important what you're doin'. We need to get word back to base camp and on to the Middle."

"I know." Jett smiles wryly. "I just wish it was someone else doin' this important job." Then he adjusts the pack on his back and turns to follow his father, back in the direction of the Lincoln Memorial.

"Watch your step," Gage calls after him.

"And may your toes always be under your nose," Jett calls back in the traditional scout greeting.

Jett picks up his walking stick, then waves one last time. Gage lifts his hand in response and suddenly feels alone. The other scouts are used to the camp life and have been scouting together for years. They have an easy rhythm about them, a pattern to their chores, a way of getting things done without having to speak.

One by one, the scouting parties are called to consult with Chief Coil and the map readers. Each party is shown a map and told which structure they have been assigned to explore.

The first party is assigned to the Capitol Building and told to watch for a white structure with a statue of a robed lady on top. Because the structure is the farthest away, the fastest walkers are sent out ahead of the others. When they disappear into the forest, fear bubbles up in the back of Gage's throat. What if he never sees these men again?

Gage's father is in the third party to head out. They've been assigned the National Archives, which is said to be a square sturdy building with images of horses and shirtless men carved into a triangle above the entrance. His father takes the lead and nods back at Gage. He doesn't shout out any last-minute advice before he disappears into the trees. He doesn't need to. He spent most of the early morning, before sunrise, lecturing.

"You do what Winch and Harley do. You do what they tell you to do. They've been scouting long as me. So don't go off on your own. Stay in their footsteps. If Winch doesn't fall through, you're sure to be safe."

Although it feels like he'll never be called up, Gage's party is ninth. He picks up his walking stick and checks to see that his machete and coil of rope are fastened securely to his belt. Although his scouting tools make him feel more prepared, his nerves are more frayed than an old goat tether. Besides these tools and the torch bundle on his back, Gage will have only his wits to keep him safe in an emergency.

Gage approaches Chief Coil. His legs are trembling so badly it takes Uncle Winch's hand on his shoulder to bring him back to reality.

"Easy there, Gage. It's not like we're gonna go rushing into someplace dangerous. Just stay behind me and Harley."

Harley smiles kindly, and Gage's stomach flips a little slower.

It's not just the danger that has Gage's nerves on edge. It's also knowing he's part of history and, more importantly, that it has taken years of the Scholars' work to get to this moment.

"Your party's been assigned to the ancient government building recorded as the Department of Human Safety and Survival," Chief Coil tells the men.

The map readers show them where the campsite is and where the structure is located. Gage leans close over the map laid out in front of them and savours the opportunity of looking at the ancient artefact, criss-crossed with different coloured lines, shapes, and words.

"You'll have to cross these major roads, then head to the centre of this circular area. We hope the structure'll be mostly intact. It was built just before the Storm Ages. The Scholars suspect it'll look different from the other buildings. It's been described in ancient books as structurally advanced and unique."

Gage wonders how he'll recognize an advanced and unique building. He's seen so few ancient buildings, they all look unique to him. But he knows Harley and Uncle Winch have more experience with such things.

"Our notes say there was reference to it being the rock star of all buildings, but we don't know if that's a symbolic term or if it'll be constructed in the shape of a star. At any rate, we're certain it's not made of rock the way the old places of worship were."

"We'll be ready for any possibility," Uncle Winch assures Chief Coil.

Gage continues to examine the map carefully and tries his best to remember road names, angles, and distances. It'll be disorienting to find their way through the forest, and the old maps are deceiving.

"This'll help you." Chief Coil hands Gage a small square of yellow parchment. "The Scholars recreated the map. It's got reference points to help you get there and back."

Gage takes the hand-drawn map and tucks it safely inside his vest. He takes a deep breath, then looks to Harley and Uncle Winch to see what will happen next.

"Good luck, men," Chief Coil says. "Be back by sundown at the latest. We don't want any parties out after dark."

Uncle Winch nods solemnly at Chief Coil, then at Gage and Harley.

"I'll be in the lead. My niece made me promise to bring you back safely."

Then he heads out past Chief Coil, in the same direction as Gage's father went. Harley falls into line next. Gage glances back at the two remaining parties waiting at the edge of the ash-filled firepit, then turns to follow his party through the waking forest.

It doesn't take long before Gage can no longer smell the lingering smoke from the campfire or hear human voices. All he can hear are Uncle Winch and Harley snapping twigs and crunching dried leaves with their feet. He's never felt so isolated. Surrounded by trees, with so few people to rely on, he begins to doubt himself and think he was a fool to come scouting. He almost wishes he was Jett, heading home.

Harley must sense Gage's discomfort. "How you doin' back there?" he asks.

Gage clears his throat. "Fine, I'm okay."

"Just checking. I remember how scared I was first time I went out scouting. It felt like the trees were closing in on me. I wanted to run back to camp."

"No, I'm good. Really," Gage says, a little too insistently. He grips his walking stick a little tighter.

Uncle Winch laughs out loud and stops completely. Harley and Gage have to react quickly to keep from walking into him.

"Yep, that's what I said my first time out. But I was shaking in my boots so bad it's a wonder a cougar didn't hear and come looking for an easy dinner."

"Winch, stop teasing the boy! You know there's no cougars around here," Harley says, then turns back to Gage. "You just let me know if you want to walk in the middle. And don't pay no attention to Winch. He likes to rile the new scouts."

"I'm fine back here," Gage says, with a little less certainty. Then he glances over his shoulder to make sure there's nobody and nothing behind him.

He follows Uncle Winch and Harley over a series of fallen trees. When they come to a thick stand of raspberry cane, Uncle Winch uses his machete to clear a path. His muscles strain against his shirt as he slices his way through the prickly branches.

Soon the forest changes completely. Instead of being thick with undergrowth and broad evergreen trees, the tree trunks are thinner and the branches are sprouting delicate green buds. There's very little undergrowth. Gage looks down and sees shoots of green sprouting through the dead leaves. He recognizes them as wild garlic and pulls a few bulbs from the moist dirt. They smell delicious and he tucks them into his vest, then catches up before the other men notice he's lagged behind.

Uncle Winch stops and looks up. He glances left and right. Gage notices the treetops are filled with hundreds of tiny brown songbirds, and generous rays of sunshine are pooling at his feet. The birds flit to the ground and then back up into the branches again, chirping and whistling. They are collecting small seeds and insects from among the dead leaves. Gage watches the birds, song sparrows and wood thrushes mostly. One lands close to his feet, tilts its small brown head, and trains a dark eye on Gage, curious but unperturbed, before flying back onto a branch. Gage can't recall seeing birds in the other part of the forest. It's like they've walked into another world.

"This will be that first road. What's it called?" Uncle Winch asks.

Gage pulls the map out of his vest and shows the others. "Seventeenth Street," he says. "Sure makes for easier walking being on the old road."

"You can say that again," Harley says. "Too bad we're just crossing over."

A few steps farther and they pass a well-worn path winding like a snake through the trees.

"Look, see? Even the deer like to follow the old roads." Uncle Winch chuckles.

"They have to worry about falling into caverns too," Gage reminds them.

It's the way the sky sifts through the trees that alerts Gage to the fact that they're approaching some sort of an opening in the forest, and he wonders if there might be a pond or a lake ahead. But even with the warning, he's astounded when they stumble into a grassy clearing as flat as the fields surrounding the Middle. In the centre of the clearing is a cluster of mushroom-shaped structures. The structures are black in colour, but they also twinkle in the sunshine, like the surface of a lake on a calm morning.

Uncle Winch pulls his hat into his hands. "What the heck? Is that a building?"

"I think so. But I hafta say, in all my years of scouting I never seen anything like that," Harley says.

Gage remembers what Chief Coil said about the building looking different than any they've seen before. He grips his walking stick tightly and takes a deep breath to steady himself.

"This must be the Department of Human Safety and Survival!"

ROOK

———

'm in the kitchen with Grandmam Ivy, helping her repot cherry tomato plants. I haven't seen her in many
years, not since I was Sparrow's age, even though she
lives in our pod. That's how I know I'm dreaming.

"If we repot them now, they'll grow another batch of
tomatoes right away," she explains patiently. "There's a
science to growing every living thing."

"That's why I like to visit the Growing Sector," I say. I
look down at my hands, which are covered in brown dirt.

"I like to visit the Growing Sector too," Grandmam
Ivy says nostalgically. "But you'll never be a Grower,
Rook."

"I know. I know. I'm a Keeper. Not a Grower. Da tells me all the time."

"You're going to be the most important Head Keeper ArHK has ever had," she says and winks.

I see the mischief in her eyes. "What makes you say that?"

"Because you're a clever bird, good at solving puzzles. You'll know how to follow the trail of crumbs I left."

"What crumbs?" I ask.

I wonder if Grandmam Ivy is losing her mind. After all, she's pretty old. In all the time I've grown older, she must have grown older too.

"They were watching me. I knew they were tracking my moves. That's why I made sure my discoveries wouldn't be lost forever."

Grandmam Ivy presses new soil into a pot with her gnarled fingers. All those years working in the Growing Sector were hard on her body.

"Who was watching you, Grandmam?" I ask.

"The Governors. They watch everything. But they can't catch you if you just look. They can only track if you make changes, the way I did."

The dream starts to fade and I try to claw it back. I don't want to lose Grandmam Ivy. I realize how much I've missed her.

"Grandmam!" I call out, trying to bring her back.

"Just follow my trail of crumbs, Rook," she says before she disintegrates into a million particles and is swallowed up by the darkness.

My eyelids fly open and I'm surrounded by black. I hold my breath and hear Sparrow breathing calmly. I sigh. I was just dreaming. I search my brain, trying to bring it back. I know there was something in it that comforted me.

Grandmam Ivy.

The dream rushes back and I blink back the night trying to figure out what crumbs are and how I'm supposed to follow them. It doesn't make any sense. I've never heard of crumbs before. But the dream feels so real I know I won't fall back asleep.

The next morning when I walk into the kitchen, Grandmam Ivy and the cherry tomato plants are gone. Mam is at the stove. She's serving corn grits for breakfast and she hands me a bowl. Sparrow is already at the table drawing faces in her grits with a spoon. I pour us each a glass of orange juice and sit down.

"How come you're not eating?" I ask Sparrow.

"I am. I'm just drawing first."

When Da walks into the kitchen Mam hands him a bowl of grits too. He sits down and douses his bowl with salt and pepper, then spreads a layer of butter over top.

"Just what the doctor ordered!" he says and takes a big mouthful.

"Yeah, the doctor of disgusting," Sparrow says, giggling.

I look at her, surprised. I'm sure I wasn't so clever when I was her age.

"I was wondering about something," I say to Da when I'm sure he's properly distracted by his oily grits.

He murmurs and waits for me to continue.

"Is there a way to track what we do in the Archives? I mean, if there was something I filed last year, like someone's death notice, but I couldn't remember the exact date or the person's name, is there a way to look back and see all the death notices I've filed in the past year?"

"Sure. You'd look at your Crumb Report," Da says.

A zap of energy shoots up my spine and makes the hairs on my neck prickle.

"Crumb Report?" I ask in a quiet voice.

"Crump Reports track all your activity on the system by your ID number so we can see what reports you created or formatted or linked to. It's a quality assurance measure. If the Governors order an audit to be sure proper procedures are being followed, they'll be able to see who made an error if one was made."

"I hope I haven't made any mistakes," I say.

"Don't worry. It's my responsibility to check all your work until your apprenticeship is complete."

"Do they track where you go and what you read?"

"No, but they track search terms."

"What else is tracked in a Crumb Report?" I ask.

"Well, every crumb is also date- and time-stamped."

"Are Crumb Reports public?"

"If you know where to find them."

"Interesting," I say, even though I am both upset and alarmed. Upset that he didn't bother to mention Crumb Reports to me after all the time I've been working in the Archives and alarmed that if he looks, he'll be able to see what I've being searching.

"I was going to assign you a project next week to get you acquainted with Crumb Reports but maybe today is a good day to get started on it," Da suggests.

On our way to the Archives, we pass our neighbours also on their way to Knowledge Level jobs. Some walk with their faces toward their feet and others, like Ruby, smile at everyone they pass.

"Rook!" Ruby calls out from across the Avenue and waves. She's with her parents, and a small group of Governors are waiting for her to step inside the Council Chamber so they can follow. I wave quickly, then gesture at my personal messenger. It's our signal to touch base later.

When we get inside, Da sits beside me. He takes me into the tracking end of the operating system, a place I've never heard of, and pulls up a long list of user IDs: RKXVII, FKXVI, IKXV, FKXIV, MKXIII, and on and on.

I point to the screen, to the first three ID numbers.

"That's me, and you and Grandmam Ivy, right?"

"That's right." He seems pleased by my cleverness. If he only knew.

"So FKXIV was the fourteenth Head Keeper, your grandda Fisher?"

"Exactly."

"Who was the thirteenth Head Keeper?"

"My great-grandda Marten," Da says. "And before Marten was his father, Quail."

"Do you know all the Head Keepers, right back to the very first?"

Da nods. "The first Head Keeper was William."

The name sounds familiar to me, but I don't let on.

"Who was the first female Head Keeper?"

"Her name was Daisy, and she was sixth Head Keeper."

"Interesting," I say. "So I could go and see exactly what DKVI did when she was Head Keeper? Even now, all these years later?"

"You can see anything anyone did on this system, by year."

"Are there Crumb Reports for the old system?"

"Not in the beginning. It was Daisy Keeper who initiated the Crumb Reports," Da says and shifts in his seat.

He's starting to look uncomfortable so I decide not to follow that line of questioning.

Da pulls up my ID number and shows me my Crumb Report for the past year. I can see that I created the Daily

Log every day last week and which files I linked. I made nine searches two days ago, and I hope he doesn't think to look at what terms I used. Then he pulls up his Crumb Report and the screen fills with an endless log of activities.

"You've been busy." I laugh.

"It can be very gratifying when you see how much you've accomplished in a week or a month or even a year."

"Do you think the Governors ever really look at these reports? I mean, who has time to go through all this?" I ask.

"I don't think they scrutinize them too closely, but I imagine they have a look from time to time to be sure productivity is steady. However, if you give them a reason to want to look, I guarantee they'd be watching everything you did, every search you made."

I shiver and try to erase the image of Governor Hawk looming in my mind. I want to ask him if that's what happened to Grandmam Ivy. But I keep my mouth shut.

"Is today an assignment day or an exploratory day?" I ask instead.

"Exploratory day. Would you like to study Crumb Reports for the morning?"

I nod. But not too eagerly.

"That's fine. But I have two Governor proposals for you to format and submit sometime today," Da says. "From yesterday's council meeting. I believe Ruby put one forward. It's her first."

"She's always said she wants to be the youngest apprentice Governor in the Official Record," I muse aloud, then wonder if I should take her to the Thrill Park to celebrate, maybe buy her a cherry-flavoured ice treat.

When Da leaves, I find Grandmam Ivy's Crumb Report. Her last recorded activity was almost thirty OT years ago. I hesitate and look around the Archives. Da has already settled himself in front of his terminal and is flying through the files on his screen, swiping left and right with a flick of his eyes. I take a deep breath and open the last of Grandmam Ivy's crumbs.

It's strange to see what my grandmam did when she was Da's age, to realize I can follow exactly what she did every day she spent in the Archives and that one day my grandchildren will be able to follow everything I did. I shake my head. It's not a comforting thought.

The first thing I notice is that on her last day as Head Keeper, Grandmam Ivy submitted the Daily Log, formatted and submitted three Fixer Reports, and linked a marriage record, two birth notices, and a death notice. She also filed a motion on behalf of Governor Ebony that was passed unanimously by Council. It's titled *Motion to Dismiss Citizen Proposal: Creation of a Research and Credibility Committee*. The title of the motion does little to grab my attention but when I see there are several links, I feel the zap of energy go up my spine again. I'm certain I've found the trail of crumbs Grandmam left for me to discover.

GAGE

Uncle Winch, Harley, and Gage stand and stare at the oddly shaped structures for a full ten minutes without speaking. Inside Gage's head, a hundred thoughts tumble like stones on the bottom of a swiftly flowing river, but they are all so slippery he can't grab hold of even one. Harley is the first to find his voice.

"It's so clear. The whole space. Wide open like the sky."

"Why aren't there any trees?" Uncle Winch asks.

"Or underbrush?" adds Harley.

Nobody moves, not so much as a flinch, or takes their gaze off the structures. It's almost as if they're afraid it will disappear if they glance away.

"You sure you've never seen something like this before?" Gage asks.

"Not with a round top like that," Uncle Winch says.

"Not with *anything* like that," Harley mutters.

The shape reminds Gage of something, but he can't quite figure out what. It's something he's seen recently.

"It looks like a row of toadstools," Harley suggests.

"Or giant top-heavy yurts," Uncle Winch muses.

Suddenly, Gage remembers the wild garlic bulbs in his pocket and pulls them out.

"Or like these," he says and holds the bulbs upside down for Harley and Uncle Winch to see.

"That's the darndest sight," Uncle Winch muses. He takes one from Gage and turns it in his hand before giving it back. "It does look like wild garlic. Who'd have thought, in a million years, it was possible to build something shaped like that."

The top of the structure reflects sunlight in all directions, while the bottom of the structure appears dense and dark. They can't see any other buildings or ruins nearby or through the distant trees. There isn't even a path leading up to the building, just a wide circular clearing the size of their base camp.

Uncle Winch grips his walking stick and prods the ground in front of him. When it seems safe, he takes a tentative step into the clearing, and his foot disappears in a thick mat of grass. Gage gasps and steps back into the safety of the trees. The sunlight dims while clouds scud across the sky, and the birds stop chirruping, almost as if they're anticipating something bad. It's like the entire forest is holding its breath along with Gage.

Gradually, Uncle Winch puts the full weight of his body on his front foot, then brings his back foot forward until he's standing with both feet in the tangled grass. He tests the ground with a little hop then looks back at Gage and Harley.

"It seems solid," he says.

Gage takes in a deep breath of forest air and exhales slowly. Some of his anxiety dissipates.

Uncle Winch turns forward again and pokes his walking stick into the ground. "There seems to be a layer of something under the grass. Something with a bit of give," he says as he jabs at the ground.

Gage and Harley take their walking sticks and poke at the greening grass in the same way. The tip of Gage's walking stick disappears but stops after a few inches. *What could be holding up the grass?* he wonders, as he watches Uncle Winch move across the clearing, step by cautious step.

"I'll let him get halfway before I start across," Harley says to Gage. "Once Winch reaches the other side, you start too."

Gage can see Harley's nerves plain as day. The corners of his mouth twitch, and he's gripping his walking stick so tight the knuckles on both hands are as white as bones.

Uncle Winch and Harley inch their way across the clearing while Gage watches from the edge of the trees. With the sun directly overhead and the clouds moving away, the top of the structure takes on the colour of the bright-blue sky. He memorizes the path of the older scouts and concentrates on every step they take. When Uncle Winch finally reaches the building, he waves and calls for Gage to follow.

When the three scouts are safely across the clearing, they approach a gaping hole in the side of the structure. Gage runs his hand over the cool, rough surface of the outside wall and feels the excitement building in him. This is the first ancient structure he's ever touched with his bare hands, and it feels like his world is expanding. He wonders if Pepper will ever get a chance to touch anything of the sort, or if Brindle will ever see anything as grand. Gage gazes up toward the top of the structure mushrooming above and blocking his view of the sun. Up close, the surface appears to be dark brown. How can the surface change colour? When Gage takes his hand from the structure he looks to see if anything has rubbed off on his skin.

From the edge of the gaping hole, Gage can see that the inside of the structure is filled with muted light. Because there are no windows on the outside, he had expected to see only pitch black inside, like a cave. But beams of dust-filled sunshine stream down from the top of the building, illuminating a massive cavern strewn with dirt and debris.

Uncle Winch whistles. "Somehow the sunlight's getting through the top of the building. Harley, have you ever seen a building with the roof still standing like this?"

Harley shakes his head. "I just don't know what to make of it."

Gage can tell both men are spooked but, suddenly, he feels calm. It's as if touching the structure has given him confidence.

"No offence, Uncle Winch. But since I'm the lightest maybe I should go in first?" he suggests. "I'll tie the rope around my waist, and you can be my anchors. Until we're sure the floor's safe."

Both men look skeptical, but Gage doesn't wait for an answer. He unhooks his coil of rope and fastens it around his waist, then hands the end to Uncle Winch.

"Don't let go! Or Pepper'll never forgive you."

Uncle Winch rolls his eyes but wraps the end of the rope around his own waist and grips it with both meaty hands. Harley grabs the rope further up and braces his feet against the edge of the door frame. Then Gage steps through the doorway with his walking stick held across his body and tightly in his hands. Because the room is filled with filtered light, Gage has to squint until his eyes adjust to the dimness. Then he can see that beyond the circle of light are rows of doorways. He can also see that the room is much bigger than it first appeared, and there are areas in shadow stretching out in all directions.

Gage taps the floor with his walking stick. It feels solid so he takes another step.

"What can you see?" Harley calls out.

"It's big in here! And there're a whole lotta doors."

He squints further into the shadows, then sneezes from the dust. "And it looks like there's an old campfire or something."

The blood turns cold in his veins.

He looks everywhere at once, in case a Lurker is hiding in the shadows ready to slit his throat, but the room is eerily still. From the looks of the floor, he's the only person who's stepped inside this building for years, probably hundreds of years. His are the only footprints visible in a thick layer of dust.

Gage moves deeper into the cavernous room. He steps slowly and every few seconds he tugs the rope to be sure Uncle Winch and Harley are holding him securely.

"Anything else?" Uncle Winch calls.

Gage glances back and sees Harley's silhouette blocking the sunny opening.

"There's a long table running across the middle of the room. It looks to be attached to the floor. And it has some sorta panel with gauges and controls. There's a few words here, but they're hard to make out. Just a minute."

Gage wipes his sleeve across the top of the table and steps away from the cloud of dust.

"Cent-ral ... Mon-i-tor-ing ... Sta-tion."

He looks around the room for other words or other signs, but all he can see are gobs of dusty cobwebs.

"Anything that says if we're in the right building?" Uncle Winch calls inside.

Gage peers behind the table.

"Dunno. Nothing yet. But there's a pile of firewood here, or something?"

Gage leans closer. He taps at a stick of wood with his toe, and when it clatters to the floor he jumps back and screams.

"Gage!" Harley tears through the door and across the room with Uncle Winch close behind.

"You okay?" Harley asks when the three of them are side by side, the way scouts are never supposed to stand.

Gage is trembling and his face is as pale as the moon in the dim, filtered light.

"Bones!" he squeaks and gulps back mouthfuls of stale air.

Uncle Winch kicks at the pile of bones, and they scatter across the floor. Dust particles rise up and float through the beams of light. Gage coughs and shudders. Harley squats down and picks up a skull.

"Don't worry. These ain't human. Just deer and wild boar from the looks of this."

Harley drops the long narrow skull back on the pile, and another cloud of dust envelopes them.

"At some point someone musta lived in here," Uncle Winch says, pointing at the pile of bones and the long-dead campfire. "Looks like they camped out for quite awhile."

Gage regains his voice. "When?"

"Probably during the Storm Ages. This woulda been a pretty safe place to hole up, I imagine."

"Not in the last hundred years then?" Gage asks.

"I wouldn't think so. I'm not even sure I believe those old stories about Lurkers roaming the ancient cities. I think people left the coastal areas when the flooding got bad and stayed in the Middle for the next three hundred years."

"Yeah, it just don't make sense," Harley agrees. "Why would anyone stay behind if things were bad as they say?"

Gage doesn't comment but squints into the shadows. He hopes with all his heart that Uncle Winch and Harley are right and that Lurkers no longer exist. But something doesn't feel quite right, and a shiver scuttles along his spine.

ROOK

I hesitate before I open the report Grandmam Ivy filed all those years ago. I worry an alarm will go off, or a notification system has been programmed into the computer to send auto warnings to the Governors if controversial files are opened.

But then I remind myself, it's better to find out now while I can pretend I didn't know better, then spend the rest of my life regretting that I was too afraid to try. Grandmam Ivy always said that not taking a risk was just as much of a risk as taking one in the first place.

I scrunch up my eyes when I open the file, but nothing happens. The Governors don't crash through the front doors, piercing alarms don't sound, and Da doesn't look up from his terminal with panic on his face. I sigh with relief. In my dream Grandmam Ivy said they couldn't trace your movements if you just read the files, and I plan to do just that.

The main problem with Governor documents is that the words are too big and complicated, and the sentence structure is awkward. I think Governors write this way on purpose, to dull the senses so nobody will be alert enough to question the decisions they make. That way the Governors can invite people to read the report, but nobody in their right mind can stay awake to the end. I mean, I'm still on the first page and I can already feel my eyelids drooping. I shake my head to bring my mind back to the task of reading.

The paper authored and put forward by Ivy Keeper, which theorizes that the last known contact with the Outside was as far back as 400 OT years, and, further, which calls for the Governors to create a Research and Credibility Committee to examine the evidence she has allegedly compiled from research conducted in the Archives, has been officially denied by a unanimous council vote.

The rest of the motion is basically a record of who said what during the discussion period and which ArHK Acts the Governors cited in supporting their decision to dismiss the paper. There's no mention of whether or not Grandmam Ivy was present or if she even had any say in the proceedings. The motion doesn't even make reference to the evidence she compiled. For a Governor document, in fact, it lacks a lot of detail. After reading the entire report, all I know is Grandmam Ivy thought she had proof that Outside contact was much further back than commonly believed then, and I have to find out what evidence she collected. I get a feeling that if I figure that out, I'll learn a lot of other interesting things about ArHK too. Maybe I'll even find a clue about where the Outside is located.

I go back to the Crumb Report to follow the links she created. This, I know, will be where I find the important information anyway. When I look at the list of linked documents, my heart races and my hands turn slick with sweat. I think of Ruby being the youngest Governor in history to submit a proposal, and it occurs to me that Grandmam Ivy knew exactly what she was doing. Of course she knew the Governors wouldn't listen to anything she had to say. Of course she knew they'd dismiss her paper and laugh behind her back. That wasn't the point. She knew that just by submitting the paper, the Governors would have to file it, and that was the only way to guarantee her ideas got into the Official ArHK Record. Grandmam Ivy was a clever woman. She left the crumbs right under their noses, and they never even noticed.

I bet it was Grandmam Ivy who linked the arrival footage of the Chosen Ones. I bet it was another of her crumbs. It was probably she who programmed my pass code into the old system so I'd have access to the restricted files.

Although I have some clear memories of Grandmam Ivy when she lived in our pod, I was only Sparrow's age when she passed over and my memories are scattered. I remember she was forever caring for her plants. She fertilized and watered them constantly. She soaked cuttings in buckets of water in the bathroom and potted them once they had roots. She even composted food scraps in her bedroom so she didn't have to lug as much soil from the Growing Sector on weekends. Da hated the dirt and the smell. He asked her why she couldn't grow her plants hydroponically, but she said the vegetables tasted better when the plants were grown in soil. One day he said he couldn't take it a moment longer: the clutter and the mess, the smell and the dirt.

"Your plant hobby is out of control, Mam. It's starting to feel like we live in the Growing Sector. We're Keepers, Mam, not Growers."

"I don't hear you complain when there's an extra batch of sweet peas or a fresh supply of tomatoes to eat," she said calmly.

Even if Da didn't like the plants, I thought they were beautiful. Grandmam had a fig tree in her bedroom and a lemon tree in the living room that grew real lemons. All my friends were jealous of me for having trees in our pod. Ruby used to come over every day after school so she could smell the leaves. Gandmam would let us touch them if we were careful. Sometimes, when Da and Mam were at the Archives, Grandmam would take me and a bucket of cuttings down to the market square and trade them for ice treats. Women would stop us in Central Park to ask for tips on how to grow this or that, and Grandmam was always happy to share what she knew. She said families deserved more independence.

I let the memories of Grandmam flow through my mind, wondering if she left any crumbs there as well for me to follow.

"Rook?" Da says.

He's standing beside me and I startle.

"How are you making out?"

"I'm good. Fine. I was just looking through the, uh, Crumb Reports," I stutter.

"If I didn't know better, I'd say you were daydreaming," he says and glances at the screen in front of me.

I quickly close the file I was reading. I don't remember what it was, but I don't want him to see that I was looking at Grandmam's Crumb Reports.

"So now do you understand how the information is tracked?" he asks.

"I think so. It's like the system takes note of everything you do and compiles that information in various ways. You can look things up by date or you can search by activity, such as the links you make or the reports you file."

"That's right. There's another way you can use crumbs too," he says and rolls a chair over to my terminal. He pulls his own, most recent Crumb Report onto the screen.

"Whenever you see a link, you can switch to the tracking view, and it will give you a report on who made the link and when. This becomes an important feature when there's more than one Keeper formatting a long report. For instance, when Heath joins us, we'll be able to keep straight who did what."

"That *is* an important feature," I say to be agreeable. "I mean, like you said, it must be good to look back and see all the work you've done. If everyone's work was mixed up, it wouldn't be nearly so satisfying, especially if one person didn't work as hard as the others."

"I don't think you'll have to worry about that with Heath." Da chuckles. "He seems very keen."

I wonder if Da is looking forward to having another apprentice. Someone new to teach, someone who doesn't daydream and ask too many questions.

"Heath's grandmam was Grandmam Ivy's younger sister, right?"

"That's right."

"What was her name? Heath's grandmam?"

"Her name was Primrose. We called her Auntie Prim."

"Was Auntie Prim upset when Grandmam Ivy had to leave the Records Sector?"

"Of course! Everyone was upset. Being banned from your home sector is a terrible punishment."

The colour in Da's face drains, and I realize for the first time how hard it must have been for him to lose his mam when he was my age, especially when he'd already lost his da. I can't imagine living in the pod alone or with such shame. I know what it means to be banished from your home sector. I've seen families moved against their wishes. Two years before I started my apprenticeship, a family was moved from the Health Sector to the Essential Services Sector. They took months to settle in. Rumour had it the mam was so upset that she didn't speak to any of her neighbours for an entire year, and the kids were teased relentlessly.

"Where was Grandmam Ivy when I was born?"

"She was still in the Growing Sector, but she joined us not long after. You were just learning to walk when she came back to live in our pod, and we were grateful for another set of hands. You were always on the move."

"Did Grandmam ever go to the Archives while she lived with us?"

"Never. When she was banned, they inserted a permanent tracking chip at the back of her neck that would set off the alarms if she even went near the Archives."

"Like what they do to Offenders?" I'm shocked to think Grandmam had been treated like a criminal.

"The chips they use today are a lot smaller. But it was the same sort of thing," Da says sadly.

"Did you visit her when she was in the Growing Sector?"

"Yes, every weekend. It was the only time we could see her. She was banned from coming into the Records Sector in those years. She couldn't even come for festival days."

"But she knew when I was born?"

"Yes, of course. We told her as soon as we knew we were expecting you. She was so excited. She even picked out your name months ahead of time. She said *Rook* was the name of a bird from the Outside. An inquisitive bird, apparently, that was good at solving problems. She insisted you be called Rook."

Da eases himself onto his feet. "Now, you should finish up with whatever you're looking at so you can format those new proposals."

"I will," I say. "Just a few more minutes and I'll be ready."

Da taps the back of my chair with his fist, then wanders away. I turn back to the computer and open the file I'd been reading. But it takes a minute for my eyes to focus. Even if Grandmam was an Offender, I loved her and so did a lot of other people. Despite the scandal, there were so many at her Life-End Celebration they had to broadcast the service onto the street in front of the Celebration Hall. People from all over ArHK turned out that day, vendors from the market square, old class-mates from her Instructional School days, neighbours from the Records Sector. Even her friends from the Growing Sector made the trip.

I return to Grandmam Ivy's Crumb Report with less energy. There's not enough time to discover as much as I want, and I'll have to wait for another exploratory day until I can start to follow Grandmam's crumbs. All I have time to do is open the first link, which takes me to a law that was proposed and passed with little notice in 2437 OT, *The ArHK Protection of People and Purpose Act*. What were the Governors up to with that? I wonder.

GAGE

B y the time they've walked around the first level of
the main hall and looked in all the smaller rooms,
Uncle Winch calls it a day.

"It's starting to get late, and it'll take a while to walk
back. Tomorrow we can go up there" — he points to a
staircase that spirals around the outside wall — "and
into the other areas."

"We didn't even find one artefact," Gage complains.
"All those rooms and nothing but rusty old cans and
disintegrating bedrolls."

Harley laughs. "Did you expect we'd find something
important on our first day?"

Gage feels foolish but nods.

"These buildings woulda been looted in the early years. Most everything of value was taken out for one reason or another. They used the wooden furniture and books for fires to keep warm, and the metal tools were stockpiled and melted down into the machetes we still use today." Uncle Winch pats the machete attached at his waist before he continues. "The only places to find artefacts these days are in the hidden rooms, the far-away corners. There's still plenty of stuff to find, but it takes a whole lot longer and it's a lot more risky."

The walk back to the scouts' camp seems quicker. Gage loses himself in his thoughts, transported by his imagination. He tries to picture all the people from the base camps and all the people from the Middle living in this ancient city. Even with everyone in the world living here, Washington would be mostly empty.

Most of the scouting parties arrive back at camp empty-handed. Only the party assigned to the White House structure has a small book with them, called *The Ultimate Crossword Dictionary*. Even by the time of the Storm Ages, when all the great societies crumbled into chaos, it would have been an old book. Chief Coil examines it closely.

"It provides definitions for words and phrases," he says. "It'll help the Scholars make sense of other written works."

He takes the book and wraps it carefully in a square of dry hemp cloth, then in a piece of greased leather. He packs it into a newly built crate to be stored in the artefact tent. Gage would trade his dinner to have a look at that book, but he knows it has to be properly catalogued and recorded on the maps for the Scholars to study, then protected for the good of humankind.

That evening the scouts gather around the fire and discuss the day. All but one scouting party are confident they located their assigned buildings. Gage's father reports that the National Archives was empty, either looted or cleared out for some purpose. The roof of the building had long ago collapsed and the lower rooms were full of ash and scraps of charred paper. The rooms and shelves were empty, and the scouting party wasn't hopeful the lower levels would turn up anything important either.

"Still, ya never know what we might find tomorrow. We've lots more to explore," Gage's father says. "We'll see if we can climb up to the higher levels safely."

Only Gage's party, it seems, found an intact building and from the expression on Chief Coil's face when Uncle Winch describes it, he doesn't believe what they found.

"Come look for yourself," Uncle Winch challenges calmly.

Chief Coil considers the invitation carefully, then smiles and nods. "Consider yours a scouting party of four tomorrow. I'm gonna see the Department of Human Safety and Survival for myself."

Gage straightens his back and squares his shoulders. Having the chief join his party is an honour he never imagined, especially on his second official day of scouting.

· · · ·

The next day, the four men arrive at the edge of the clearing and, as before, stand and stare for several minutes before anyone speaks.

"When I woke up this morning I thought maybe we dreamed it," Gage whispers. "But there it is and it's real."

"That is the oddest structure I ever seen," Chief Coil murmurs. "If I didn't see it with these two eyes, I'd never believe it."

Uncle Winch and Harley share a smug look.

"We been inside and scouted the first level of the tallest structure, but that's as far as we got," Uncle Winch says.

"And what about this clearing? Have you figured out why there's nothing growing?" Chief Coil asks as he spreads his hands out before him.

"There seems to be a layer of something under the grass. If you press hard enough, you can feel just a bit of give."

"I think they did it on purpose. So the light would get to the building and the sunshine would keep the inside lit up," Gage says.

The other men turn and stare at Gage until his ears burn red.

"We'll have to excavate and see what's there," Chief Coil says finally. "It could be an important discovery."

As they did the previous day, the men cross the clearing in single file and step into the cavernous sun-filled hall. They see yesterday's footsteps tracking across the dusty floor, then show Chief Coil the Central Monitoring Station and the small empty rooms around the edges. Chief Coil glances only briefly in each room, though; his attention is focused on the domed ceiling above and the filtered light streaming down upon them.

"We're planning on exploring the upper level today," Uncle Winch says and leads them toward the spiral staircase.

"And the other areas on this level," Gage adds.

Again the men turn and stare at Gage, and he wonders if he's supposed to keep his thoughts to himself. His father never warned him about not speaking, but maybe he figured Gage knew better than to offer unsolicited opinions.

Chief Coil looks down a wide corridor into another cavelike room.

"Let's finish exploring this level first," he says and wanders toward the adjacent cavern.

Uncle Winch and Harley follow Chief Coil. They hold their walking sticks at their waists, even though they're confident the structure is solid.

The other areas on the first level are also dusty. Beams of muted light fill the second domed expanse, but there are no piles of bones. On the far wall are four doors, each with words above. The men stand below the words, then look at Gage. Gage points and reads them aloud.

"Lower Level A. Lower Level B. Lower Level C. Restrict-ed Level."

"We need to find a way to the Restricted Level," Chief Coil says.

Harley steps forward and pushes one of the doors with his shoulder, but it doesn't swing open. Uncle Winch adds his weight but, again, there's no give.

"They must be blocked," Chief Coil suggests. "Maybe there's another way inside. A back door perhaps?"

The other men begin to explore the second cavern-ous area while Gage examines the doors in front of him. Each door is made of two metal panels, but there are no handles, unlike the other doors in the building. One door has a circular symbol in the middle with spokes running through the outer circumference. He steps close and runs his hand along the join where the two panels meet. He can feel cool air seeping through.

If air can get through, they must open, he muses.

He leans his walking stick and machete against the wall, then, with his hands working in opposite direc-tions, he applies sideways pressure on each metal panel. They don't open, but he's sure he feels a slight movement and pushes harder. When the panels move a little, he pries them apart with his fingers until there's enough of an opening to squeeze his hand inside. Then he leans against the far panel with all his weight, and they move apart even more.

"Uncle Winch," he grunts, hoping the other men will come and help.

Gage holds the panels apart while he squeezes his head through the opening. The room is too dark inside to see a thing, so he pushes his shoulder through for a better look. He can feel cool air on his face and the panels pressing against his chest and back. He squeezes his hip through the narrow opening, then his bent knee.

"I can just about step inside," he speaks aloud, as if to make his decision official.

Gage pushes his weight forward so he can bring the rest of his body through: his whole leg and both hips, his second shoulder. He puts his foot down in front of him for balance but realizes, too late, that there's no floor beneath him.

"A cavern!" he realizes at the same moment he loses his footing.

As Gage plummets through the darkness, he twists around in time to see the panels snap closed above him. It feels like he's falling for five minutes, but even as he thinks this he knows it's only been a second, or maybe two. He also has enough sense to realize he can't fall forever. Then he lands heavily on a hard, flat surface. The landing jars every bone in his body, and pain shoots up his back into his head. He wonders how badly he's hurt himself and starts to panic. He gulps and tries to cry out, but the darkness takes over his brain.

ROOK

After Da glances up at me and clears his throat for about the tenth time, I decide I better get working on formatting Ruby's report. It's short but, from what I can tell, well written and well argued. She proposes that all pre-apprentice-aged children be permitted an extra day per year to explore the sector of their choosing. It's a twist on the Instructional School Field Trip Policy, but instead of forcing kids to spend an afternoon in a sector or service they have no interest in, they get to have some say in their rounding-out, which is pretty open-minded if you ask me. I'm impressed.

If I'd had that opportunity when I was in school, I would have chosen to spend all of my days in the

Growing Sector. I already know I want to recommend my secondborn transfer there, so that some of my grandchildren will have the chance to be Growers.

My favourite memory of the Growing Sector was when I went with Grandmam for the first time, just the two of us. Sparrow was a newborn, and I was feeling left out because of all the attention she was getting. We couldn't leave the pod without someone gushing over her, saying she was so cute and precious. I couldn't understand what all the fuss was about. Her constant crying made me angry and Mam uptight. So when Grandmam suggested taking me for an excursion to the Growing Sector the next day, Mam looked at her with exhausted relief, and I started bouncing around with excitement.

The next day, Grandmam held my hand while we walked along the streets and avenues together. She showed me parts of ArHK I'd never seen. We passed the Entertainers' studios and watched through the window as Animators worked on scenes for a cartoon. She took me past the New Technology Sector, and we saw apprentices being fitted for their personal messengers. She walked me around some of the areas of the Manufacturing Level and told me it was where all of the household and human goods were created, and she let me stop and watch the Clothiers in the garment room making new shirts. She even took me down to the Recycling Sector, where we walked under a big arch

that said *materia nunquam destruuntur*. Grandmam
said it meant that nothing in ArHK is ever destroyed
and everything is always made new, and we saw with
our own two eyes how they composted kitchen waste to
make soil for the Growers.

When we arrived at the security gate for the Growing
Sector and stepped into the brightly domed fields, my
eyes popped wide. We were on the edge of the night-
shade gardens, with rows and rows of ripening tomatoes, sweet peppers, and eggplants. It was love at first
sight. The plants were unbelievably green and the air
warm and moist. I drank in the smell of dirt, growing
plants, and vegetables. It was glorious.

But what was most surprising, even to my child's
powers of observation, was the immediate change in
Grandmam. Her face radiated calm, and she smiled
more easily than she did around Da and Mam or when
she was walking the streets near our pod. Her shoulders
slid away from her neck, and her grip on my hand loos-
ened. She reached out and plucked a leaf from a tomato
plant, crushed it between her fingers, and handed it to
me.

"Smell that, Rook. If that doesn't smell like freedom,
I don't know what does."

I didn't ask how freedom could have a smell, but I
took that leaf, inhaled the scent, and rubbed the rough
foliage between my thumb and fingers until my skin
turned green.

"Ivy!" a man called out from down the row of eggplants and approached with open arms. "So good to see you!" he said as they embraced. "It's been too long."

I watched as they hugged for what seemed like forever and wondered if she'd forgotten about me. But when their greeting was over, she stepped back and beamed down at me.

"I brought my granddaughter for an adventure!" she said brightly and placed her hand on the top of my head. Her touch was gentle and soft, and it claimed me too.

The man's face split into a wide smile and he kneeled down to look at me.

"So this is little Rook, at last." He reached out a hand and took mine in a firm handshake. "It's such a pleasure to meet you," he said and pumped my arm.

I looked up at Grandmam and laughed. Nobody had ever shaken my hand before. It was not a common greeting on the Knowledge Level.

After that, it seemed like the whole Growing Sector appeared. Suddenly, I was surrounded by people hugging Grandmam and smiling at me, commenting on how intelligent I looked, what mischief I had in my eyes, how Grandmam was right, and I was a special one all right. There were adults and apprentices crowded around. Some had dirt-stained hands, and others were carrying odd tools and balls of bamboo twine. I felt like a celebrity.

It wasn't a school day so there were other children around, kids I recognized from Instructional School.

While Grandmam chatted with her old friends, I sidled up to a group of kids playing with the plant clippings. They were weaving stems and leaves together and making green crowns. A boy about my age took the crown off his head and put it on mine.

"Here you go," he said. "Now you can be a ruler too."

Grandmam and I spent the whole afternoon with her friends. She picked up pruning shears and started down a row of plants, snipping off stocks and shoots and collecting them in the bucket at her feet. She didn't work as hard or as fast as the other Growers, but even the little bit she did brought a smile to her face. At first I followed her down the row and watched, but when I started to fidget she sent me off.

"Go play, little Rook. Run with the other children and enjoy the freedom to roam."

I hesitated but she shooed me away. "Go! Go! Have fun!"

I ran back up the row to where the children were twining sweet pea vines around their necks and waists. When we were dripping with greenery and our royal costumes were complete, we ran up and down the empty rows in a never-ending game of tag. We squealed and shouted, ran and dodged, and stopped every so often to adjust our leafy crowns or belts. I wasn't used to the freedom to run and scream. On the Knowledge Level, parents don't let their kids chase one another unless they're at the playground in Central Park.

But that day, once we'd run ourselves breathless, we flopped down at the end of a row, stretched out in the grass, and pondered the bright blue dome above us.

"Do you get to play with the leaves whenever you want?" I asked the boy lying beside me.

"Only on pruning days," he said soberly, his dark eyes full of kindness.

"Do you always get to play tag?"

He nodded, but looked at me with a strange expression. "You don't play tag on the Knowledge Level?"

"We do," I said. "But it's not the same. The Knowledge Level is boring."

I thought of the structured games we played in Central Park on holidays, always under the supervision of parents or childminders. The games never lasted long and somehow the rules turned everything sour. I didn't know how to explain the difference to him, how everything in my world operated with precision and control.

"But you have Central Park so close. You can see the ponds and take the Thrill Rides any time you want!"

I recognized the envy in his tone, and I never forgot how I felt when I sat up and looked at the great expanse of fields around me, stretching farther than ten Central Parks. I would have traded him spots in a heartbeat. The idea of working with so many other people gave me a thrill. Even by then, I recognized how quiet and lonely the Archives were.

I was so tired on our walk home that Grandmam carried me part of the way on her back with my feet threaded between her torso and arms. I fell asleep with my head against her shoulder and my bottom sagging low. When we got to our pod she put me on the street and kneeled down so that our noses were almost touching.

"Did you have a good time today?" she asked while she picked bits of tomato plant out of my hair.

I nodded vigorously. "I love it in the Growing Sector! How come we have to be stuck up here in the stupid Records Sector? Why can't we go live there with your friends?"

"It's just the way things are, Rook," she said sadly and pulled up my socks, straightened my pants, tucked in my shirt.

I didn't like her explanation, and even though I could see the tension creeping into her expression I pressed for a more satisfactory answer.

"I bet Mam and Da would like it down there too. We just need to tell Mam how much more fun it is than up here. She can convince Da."

Grandmam smiled, but it was one of those trick smiles. The kind that hides sadness. "Let's not tell them too much about all the fun we had today, okay? We wouldn't want them to feel left out."

I nodded sullenly, but I didn't really understand. She must have sensed I was struggling with the injustice because she kissed the top of my head, then stood up to open the door.

"Everyone will tell you we're Keepers, Rook. Not Growers. But that doesn't mean we can't dream."

"And visit?" I asked, hopefully. "You can take me back there sometimes?"

"Of course, I can! And when baby Sparrow is big enough we can take her too."

"Maybe we can go tomorrow," I suggested.

Grandmam chuckled. "Not tomorrow, but soon."

Then she opened the door and we walked into our pod to find Mam and Sparrow curled up on the couch asleep. I tiptoed over and kissed the soft dark fluff on Sparrow's head. I couldn't wait for her to hurry up and get big so we could take her for a visit to the Growing Sector too.

I shake the memory from my mind and finish formatting Ruby's report. I insert the links, tag the content, and submit it to the Official Record. Then I stand up and make my way to the front of the Archives on my way to lunch. Before I head out onto the busy Avenue, I watch the activity from my quiet vantage point. A group of kids roll by on kick-scooters, kids a year or two older than Sparrow. It's obvious from their excited voices that they're on a field trip, and I think nostalgically of all the school trips Ruby and I went on together. Their teacher brings up the rear, shouting directions about staying together, watching for pedestrians, and keeping to the right. Most of the children are too far ahead to hear, and the rest are too busy talking and laughing to care what she's said. I wonder where they're headed and make a mental note to ask Sparrow how school has been going and if she has any field trips coming up. I've been so preoccupied the past couple of days, I've barely heard a word she's said.

GAGE

Waking up in the pitch black is disorienting, and it takes Gage a few moments to remember he's somewhere in the bottom of the Department of Human Safety and Survival. The first thing he does is reach for his talisman. He rubs his index finger over the engraved symbols and takes a deep breath. When he moves his legs, pain radiates up his back.

"How long've I been here?" he whispers.

Then all his senses come to life at once. He notices the air feels cool to his skin, his head is throbbing, his left leg hurts near the ankle, his mouth is dry.

"Uncle Winch?" he calls out, but his voice is too weak and it hurts to yell.

"Chief Coil?" he tries to call out again but stops when his voice breaks.

He lies still and listens for sounds from the other scouts. He knows they must be looking for him. He knows they will pry open the doors and, when they do, he'll call to them and they'll throw down a rescue rope. But no matter how hard he strains his ears, even when he holds his breath, he can't hear anything above his own heart pumping blood at double the normal speed.

Despite the pain screaming up his spine, Gage scuttles backwards until he feels a wall. Then he props himself up and feels his way to the torch bundle, still secured to his back. He tries to see in the darkness, but there's not a ray of light anywhere. Even when he puts his hand in front of his face he can't see a thing. He pulls out the fibre cloth and the small leather pouch of pine pitch and fumbles in the dark. Twice he has to run his hand over the dusty floor to find what he's dropped, and by then fear is frothing inside him.

"Breathe, Gage. Just calm down and breathe," he coaches himself.

His voice echoes in the cavern and startles him.

It takes patience but finally he fashions a small torch. He knows he has a few hours of light, maybe five or six tops, if he doesn't find more flammable material. He locates his flint and a small metal knife blade in the bottom of the bundle and strikes them together as quickly as he can without being able to see. Finally, a small spark ignites the torch. He has never been so happy to see light.

Gage climbs to his feet and winces at the pain in his left leg and back. He looks around the small square space, then up at the distance he fell. He can't make out the doors above him and has no idea how far down he has fallen. What he can see though, is an opening on the other side of the narrow space and he steps carefully through, onto solid ground and into a long corridor.

"Harley?" he calls out.

"Uncle Winch?" he croaks hopefully.

The corridor smells dusty but the air is dry. Gage shivers again from the chill and wishes he had his over-coat with him. He runs his hand over the surface of one wall. It's cool and hard, like stone. The ceiling and floor seem to be made of the same hard material. Gage limps along until he comes to a juncture, then he waves his torch in both directions. The corridors stretch farther than the light.

"Left or right?" he asks himself before hearing his father's words in his head: "If you go right, you can't go wrong."

Gage turns to the right. He wishes he had his walking stick with him, that he didn't leave it leaning against the wall with his machete. When he feels for the coil of rope, he realizes that it is missing too. He feels vulnerable without his scouting tools.

After hobbling a few more paces Gage comes to another juncture.

"Let's try going right again," he says.

Although the idea of making a sound terrifies him, he knows it's the best way to draw the attention of the others if they're within hearing distance.

"Steady there, Gage. Everything's gonna be fine. Just keep putting one foot in front of the other. One step at a time," he says loudly into the void, the torchlight wavering with the force of his voice. He has no idea how long it will take him to limp up and down every corridor but he's determined to try.

• • •

It feels to Gage as if he's hobbled up and down corridors for hours, and all he's found are empty rooms, locked doors, and dead ends. His ankle throbs and his torch flickers as it burns low. Discouraged, he sinks to the floor with his back against the cool hard wall. The silence envelops him, and the beat of his heart echoes in his head. It's been a long day, and the exhaustion is numbing his limbs, confusing his thoughts, slowing his breathing. Although he knows he shouldn't let himself fall asleep, he can't resist the comfort and escape, and he embraces the blackness.

• • •

When he wakes up, it's dark again. The torch has gone out and he has no idea how long he nodded off. He feels for the torch lying by his leg and retrieves the flint and knife blade from his pack. The torch is burnt almost to the bottom, but it catches fire and the light is as welcome as a breath of fresh air. He pushes himself to his feet again and waits while the feeling returns to his lower limbs.

Gage limps to the next juncture and squints one way down the corridor, then the other way. He blinks his eyes and shakes his head to be sure what he's seeing is real. He even snuffs out the torch. But it *is* real: a faint glimmer of daylight coming from the left corridor.

"There's definitely something down there," he says and hobbles toward the light.

For the first time since he regained consciousness, Gage feels hopeful, like he might not die alone in the dark cavern after all.

"Maybe it's the back way to these corridors. Maybe it's connected to the outside," he mutters and limps as quickly as he can, drawn toward the possibility of finding his way out.

At the end of the corridor, Gage sees that the faint light is seeping from beneath a door, a crease of blue that spills across the floor. On the door is the same circular symbol he saw in the cavern above. There are also words.

"APE Monitoring Room. Restricted Access," he reads slowly to himself.

He reaches out and feels the raised shape and letters. They feel cold to the touch, like a knife blade on a
winter's day. Encouraged by the light pooling at his feet,
Gage pushes on the door, first with his hands and then
with his shoulder. It's heavy and stubborn, but with
all his weight behind him he's able to open it and step
through. This time he sweeps his eyes across the blue-lit
floor, to make sure he has something solid to step onto.

The room is not connected to the outside the way
Gage had hoped. In fact, it's completely enclosed, and
the far wall is covered in dusty gauges and panels, dials
and black squares that look like the ancient windows
he's seen in his mother's picture books. In the centre of
the far wall, one of the squares is glowing. It emits a pale
blue light, the way the horizon does just before the sun
rises on a cold clear morning.

Gage crosses the room to examine the source of
light. It looks flat and smooth and he reaches his hand
toward it, tentatively, afraid to touch it but too curious
not to. He wipes his hand across it and clumps of dust
tumble to the ground. He takes the bundle from his
back and uses it to wipe the entire square clean, until
the room is filled with a cloud of ancient dust and pale
blue light. He sneezes, then freezes in place. The square
of light has suddenly come to life. It brightens until it
seems to Gage he should be able to see through to the
outside. He puts his face close, but he can't see anything.
The square is not transparent like windows were said to

be in the ancient buildings, the way the ice freezes on a pond in early fall. Somehow the square produces its own light, enough to illuminate the room. Gage puts his pack and torch on the ground, then looks around at the controls, gauges, and dials. There are numbers, letters, and words, all jumbled together.

None of the words look familiar, but Gage tries to sound them out anyhow, hoping the meaning will emerge when he hears them said aloud.

"Bar-o-met-ric press-ure," he reads, but it means nothing to him.

"Dopp-ler rad-ar." Again, even with the sound of the word in the room, there's no meaning he can attach to it.

"W-in-d," he says, relieved to hear one word he recognizes. But then he reads "vel-o-city" and can't understand what it is saying about the wind.

"It's no use," he mutters to himself when he realizes it will take him hours to decipher it all, and even then it won't help him figure out how to get out of the cavern.

Gage explores the rest of the room. In the far corner is an old bedroll on posts, like the cots they have at base camp. There's a chair with a tall curved back, shelves of rusty cans, bottles, and rows of books that stretch across an entire side of the room. Gage has never seen so many ancient artefacts. He's afraid to touch anything; yet he can't contain his curiosity. He wipes his hands on his sweater to clean off the dust, then runs his fingers softly along the spines of the books. His fingers tingle when he thinks of what he's touching. So many books! There must be a thousand in this one small room. He's not sure the Scholars have even seen this many books in one place.

Wait 'til I show the others, he thinks hopefully. *I'm gonna be a legend in all the scouting camps. Even back in the Middle everyone'll know my name.*

When he's taken inventory of the room, Gage turns back to the magic square. He stretches out his fingers and rests his hands flat on the surface. He's surprised it isn't hot, even though it's so bright. Again the square changes from his touch. This time rows of letters and numbers appear. Surprised, he jumps back. But when nothing more happens, he inches close again. He traces the letter *H* with his finger, the way he did when he was a small child and was allowed to touch his mother's books for learning. He moves his finger down one vertical line, then the other, and finally he connects them with the small horizontal line.

At the top of the square an *H* appears.

"Did I make that happen?" he asks.

He traces another letter: *E*. At the top of the square an *E* appears: *HE*.

"I *did* make that happen. This is some sorta ancient writing machine!"

He traces a random series of letters and they all appear in the row at the top: *SALKAPODJ.* Gage has never seen anything like this and wonders if it's one of the ancient computing machines he's heard about. The Scholars said computing machines no longer existed and even if one was found, it wouldn't work. But here he is, staring at the most extraordinary object, and he has nobody to tell.

"Harley!" he calls out again.

He goes back to the doorway and summons as much of his voice as he can.

"Uncle Winch! Chief Coil!"

His voice echoes down the corridor, but when the sound dies away there's nothing left to hear except his ragged breathing.

He returns to the square on the wall, and his breath leaves him completely, the way it did when he landed at the bottom of the cavern. On the square are letters, letters that weren't there before, a word he is sure he didn't make. It's a word he knows by heart.

"Hello," he reads the word aloud.

"The computing machine must know I'm here," he whispers and looks over his shoulder uneasily.

He examines the rows of letters on the bottom of the square and realizes there's one for every letter in the alphabet, plus a row of numbers on top, so he starts to trace out a message to the computing machine.

"Hello," he finally writes back, then smiles to himself. "Look what I just did! I wrote an actual word!"

The square responds, "How are you?"

It takes awhile to find all the letters and to remember how to spell the words, but after a few more attempts at tracing, he realizes he only needs to tap the letter to make it appear.

"Im good. How are you?" he taps.

It takes only seconds for a reply. "I'm fine. Can I help you with something?"

"Can you help me with something?" Gage says aloud, then wonders where to begin. After a moment he types, "Can u tell me wen was sum one here last?"

He steps back and watches the square until more words appear.

"Where is here?"

Gage concentrates on the letters and types, "I thot u wud now."

Once the message is up there, he second-guesses himself. He's not sure if he spelled *know* correctly, but hopefully he was close enough for the computing machine to respond.

There is a pause before the square lights up. "I don't know. Can you give me a clue about where you are?"

Gage takes a deep breath and sounds out the words he doesn't recognize. Then, when he's sure of the message, he steps quickly over to the door to read what room he's in. It takes him a minute to find all the letters, and he has to take three trips back to the door to remember all of the words.

"APE Monitoring Room."

"What is the APE Monitoring Room?" the computing machine asks after a moment.

Gage searches desperately for each letter. "How shud I now?" he types slowly.

"Who is this?" The words pop up quickly.

Gage types, "My name is Gage. Who are u?"

ROOK

When I return to the Archives after lunch, Da is standing at the counter talking to Governor Hawk, and my first impulse is to turn and run. It takes all my energy to open the front doors and walk inside. Da glances up and I try to interpret his expression. Is he angry? Upset? Afraid?

Governor Hawk turns around too and pins me in place with his shiny black eyes. He tilts his head, tracks my movements, measures my panic. I glance over my shoulder. I'm closer to the front door than to the counter if I need to bolt.

"Rook!" Da calls out with the fake cheerfulness he reserves for interactions with Governor Hawk. "The

Governor stopped by to see how we were making out with Ruby's proposal. He wants to present her with an award this afternoon so he wants to be sure it's been officially filed."

"I finished just before lunch," I say cautiously.

I swear Governor Hawk is glaring at me, and a shiver scrambles up my neck and down again.

"There you go!" Da says and wipes away a line of sweat that has bubbled up suddenly on his forehead. "You should be able to pull it up in the Council Chamber for everyone to see. I bet Ruby is a real asset to the team. So young and already in the Official Record!"

"Yes, she is. A real asset," Governor Hawk replies coldly. "Thank you for filing it so quickly."

He nods at Da before he leaves. I swear I feel a chill when he passes by me.

"That was weird," I say to Da when Governor Hawk is out of earshot.

Da is finishing something on his terminal.

"What do you mean?"

"You don't think Governor Hawk was a little intense just now?"

Da motions for me to lean close. "He's always a little intense if you ask me." Da turns off his terminal and unfolds himself from the chair. "I'm going for lunch now. I hope you didn't finish all the apple tarts."

"I left you one, but you might want to hurry because Mam was eyeing it when I was leaving."

"Don't forget to submit the Daily Log this afternoon," he says as he pulls open the front door.

I roll my eyes as he disappears onto the Avenue.

"How could I forget?" I mutter. "I do it every single day."

When I power up my terminal, the first thing I do is open the Daily Log screen. I'm about to input the population and link a birth and death notice when a letter appears at the bottom of the screen: *H*. I stare at the letter and wonder how it got there. I don't think I input it accidentally. Before I'm finished wondering about the *H*, though, an *E* appears next to it.

"He?" I wonder aloud. "He who?"

I look around the Archives to see if Da returned or Mam arrived without me noticing, but I'm definitely alone.

When I turn back to the terminal, another series of letters appears: *SALKAPODJ*.

"Sal-ka-pod-j? What's that supposed to mean?"

I'm sure nobody in ArHK has remote access to the Daily Log. At least Da's never told me the application is linked to another terminal. And after a year, I *know* I've never seen any words at the bottom of the Daily Log screen before.

I assess my options and decide the best thing is to confront whoever is fooling around on the Archives computer. I type *Hello*, then sit back in my chair to think. Maybe someone has hacked the system. Maybe

I caught them just in time, and when Da finds out he'll present me with a special Keeper award. I know hackers haven't existed in my lifetime, but Da told me about them when I first came to apprentice. Back before Grandmam Ivy was Head Keeper, someone hacked the system from a remote location and downloaded twenty OT years' worth of Governor Reports from the restricted files. The programmers added a layer of security after that.

After receiving a polite *Hello*, I shoot off a new line of text: "How are you?"

I might as well keep the conversation going until I figure out my next step.

Suddenly another line appears at the bottom of my screen: "Im good. How are you?"

Although the conversation is a bit mundane, there is nothing to do but play along. "I'm fine. Can I help you with something?"

"Can u tell me wen was sum one here last?"

Again I turn and look over my shoulder but the Archives is empty. I'm the only person in the entire hall.

"Where is here?" I input.

The reply takes a long time but eventually the words appear: "I thot u wud now."

Based on the spelling, whoever is writing is clearly not an intellectual. This makes me think it could be someone from the Waste Management Level. What if someone built a supercomputer from discarded parts?

Could someone without any computer engineering training learn how to build a computer? Could they have had access to knowledge not normally available to their level and sector, the way Grandmam learned how to be a Grower?

I start to type a couple of different replies but delete them. Finally, I send this message: "I don't know. Can you give me a clue about where you are?"

It takes a while, but eventually the reply appears: "APE Monitoring Room."

"Huh?" I say out loud. I've never heard of a place called the APE Monitoring Room and although I realize there are places in ArHK I've never been, I'm surprised to know nothing about what this APE room is, or where it is.

"What is the APE Monitoring Room?" I write.

"How shud I now?" comes the reply.

"Well, if you don't know, then how would I know?" I mutter. "I swear, people think we Keepers know everything, just because we work in the Archives." By now I'm even more convinced my instincts are right: someone is writing from somewhere down in Sorting or Recycling.

I wonder if I should log off the terminal before I get myself into serious trouble. Then a thought crawls into my mind from nowhere. What if I'm not talking to a hacker? What if Governor Hawk is spying on me from the Council Chamber, or Da is testing me? Still, I can't help but reply, hoping that Da will reveal his ploy, or the writer on the other end will make a mistake and give themselves away.

"Who is this?" I type quickly.

The reply that comes back is even more baffling: "My name is Gage. Who are u?"

I've never heard of anyone by the name Gage, not even from the Growing Sector, where they tend to use unusual names, like Strider, my friend from school. I switch screens and type *Gage* into the ArHK Locator Database. It comes up with Person Not Found. When I try again, checking the filter for nicknames as well, it still comes back blank.

"I'm Rook. What sector are you from?" I ask, even though I'm pretty sure a hacker is not going to tell me what sector they're from. It would be like announcing on the ArHK intercom that you're about to commit a serious offense.

"What's a sector?"

My pulse races so quickly I feel dizzy and grip the edge of the desk for balance. Everyone in ArHK knows what a sector is. Even the smallest child knows what sector she's from. It's something parents begin drilling into their children's heads as soon as they can walk.

I swallow hard before I ask, "Is this a joke?"

"No joke. Are u a computing mashine?"

"Am I a computing machine?" I say it so loudly the words echo through the Archives. I glance around, grateful I'm still alone.

"I'm a person. A Keeper," I type. Then I add, again, "What sector are you from?"

I'm so anxious waiting for a reply that I begin to chew my fingernails and tap my foot on the floor. Either something really big is happening or someone is playing the best practical joke ever. But who would risk so much on a practical joke? Certainly not Ruby or Heath. Definitely not Strider. The Entertainers wouldn't even attempt something this serious for their *Walk the Prank* series.

"I dont now. What sector are u from?"

"I'm from the Records Sector," I write.

"Ware is the Records Sector?"

I want to ask, Are you for real? I mean, asking where the Records Sector is, is as ridiculous as asking someone, Where is your nose? Instead I type, "Are you from ArHK?"

I hold my breath until the words appear: "I dont now. How wud I now?"

I laugh aloud, then almost cry. I reply, "You would know. Trust me."

The next sentence appears: "Were is ArHK?"

I don't hesitate and type, "That's a good question."

GAGE

E ven though he sees the words with his own eyes, Gage has a hard time believing he's talking to a real person on the computing machine, a real person named Rook who lives in a place called ArHK. He's read a few books in his short life, he's been lucky enough to see maps with his own eyes, and he's spent hours listening to the scouts talk about the ancient cities they've explored and the ones they hope to explore. He's even met some Scholars in the Middle, but he's never heard of an ancient city named ArHK. He has so many questions fighting to get out of his brain, his fingers have a hard time keeping up.

"Im a scowt ecsploring the anchent city of Washington. I fell down a cavern."

When he finishes putting the words on the square he waits. The minutes drag, and he gives up hope of getting an answer when the sentences pop up suddenly before his eyes.

"Washington was one of the great cities from the Outside. From before the time of winds, fires, and floods. We learned about it in school. I didn't think it was real."

Gage takes a deep breath and deciphers all the words he doesn't recognize. Then he replies, "It was real. U now about the Storm Ages?"

He waits for a response.

"Yes, that's why the Chosen Ones were sent to ArHK. Are you really from the Outside? Are there many people there?"

Gage isn't sure what Rook means by *Chosen Ones* or *the Outside*. Her words make sense, but he can't quite grasp the meaning of what she's asking. Still, he has to reply so he taps out, "There are many thowsands of pee-ple on Earth. If thats wat u mean. Nobody nows for shur how many. There are thowsands in the midel alone. There may be more in other lands."

"Do you mean Earth like in the Creationist legends of the planets, stars, and sun?"

Legends, Gage thinks to himself. Why would Rook think the sun is a legend? Finally, he taps out, "There not legends."

"Have you seen them?" Rook asks.

Gage nods as he taps out the words. "I see the stars at night and the sun in the day. Can u see them?"

"No."

"Why not?"

"I don't know."

"Are u blind?"

"No."

"What can you see ware u are rite now?"

"Desks, computers, chairs, walls, the sky turning dark blue."

"U can see the sky but not the sun or stars?"

"It's not the limitless sky. The sky in ArHK stops a few metres above our heads. Except in places like Central Park and the stadium. Then it's much higher."

Gage stumbles through the words and when he's finished, he thinks of the cavernous rooms far above him, filled with filtered sunshine.

"Are u in a bilding?" he asks.

"I don't know."

"A cavern?"

"I don't know."

"How many peeple live in ArHK?"

"5,028. My Da is coming back from lunch. I have to stop now. Will you be here later?"

"I think so. Im lost. I have no ware to go."

"I'll write as soon as I can."

The words disappear, and Gage stares at the blank glowing square. He reaches out and touches it again with the palms of his hand. Although he expects it to have grown warm, the way the coals of a fire build heat the longer they burn, it still feels cool.

He limps over to the bedroll and flips it over, then chokes on the dust that rises up in his face. The bedroll is not made of hemp cloth stuffed with feathers, like his bedroll at base camp. It's lighter and stiffer. Gage squeezes it with his finger and instead of leaving an impression, the bedroll springs back to a smooth surface. He looks under the bedroll at the platform. It has six legs and thin slats that run from one side of the frame to the other. Despite being made of some type of plastic, which Gage finds surprising, it looks as sturdy as the wooden platforms they use in the Middle.

"It looks like it'll hold my weight," he muses, then sits down carefully.

The bedroll gives slightly but doesn't collapse. In fact, it feels good to be sitting, resting his throbbing leg. He pulls up his pant leg to check for damage. He didn't split his skin so there's no blood, which is good news. And he knows he hasn't broken a bone. Still, he expects it will look as nasty as a storm cloud by morning. Gage pulls his pant leg down again. There's no sense dwelling on what he might have done differently. The facts are the facts. He hurt his leg, but at least it's not so serious he can't walk. And his back has stopped bothering him as much as it did when he first woke up after falling.

Gage turns his mind back to Rook and ArHK, and he thinks about what it would be like to live in a place with a sky that stops.

"If she isn't in a building, where else could she be?" he reasons aloud, then continues to chase his logic. "And if she doesn't know she's inside a building, she must never have gone into it."

Gage wonders if Rook is in a building like the one he's in, a building created to survive the Storm Ages. Where would such a building be? Somewhere in Washington? The questions multiply in his head but are interrupted when his stomach growls. He remembers the wild garlic and digs it from his pocket. It isn't much, but enough to stop his stomach from complaining for a little while anyway.

With silence filling his head, it doesn't take long for him to approach the shelves of books. He knows he shouldn't touch the artefacts without Uncle Winch or Harley supervising, but he hasn't heard a sound except his own voice in hours, and the draw is just too great. Besides, if he's careful when he handles the books, and he places them back on the shelves in the exact same position, who will ever know he's touched them? He scans the spines of the books, selects one called *World Atlas*, and takes it to the bedroll. He lays it flat on his lap and runs his hand over the smooth blue and green cover. Then he opens it and turns the pages, carefully, one by one.

The pages are filled with maps of all the countries in the ancient world. He's never seen so many maps, and he wonders if the Scholars have ever seen a book dedicated to maps. He finds a map of the United States of America and looks for the city of Washington.

I'm here, he thinks to himself when he locates Washington, DC, on the edge of the United States, beside the Atlantic Ocean. *But where's Rook?*

Gage starts back at the beginning of the book, on the very first map, and looks at every word, searching for ArHK. He flips from page to page and even scours the index pages, but he can't find any reference to ArHK. He finds Argentina and Aruba. He finds Arctic Circle and Armenia, Arkansas and Arlington, but he does not find ArHK. He closes the book and thinks. What he needs more than anything is to find Uncle Winch and Harley. He needs to find Chief Coil and the map readers. They'll help him figure out where ArHK is located.

His torch doesn't have much life left, but Gage lights it and returns to the corridor. He wants to be sure he didn't miss any doors when he first started exploring. He has to find a way out. And this time, to be sure he searches every direction and every corridor, he uses ash from his torch to smudge arrows at each juncture.

When he gets back to where he landed from above, he searches the ground and finds the coil of rope on the far side of the cavern.

"It must have come loose when I fell," he says aloud, then startles at the echo as his voice ricochets above him.

He picks up the coil of rope and secures it at his waist. If nothing else, he can cover the rope fibres with whatever pine pitch he has left and use that as a torch. It won't offer the same quality of light as the dense woven torch fibre his mother makes, but it will be better than nothing.

As Gage hobbles down each corridor, he quickly realizes how hopelessly lost he'd be if he hadn't thought ahead. At the end of each corridor are heavy metal doors that won't budge, no matter how hard Gage pushes. There are six end doors in total and none of them have light coming from the bottom. Discouraged and with his torch flickering weakly, Gage returns to the room with the glowing blue square. He checks the computing machine but there are no more words.

Gage is drawn back to the shelves, and he looks again at the spines of the books. The books on the top shelf are the smallest and have soft covers. Gage can tell by the titles they are ancient stories: *Riddley Walker, City of Ember, Nineteen Eighty-Four, The Hunger Games, Brave New World, The Room, Lord of the Flies, The Swiss Family Robinson, The Giver*. The colourful spines go on and on and behind the first row is a second row of books. The books on the second shelf are taller, with hard covers, like the *World Atlas* he looked at earlier.

In fact, there are several map books, one devoted entirely to ancient cities in the United States of America. Another book is all about plants, complete with pictures of every type of plant as well as a description of when it grows and a map of where the plant is found in North America. There are books on animals and birds, fish and vegetables, trees and flowers. There are books about ancient machines, even flying machines, and narrow linked machines called trains that ran across the land on long straight rails.

There's a book on ships and Gage studies it for a long time. He scours every page hoping to find a clue about the Ship of Knowledge, but there's no mention of such a vessel. There are even books about people and historic events from the last millennium. Gage studies each picture carefully and sounds out the words below. He's so absorbed he almost misses the new words on the glowing blue square.

ROOK

When Da steps inside the Archives, I'm pacing in front of my terminal, chewing on the nail of my left thumb. It's already down to the quick and I want to stop, but I can't. As soon as he steps behind the counter, I rush to the front door and lock it manually. I draw the shades so people walking by cannot look inside.

"What are you doing?" he asks.

I continue to chew on my fingernails. I'm trying to decide whether or not to tell him about what happened while he was at lunch. But how can I not tell him? I pace and think.

"Rook, what's going on?"

I stop and assess him for a full minute before I open my mouth.

"I have something important to tell you. But I'm afraid."

"Are you in trouble? Have you done something to upset the Governors? Did Governor Hawk come back after I left?"

Da's questions come out in rapid succession, and I hold up my hand to stop him.

"I'm not in trouble. Not that I know of anyway."

I watch panic rise in Da's face. His neck turns prickly red and hot blotches travel to his cheeks.

"You know what will happen if you breached protocol! We'll both be in trouble," he says. "Governor Hawk has been watching —"

"It's nothing to do with the Governors. Well, not exactly. But you have to promise me you won't get angry."

"I can't make any promises, Rook. But I have no idea ..." he stammers.

"Da!" I say sharply. "You have to promise you'll stay calm."

"Of course, Rook. Just tell me what's going on."

I grab Da's arm and drag him over to the terminal where the Daily Log is still up on the screen, unfinished.

"You didn't do the Daily Log yet?" he asks and raises his left eyebrow the way he does when he's trying to solve a puzzle.

"No. But that's not what I want to show you."

"Then what?"

"Sit down," I say and press him into a chair.

I sit beside him and look straight into his eyes. I hold his hands tightly in mine to keep him still.

"Someone from the Outside just contacted us." I say each syllable slowly and with purpose.

Da looks at me. His eyes search my face. He opens his mouth then closes it again. Finally, he shakes his head.

"That's not funny, Rook," he says.

I'm speechless for a moment. I never considered he wouldn't believe me.

"I'm serious," I say and squeeze his hands to make my point.

Da looks at the screen, then back at me. He screws one side of his mouth into a twisted smile.

"Is Mam in on this?"

"Da, seriously. This is not a joke. Some person named Gage says they're in the bottom of a cavern in the old city of Washington. In a room called the APE Monitoring Room," I explain as patiently as I can with blood gushing through my veins like when the kitchen tap is on full.

The expression on Da's face turns from amused to confused to terrified. By the time I take a breath, his complexion is the same shade of grey as the Avenue. In fact, he looks like he might faint. He leans over and puts his head on the top of the desk. I rub his back the way he does when Sparrow or I are sick.

"Does this mean anything to you?" I ask. "Have you heard of an APE Monitoring Room? At first I thought it was a joke. You know, like a hacker? Or I thought it was you or Governor Hawk messing with the computer system. But then I didn't think it was possible anyone outside the Archives could access the Daily Log."

Da is rolling his head back and forth on the desk.

"I don't believe it," he moans softly.

"Look," I say to get his attention. "I'm going to show you. I'll send a message and see what Gage writes back."

Da lifts his head. He looks dazed, but he watches the screen as I write.

"Gage? Are you still there?"

Nothing happens and Da looks relieved. Then words appear at the bottom of the screen.

"Still here. No way owt."

Da chokes and I slap him on the back. Then I reply to Gage.

"Da is here with me now. He's Head Keeper. He's shocked to hear from someone from the Outside. It's been hundreds of years since we had contact."

"Hello Da," Gage writes. "Is yur name Da or are u Rooks father?"

I turn to Da, apologetically. "Gage writes phonetically."

Da looks at me and nods numbly. Then he turns back to the screen and watches me type.

"He is my father. His name is Fern."

"Hello Fern," Gage writes.

Da stutters for a moment, then says, "Ask how Gage contacted us."

"Da wants to know how you contacted us?" I write.

"I fownd a glowing square in the bilding ware Im trapped. I think its a computing mashine. It had letters so I tuched them and you rote me back."

Da looks haunted, as if he's been told he has a terminal disease and only a few hours to live.

"Gage contacted us by accident?"

I shrug and screw up the corner of my mouth. "I guess so. At least it sounds like it."

I turn back to the Daily Log screen.

"Tell us more about the Outside. What is Washington like? How long have you been there?"

Da and I wait for Gage's reply. When nothing appears on the screen for several minutes I panic, but the colour returns to Da's face and his breathing becomes regular again. Then the screen comes to life with several lines of writing.

"Im part of a scowting kamp. Weve been serching for Washington for many years. Weve only bin here a few days. Its the first ancient city Ive ever seen. There are many old rewins, walls, briges, and even monamints."

Da and I decipher the words on the screen, then look at each other with puzzled expressions.

"It seems like they're rediscovering Washington," Da says.

I write another message. "Have people lived in the Outside forever?"

"Yes."

"Humans survived the times of the winds, floods, and fires?"

"Many died. The scolers in the midel say hole sosi-etees fell."

Da shifts in his seat and straightens his reading glasses. "Ask what the midel is," Da says.

"What is the midel?" I write.

"The midel is the senter of our sosietee. Ware food is grown. Tools made. Cloth wovin. Its ware scowting parties are sent from. Its ware the scolers study the anchent artefacts and human nowlege the scowts colect."

"Maybe Gage means to say *middle*," I suggest. "You know. *M-i-d-d-l-e*?"

Da bumps my chair out of the way and takes control of the terminal.

"This is Fern Keeper writing. Let me get this clear. You're looking for human knowledge?"

"Yes. We now anchent humans culd do things we cant even imajin. Were serching for the ship of nowlege. Our scolers say if we find it we will find the seecrets to humankinds gratest akomplishments and improov our lives. Thats our mishin in Washington. To find a cloo abowt this grate ship."

"The Ship of Human Knowledge?" I say to Da. "I've never heard about that in the Creationist legends."

When Da doesn't say a word, I look away from the terminal and at him. He's staring at the floor and rubbing his temples. His scalp and hair move at the same time, and he rubs so hard I think he's going to wear a hole in his skull.

Finally, he looks up and blurts, "We have to tell the Governors."

My heart clenches and I bunch my hands into fists. I can't say for sure why this is a bad idea, but my gut tells me to fight back.

"NO!" I pound the desk. "No. No. No. It's not time to share this news. Not with the Governors. Not with the rest of ArHK."

I feel a surge of hope when Da doesn't move, like maybe my outburst worked. Even when he stares at me with eyes as wide open and round as an ArHKball, I feel like I might finally have a say about what happens next.

GAGE

When no message returns, Gage worries he's broken the computing machine, so he tries writing a new sentence.

"Do you now ware the Ship is?"

There's another long delay, and Gage is about to go back to looking through the books when words appear.

"I think we might be the ship you are seeking."

Gage's chest contracts so hard he can't breathe for a moment, then he coughs and chokes back a lungful of stale air.

"Yur in a bowt?" he writes.

"We are in ArHK. Archives of Human Knowledge. Our ancestors were sent here five hundred years ago to protect human knowledge and ensure the future survival of humankind."

When he sees the message, Gage's stomach twists into a knot. The words are long and complicated, and each one takes time to sound out. But when he finally finishes reading, he gets another kind of feeling in his stomach, a rush of excitement that radiates from his centre and up through his beating heart. Gage knows his father was assigned to explore the National Archives, so some of what he's reading makes sense. Still, not everything adds up. He shifts from one foot to another and feels pain shoot up his back. More than anything he wishes he had something to drink.

"Maybe yur on a ship. The scolers said we need to find a ship. Ive seen pikturs of wat a ship looks like. Its a very big mashine that flowts on the water. They sid Washington wud hold a cloo as to the ships ware abowts."

Thinking of how to spell each word and tapping them out using the square is time-consuming, and Gage begins to think that maybe the ancient people didn't have it so great after all. When he was exchanging short messages, it was one thing, but his brain is starting to hurt, a throbbing that reaches like fingers around his skull and squeezes.

"An ark is a type of mythological boat and as big as a ship. Maybe your Scholars misunderstood?" the reply says.

Gage doubts the Scholars could misunderstand anything. The Scholars are the smartest and most educated people on Earth. It is said the original Scholars travelled from the far north, collected people into the Middle, and organized a new society. They've spent their lives reading books and gathering knowledge. Still, Gage doesn't have the energy to explain, to think of all the words and spell them out. He doesn't even have the energy to keep standing at the magic square.

"Im very tired. I need to rest. I hurt miself wen I fell into the cavern and its been many howrs sins I ate or slept. Will u be here later?" Gage writes.

The response comes quickly, and Gage feels relieved when he reads it.

"We'll be here. Maybe by then we'll have more answers for you. But one more question. Have you had your gender confirmation yet?"

Gage ponders this question and is confused. Eventually he replies, "I dont no wat u meen."

"We are trying to find out if you identify as male or female, or where you fall on the gender spectrum?"

"What the heck is a gender spectrum?" Gage mutters to himself before tapping out his reply.

"I'm male. Wat abowt Rook?"

"Rook is a girl."

Gage limps over and sits on the bedroll. He pulls up the leg of his pants. His left ankle is swollen and purple, so he lies down and stretches out. The bedroll smells old and dusty but is softer than the floor, and warmer too. He wonders how many hours he's been in the cavern and where the other scouts are. He didn't let himself consider it before, but he wonders if they assume he's dead? Didn't his father say that sometimes scouts fall into caverns and are never found? Didn't Jett say the same thing happened to his uncle? How many scouts have died waiting for help that never came? He wonders about his mother and how she'll take the news when the messengers arrive at base camp and tell her that he's missing. He wonders about his father, above him some-where in the ancient city of Washington, doing what? Gage shivers and rolls onto his side. He grasps his tal-isman in his fist, curls into a ball for warmth, and falls asleep.

Gage sleeps so deeply he doesn't move or dream. When he wakes up, it takes a few moments to pull all the information back together again. He recalls with a shudder that he's lost in a deep cavern, then he remem-bers the computing machine and sits upright.

The square is still glowing blue, but the rows of let-ters are gone.

"Please don't be a dream," Gage says as he hobbles over and places his hands flat on the square.

As it did before, the square brightens and the rows of letters and numbers appear.

He writes, "Are u stil ther?"

When nothing appears for several minutes, Gage hobbles around the room. He glances at the square often but it remains blank, except for his last sentence.

He examines the rusty cans and bottles. There's clear liquid at the bottom of the bottles, but he's not sure what it might be. Hoping it might be something to relieve his intense thirst, Gage cracks the top of the bottle against the wall and winces when the glass shatters. He puts his nose to the broken bottle and sniffs, but he can't smell anything. He pours a few drops into his hand and touches the liquid with his tongue: all he tastes is water. Just to be safe though, Gage pours more of the liquid into his hand and takes only small sips at a time. It's a relief to wet his mouth and throat.

With his thirst satisfied, Gage goes back to look at the bottom row of books. These are not like the softcover books on the top shelf or like the picture-filled books on the middle shelves. These books do not have words on their spines, and all of them are bound in the same hard black covers. Gage pulls the last one from the bottom shelf. On the front is the circular symbol with spokes running through the outer edges. He flips through the book and sees page after page of handwriting. Each entry is short and contains lists of numbers and names in short form. He knows it would take too long to read all the entries, so he flips to the last few pages.

April 22, 2359

The people in ArHK continue to fulfill their mission. They are protected and safe and the

*population grows at a predictable rate. The Daily
Log comes through every day but contact is no
longer actively maintained as per the instructions
received from their leaders.*

*Washington, DC, is almost empty now. I'm not
sure how much longer we can survive. Only this
building continues to function and provide shelter.*

*We will remain as long as we are able but the
ongoing monitoring of ArHK is at great risk and
is no longer consistent. It is our hope that those in
ArHK will stay true to their purpose for the future
benefit of humankind.*

Next he turns to the last page. The entry is short and
the handwriting is shaky.

October 12, 2360

*Not much hope of anyone finding this log but I will
make a final entry regardless. Monitoring of ArHK
can no longer continue. I have breached ArHK
protocol and made contact to notify the officials
there of this unfortunate development. I regret
to say, the monitoring of the ArHK Preservation
Experiment is at an end. Over and out.*

Gage turns to the front of the book and flips through
all the journal entries. Each one looks the same. They

record the population of ArHK. They report on the internal and external temperatures. They report on the integrity of the outer shell of ArHK. Every entry looks exactly the same. Gage pulls out another journal and flips through it. Again, the book is filled with handwritten entries in the same style and format.

The journal for 2350 has a small white dot on the spine, so Gage pulls it out and looks through until he finds an entry that is slightly longer than the others. At the end of the list of regular details is a short passage of writing, starred and underlined: *Due to the social upheavals regularly experienced in ArHK, the officials there have requested direct contact with the Outside be discontinued. They have requested that Monitors no longer send comments through the Daily Log.*

Gage pulls out several of the black-covered books and sees that for over one hundred years, the only thing that changed was the date and population of ArHK. He looks around the room and shivers. To think someone, or several people, spent years within these four walls, sleeping on the same bedroll, reading these same books, writing their observations.

He thinks about the Monitors and what their lives were like. Did they ever leave the room or were they trapped like he is? What happened to the last Monitor after the last journal entry was written? Did the last Monitor leave the building and become a Lurker or add to the pile of bones in the great cavern above?

Gage shivers at the thought of being one of the last humans in the city of Washington, of being left behind when the other people fled to safety. He wonders what would make someone persevere alone, when all hope was gone? Then it dawns on him. He really has discovered the Ship of Knowledge! Rook and her Da are the Keepers of Human Knowledge. They've been in ArHK protecting the secrets over the centuries.

If only I could tell the others, he thinks to himself.

Then he notices a flicker on the square and hobbles over to read what's written.

ROOK

Da and I argue about what we should do next. Normally I accept Da's authority as Head Keeper, the way firstborns are taught. I trust him because he's my da, and I know he loves me and Sparrow more than anything in ArHK. But this time it's too important to sit back the way I've done all my life.

"I know we have to tell them, but not yet. We need to figure things out first. We have to follow Grandmam's trail and find out what the Governors have been hiding. Otherwise, who knows what they'll do with this information? What if this is our only chance to learn the truth?"

I'm walking laps of the Archives, and Da is still sitting beside his terminal, his head tilted back, staring up at the sky as it changes hues.

"Grandmam's trail?" he asks.

"Grandmam Ivy figured out a lot of things about ArHK. Things she didn't want the Governors to know, but she wanted us to know. That's why they sent her to the Growing Sector. She found out what they were keeping to themselves. She might have found out where ArHK is. Whatever she discovered, we have to find out too."

Da continues to stare at the sky, as if in a trance. I wave my hand in front of his face to get his attention.

"Da! Da! We have to go into the restricted files."

Da shakes his head sadly.

"If we start searching through the restricted files, Governor Hawk is going to be alerted. We have to tell them now, before we get ourselves banned from the Records Sector altogether. If that happens, we can't help Gage or ourselves."

"How long does it take the system to generate a report to the Governors?"

"A few hours. They'll get a report on all of our search terms first thing in the morning. I don't know how long it'll take before they review it."

"Then we have maybe ten hours to figure everything out. We need to start now and we need Mam's help."

Da hesitates so I say with as much force as I can muster, "We need Gage as much as Gage needs us. We have to help each other, but I'm not sure the Governors will see it that way. This is the biggest news in the history of ArHK. We need to figure this out first, before we tell anyone."

I'm startled by my own passion. And I'm not ready to let Da talk me out of anything either.

Lucky for us both, Da finally agrees. He beeps Mam and tells her to bring Sparrow to the Archives with enough snacks and drinks to last until morning. Then he promises to explain more when she arrives.

While he tries to convince Mam that he's serious, and implores her not to panic or stop and talk to anyone on her way, I power up the old computer and start following Grandmam's crumbs. I go back to 2437 and open the original version of *The ArHK Protection of People and Purpose Act*.

The Governors of ArHK, who find it increasingly difficult to maintain <u>order and control</u> within ArHK, and who have as their responsibility the best interest of the citizens of ArHK and the <u>ultimate survival of humankind</u>, hereby pass into immediate law The ArHK Protection of People and Purpose Act, whereby:

a)   The practising of all <u>religions from the Outside</u> shall be banned in all forms, whether a gathering of people, a recitation, a reading of <u>Outside writing</u>, or the <u>keeping of symbols</u> directly related to said religion.

b)   All files created and stored in ArHK from before
     2352 OT will be secured in a <u>restricted section
     of the Archives</u>. Access to these files will be
     limited to Head Governor and Head Keeper,
     with <u>Head Governor directly monitoring access</u>.

c)   All <u>Revolutionaries</u> currently identified in ArHK,
     and all those who are identified in future years,
     will be banned from public meetings and con-
     fined to their home sector, unless the home
     sector is located in the Knowledge Level of
     ArHK, then said offenders will be banned to a
     level and sector as chosen by the Governors.

d)   All <u>Outside artefacts</u> housed in ArHK will be
     elevated from restricted access to banned ac-
     cess, including all artefacts in the Great Hall,
     the ArHK <u>jet plane storage facility</u>, and the
     Governors <u>historical document room</u>. These
     areas will continue to be monitored for appro-
     priate environmental factors.

e)   All school curriculums will be reviewed and
     revised. All <u>photos</u>, <u>videos</u>, and <u>past communi-
     cations</u> from the Outside will be <u>removed from
     all learning materials</u> and placed in restricted
     access files in the Archives.

This Act will ensure the original purpose of ArHK,
which is to protect human knowledge for all time.

Although I know we have a lot of information to uncover in a very short time, I read the Act through several
times before it sinks into my head.

"The Governors control everything!" I say aloud.
"They don't want us to think for ourselves. They've
compromised the entire purpose of ArHK."

When I examine the document more closely, I see
Grandmam Ivy created links to files in various years,
spanning almost 300 OT years in total. I also see from
the dates captured in the Crumb Report that DKVI
made some early, preliminary links.

"Da!" I call out. "Look at this! Daisy Keeper also left
a trail of crumbs. Grandmam must have been following
Daisy Keeper's trail when Grandmam got banned."

Da comes and looks over my shoulder. He's mut-
tering nonsensical syllables to himself, and his hair is
so dishevelled I'm beginning to worry. He's unravelling
before my eyes.

"Da! We're committed to this. We've already started
down Grandmam's trail. Even if we stopped this minute
we'd be deemed Offenders by tomorrow afternoon. The
best thing we can do now is compile enough proof to
convince the other Governors to overthrow Governor
Hawk."

"That would be the best-case scenario," Da says.
"Worst-case is we need to overthrow all the Governors."

"Hopefully it won't come to that," I say and think of
Ruby.

When Sparrow arrives, I can tell with one quick glance she's not happy. Mam is doing her best to calm her, but I can see a temper tantrum brewing, and the last thing we need is to draw attention to ourselves.

"Hey! Sparrow!" I call out as she pouts by the front door with her arms crossed and her head lowered. "Come here. I want to tell you something."

"What?" Sparrow shouts, trying her best not to sound interested.

"You have to come here first. Then I'll tell you. It's top secret."

While I try and tempt Sparrow to join me by making silly faces at the computer screen and then at her, I also keep an eye on Da and Mam talking near the front of the Archives. Da moves his arms wildly as he talks, and the expression on Mam's face turns from amusement to disbelief and finally to fear.

"You don't seriously expect me to believe …" I hear Mam say.

Da nods solemnly.

"That's the most ridiculous thing I've ever heard. She's having you on —" Mam turns her head and the rest of her words are lost.

Dad continues his explanation until finally Mam's shoulders droop. The shape of her spine changes from straight to slumped. Finally, she crumples into a chair. Like Da, her face pales while she absorbs what she's heard.

A gentle tapping on my shoulder brings my mind back to Sparrow, who has finally appeared at my side.

"What did you want to tell me?" she says in a soft tone.

"What's got you all bent out of shape?" I ask. "Did you see Governor Hawk? Did he stare at you with his evil little eyes?" I ask and imitate Governor Hawk.

Sparrow laughs. "No, I didn't see Governor Hawk. But Mam says I have to spend the afternoon here, so I'm going to miss practice for the Day One Celebration play. I'm the Welcoming Governor. I even have lines to say."

Sparrow puffs out her chest and puts on a deep voice. "People of ArHK, I welcome you!" She sweeps her hand across her chest. "Never again do you have to worry about poisonous air, floods, fires, or winds. ArHK is the safest place you can imagine, and you are among the lucky few who have the opportunity to live here."

"Nicely done!" I say. "You're going to be the best Welcoming Governor in the whole history of ArHK. And I can show you something that will help you play your part even better."

"What? Show me!" Sparrow says.

"Go tell Mam and Da to come back here so I can show you all together."

Sparrow looks at the clunky old computer. "That thing actually works?" she asks.

"Surprising, isn't it? But yes, and it has foot-age of the Chosen Ones arriving in ArHK. It even shows them coming down from one of the five flying machines."

"Really?" Sparrow asks. Her eyes are as round as pot lids.

"Yes. Hurry and bring them back."

Sparrow collects Mam and Da while I find my way to the arrival footage.

"What do you want to show us?" Mam asks when she joins me. Some colour has returned to her face, but her hands are trembling.

"Arrival footage of the Chosen Ones. Real video. The quality is a bit rough, but it's clear enough to see. I found this the other day when Da's assignment was to find out what decision the Governors made in 2412 that impacted our Day One Celebrations. I think Grandmam Ivy made the link."

"Are you sure this is a good idea?" Mam begins to protest, but Da puts his hand on her quivering wrist to quiet her.

Da and Mam are standing behind me when I start the video. Sparrow leans in for a better look, then climbs on my knee. Mam gasps when she sees the people climbing out of the side of the jet plane.

"Is that real?" Sparrow asks.

"No," Mam says.

"Yes," I counter. "We're in this together. Whatever happens it's going to affect her too. She deserves to know what we're up to."

"What are we up to?" Sparrow asks. Her voice is quiet, conspiratorial, like she's telling the secret of her best friend.

"Just keep watching and you'll find out."

When the footage ends, Da tugs at his hair for what seems like forever, then finally finds his voice. "Things are starting to make more sense now."

Mam looks shocked: her mouth is agape, her eyes caught in a wide-eyed stare. She's piecing together information in her head, and I know things can go one of two ways. Either she will reject what she's seen and find every excuse possible to discredit it, which means we are sunk, and without Mam on board, I might as well walk out to the Avenue and start insulting the Governors — anything to focus the blame on myself — or she can find a way to take the leap of faith that Da and I have already taken and back us completely. She's always been an all-or-nothing type of person.

I watch Mam's face as emotions flicker across it. Time stops. My heart stops. Even Sparrow's squirming on my knee stops. It feels like the sky stops changing colour too. Finally, though, she nods and bites her bottom lip. She scrunches up her eyes the way she does when she's determined. That's when I know she's on our side. There's nothing like live footage to change a person's outlook. No wonder the Governors banned it.

"I can't believe Grandmam Ivy was telling the truth. I thought she'd lost her mind. I feel so awful."

Da takes her hand and squeezes it. "You weren't alone. She wouldn't blame you."

I clear my throat to break their moment of reverie.

"We don't have a lot of time and we have a lot to do. So if we could focus …"

They both look at me, surprised. But they don't scold me. Instead they listen closely to what I'm saying, which I find strange, like our roles have reversed suddenly and I'm in charge.

I stand up and pace the Archives, deep in thought. Mam, Da, and Sparrow trail behind me.

"There are a few questions we need to answer. I figure there are at least three main things to find out. If we each concentrate on one thing and itemize the proof, we should have what we need to convince the Governors that the Outside is real and humans still exist there."

"What's on your list?" Da asks.

"We need to find out where ArHK is. I *think* ArHK is part of the Outside, but we need to know for sure. Wherever we are, I found reference to the fact that it took six hours to fly here in a jet plane."

"Where did you find that?"

"In an old e-letter from the Outside, from right after our ancestors arrived."

I stop near the terminal at the front counter and turn to face my parents. Da and Mam exchange glances but remain focused.

"What else do we need to find out?" Da asks.

"We need to find out *what* ArHK is. Gage asked if we were in a building or in a boat, a ship. I read a script from an old campaign that was used to recruit people to come to ArHK. It referred to ArHK as a purpose-built facility."

Mam sits down slowly in a chair beside me. Her eyes are bleary, her expression veiled.

"A facility!"

"Yes, the script made it sound like ArHK was a laboratory or something. I don't know. I haven't got much to go on yet. That's why we need to find out as much as we can about ArHK."

"What else?" Mam asks while Da is deep in thought.

"We need to find out how to get out of ArHK. If our ancestors got in, there must be a way out. If we can find that, nobody can tell us we're wrong."

I let Da and Mam absorb the enormity of what they've just learned and what we have to accomplish. I can barely look at their faces. It's not right, I realize suddenly, to see so much fear in the two people who have always protected me. I drop my gaze to the terminal. That's when I notice a sentence waiting patiently on the Daily Log screen.

"Gage!" I shout. "He's back online. Someone needs to monitor this station. Someone needs to learn everything Gage knows. Like the poisonous air. We don't know if there's still poisonous air in the Outside."

"Heath," Da and Mam suggest at the same time, snapping out of their confusion.

"Heath?" I say. "Are you kidding?"

Even though he's my cousin, I don't know him well. But he seems like the kind of boy who would report every little misdemeanour to the Governors.

"I don't know about Heath," I say.

"He's going to be one of us, Rook," Da says. "Plus, he's smart."

"And he's all we've got," Mam adds.

I sigh. They have a point. I can't exactly bring Ruby on board, and who else is there?

"Give him a beep and see if he's willing to come," I say.

Then I sit down at the terminal to write Gage.

"Gage! I'm sorry we were delayed. I'm back now and getting someone to monitor you more closely. Are you okay? Have you found a way out of the cavern?"

GAGE

G age reads the words on the square and shakes his head miserably. Then he types: "Ther is no way owt. Ther are many dors, but none of them open. My torch burned out. So I have no lite. I have to wate here and hope the scowts find me."

He hobbles over to the corner of the room and drags the chair to the front of the square. He gets tired standing for long, and the square is at an awkward angle. When he sits down, though, he realizes the rows of letter are at the perfect height.

"Maybe we can help," comes the reply.

"I dont now how, but I hope so. I found some books called ..." Gage grabs the journal to check the spelling, then continues to tap letters, "journals. They hav informashun about ArHK. The last time was 2360. It sid the monitoring of ArHK culd no longer continue and the person in charje notifide your offishials. That must have bin the last time any one was in this room and the last time any one contakted u."

While he waits for a reply, Gage re-examines the controls on the wall in front of him. Because some of them show numbers and others are blank, he isn't sure if they are working or frozen in the past, like everything else in the room. Beside each gauge are lines and numbers which, he comes to realize, indicate optimal ranges and dangerous ranges, both high and low. The Outer Shell Temperature panel shows -20°C and he wonders if that means it is cold like a winter day or hot like a summer day. When words flicker on the blue square, however, he turns his attention away from the wall of controls.

"I'll do a search on that date. What else did the journals say?"

"There are many, many journals. Too many to count. All the dayly informashun is the same until the end. The last paj said it was the end of the *ArHK Preservation Experiment*." Gage looks back and forth between the journal entry and the square to get the spelling right. Some words are worth the extra effort.

Rook replies, "ArHK Preservation Experiment! That must be what *APE* stands for. Wait until the citizens of ArHK learn we're part of an experiment."

Gage wonders what it would feel like to find out his entire existence was based on an ancient experiment, and the thought makes him more determined than ever to help Rook and her family.

"Ther are othr books too. Books about plants and animals and countrys of the world. Books full of maps."

"Is there anything that mentions the location of ArHK? We need to figure out where ArHK is. I read that it took the Chosen Ones six hours to fly to ArHK by jet plane, and I know my ancestors left from the ancient city called New York."

Gage glances over at the bookshelf that stretches across an entire wall of the small room. He remembers seeing something about jet planes. He remembers because it made him wonder about Jett and his father, whether or not Jett had seen Brindle and his mother yet, or Pepper, while he was back at base camp for the night.

"Ther's a book on flying mashines. Ther is also controls in the room. They seem to show informashun about ArHK. I cant read most but one is called ..." Gage hobbles over to check the spelling, "Outer Shell Temperature. It shows -20°C. Duz that meen anithing to u?"

The response is rapid.

"It means some part of ArHK is really cold. Stay close while we try to figure that out."

When the square goes blank, Gage retrieves the book on flying machines. He sets it on his lap and starts flipping through, page by page. He examines a picture of a great round machine that floated through the sky and slick triangular machines that travelled at great heights and great speeds. When he turns to the page on jet planes he freezes and listens closely.

What was that? he wonders. *Did I just hear something?*

Gage holds his breath and listens hard until he hears it again, a faint thumping sound. It's the first sound he's heard since he woke up at the bottom of the cavern. He puts the book on the floor and stands up as quietly as he can, then he tiptoes to the door. He hears it again, a distinct but distant thumping sound.

Gage hobbles into the corridor, stopping again to listen. Then, in the darkness, he travels toward the sound. He runs his hands along the wall to guide himself, tracking turns so he'll be able to find his way back. The sound draws him nearer, and the closer he gets the louder it becomes. Finally, he comes up against one of the doors and places his hands flat on the cool hard surface. He can feel a vibration.

"Chief Coil?" he shouts as loud as he can. "Uncle Winch? Harley?"

He listens close and thinks he can hear distant muffled voices, which makes him shout even louder.

"It's me. I'm in here! It's Gage!"

He pounds on the heavy door with his fists, but the effort is feeble. Then he lies on his back and kicks with the bottom of his good foot. He kicks a pattern with the sole of his boot: thump, pause, thump, pause, thump, thump, thump. He stops, listens, and hears the pattern returned from the other side. He kicks the pattern again — and again the pattern is returned.

Gage is torn between hobbling back to the computing machine to tell Rook the good news and pounding on the door to make sure the men on the other side don't give up. Then he hears the sound of particles hitting the floor around him. He feels bits of dust falling on his face and scurries back from the door. His timing is good because just then part of the ceiling collapses and a ray of light slices across the dark corridor.

"Uncle Winch!" he screams up at the hole in the ceiling. "I'm down here. Watch out, there's a cavern."

Gage's words are drowned out, however, by an enormous crash as a body lands in front of him, among a pile of rubble and dust. A torch lands a split second later. Gage picks himself and the torch up at the same time. He illuminates the corridor and limps forward to help.

"Dad!" he shouts when his father stands upright and shakes the debris from his head and shoulders.

His father steps close and wraps his arms around Gage.

"I knew we'd find you."

They hold tight onto one another and let time wash over them. Never has a hug felt this good. Gage sinks deeply into his father's chest and feels safe for the first time in, well, he's not sure how long.

When Gage looks beyond his father's shoulder, he sees Uncle Winch's and Harley's dirt-smeared faces peering down through the hole in the ceiling. Both men are sweaty but smiling broadly.

"It's him all right. We found Gage," Uncle Winch calls over his shoulder.

Gage hears the message travel like a gust of wind from mouth to mouth until the sound disappears in the distance.

"We found Gage!"

"We found him."

"He's down there!"

It sounds like every scout in camp is up there.

Gage pulls himself free of his father. "How long've I been down here?"

"Three days."

"It's hard to tell without the sun. What time is it?"

"Afternoon. Now let me look at you. You look a mess. Are you okay?"

Gage's father turns him slowly.

"I hurt my leg when I fell. But I think I just twisted my ankle is all. I'm hungry as a bear though."

His father looks up through the hole in the ceiling and shouts. "Someone throw down something to eat. The kid's starving."

Before long a bundle is lowered through the hole.

His father unties it and hands Gage a hunk of bread. Gage looks surprised but tears off a piece with his teeth and chews. Bread has never tasted so good.

"Who made this?" he asks with his mouth half full.

"Your mother sent it back with Jett."

"They're back already?"

"They didn't spend a night in base camp. Just delivered the message and headed straight back. Apparently Jett missed you," his father teases and ruffs up his son's hair.

"This bread is good," Gage says, then swallows.

His father hands him a flask of water, and Gage gulps half of it back before he takes another bite of the bread.

"How'd you find me?"

"Luck," his father says. "And stubborn determination. We were scouring the area for any signs of you falling through a cavern. Then Harley, well, he found an entrance in the forest. He followed a passageway leading down into the ground, and it led to here. First, we thought it was an old storm shelter. But it musta been an emergency route to the bottom of this building. We ended up somewhere on the other side of that door." Gage's father nods at the door beside them. "But we couldn't budge it no matter what we did. So I said, 'Boys, we're going through the wall if we have to.' I had no idea it was the roof 'til I fell clear through and almost squashed you."

Gage swallows the last of the bread and takes another long drink of water. It feels good to be full. Hunger, he realizes, is one of the worst types of deprivation. Even worse than no sunlight.

"But didn't they see my walking stick and machete leaning against the wall in the upper cavern? Didn't they realize I fell through one of them metal doors?"

Gage's father tilts his head to one side. "You fell through from inside the building?"

"Yes, through the restricted access doors."

"They brung back your walking stick and your machete, but they said your footprints went back outside so we started searching there."

Gage shakes his head. He can't make sense of what his father is telling him. Perhaps with all the footprints tracking across the floor, the older scouts got confused.

"Thanks for not giving up on me," he says.

His father pulls him into another hug and whispers into his hair, "I'd never give up."

Uncle Winch and Harley lower thick hemp ropes down through the gaping hole.

"Tie Gage on first and we'll haul him up. Then we'll bring you through," Uncle Winch says.

The ropes snake down around them, and his father starts to form a harness for Gage's legs.

"Wait! We can't go yet. I hafta show you something." Gage starts limping down the corridor.

His father sizes him up but doesn't speak.

"This way. C'mon," Gage urges, then turns and hobbles away with the torch burning in his hand. His father hesitates only briefly before he calls up to the other scouts. "Hang on a minute. Gage wants to show me something."

His father glances around at the dark corridor before he follows Gage's light through the maze of corridors, through a heavy metal door, and into the APE Monitoring Room.

Gage watches his father's face as he scans the room. He sees his father take in the shelves of books, the cot, the broken bottles, the wall of controls. His father looks confused when he sees the glowing blue square.

"This's where you been all this time?" he asks.

Gage nods and sweeps his arms around the room in a grand gesture, as if he's unveiling a brand new yurt.

"I found the Ship of Knowledge."

ROOK

Heath arrives within the hour, out of breath and looking flushed. Da unlocks the front door and pulls him inside. Most people don't give the Archives a second glance, except the Governors. Many people in ArHK never visit, not once in their whole lives. Still, if a passerby were to see someone going in when the blinds were closed, it might raise suspicion.

"What's going on?" he asks brightly. His blue eyes are wide with purpose.

I pat the chair beside me. "Come sit with me, Heath. I think I'm probably going to blow your mind, but there's no time to break it to you gently."

"Break what gently?" Heath asks, looking suddenly concerned, his eyes scanning in all directions.

"Are you sure you want to be a Keeper?" I ask.

"Definitely. I've wanted to be a Keeper since I could read. Mam says I have an aptitude for —"

"That's great," I interrupt. "But what if it means keeping more than just information? What if it means keeping secrets? Keepers have to keep some pretty big secrets. Even from their families."

I expect Da or Mam to object, but they stand nearby with hesitation in their faces and postures, and add nothing. Mam is tapping her forehead with her index finger, and Da is rubbing his hands together.

"I can keep a secret," Heath assures me.

"This secret is going to change the rest of your life. Nothing will ever be the same for you again," I warn.

Heath fiddles with one ear but nods. "Okay."

I look at Heath and almost feel sorry for him. He has no idea what he's getting himself into.

"So here it is. We've just had contact from the Outside, and we need you to monitor this terminal. You have to communicate with the person on the other end while we figure out what to do next."

Heath looks from me to Mam to Da, then over at Sparrow who's perched on the counter listening quietly for the first time in her life.

"Is this some sort of Keeper initiation?" Heath asks. The corners of his mouth twitch like he is trying to decide whether or not to smile.

"This is no initiation. This is completely serious."

"It's some kind of prank? Right? Like something the Entertainers are filming?" He starts scanning the room again, but more closely, as if he is expecting to find a hidden camera.

"It's not a prank."

"But we haven't had contact from the Outside in over two hundred OT years. Have you told the Governors?"

"No. That's the tricky part. It turns out the Governors have been hiding the truth about a lot of things from the citizens of ArHK. They probably don't even know what they are hiding or why."

"The thing is," Da speaks finally, "we're not sure how they're going to react to this news. We could get into a lot of trouble. We could all be banished to a lower sector, like my mother was. So think about this carefully. You can still walk away."

Heath turns his face from me to Da to me again. He narrows his blue eyes in concentration. Then his face brightens. "Da and Mam have always been suspicious of the Governors, ever since Mam's Auntie Ivy got sent away. So I'm definitely in."

"Then we need you to stay online with this young scout named Gage, who seems to be some sort of explorer. Find out anything you can about ArHK and the Outside. And keep notes. But not on your personal messenger."

I hand him a pad of plexpaper, the kind Da and I use to write work plans on or to track sequencing when we format complicated reports. "You can use this."

"What do you want to know? I mean, is there anything specific I should be asking about?" Heath asks.

"Find out everything. But maybe start by asking if the air in the Outside is still poisonous, and let us know what he says."

Heath settles himself in front of the terminal while Mam and Da set up at computers farther back in the Archive Hall. Sparrow follows so quietly I barely notice her.

"Da, find what you can about where ArHK is. Every little piece of information will help."

Da logs onto a terminal and begins to search.

"Don't forget to look at Crumb Reports. Follow anything Grandmam Ivy linked," I remind him.

Then I turn to Mam. She's pulled her hair back into a tie to keep it off her face and is picking at her cuticles the way she does whenever she's anxious.

"Mam, you should find out whatever you can about *what* ArHK is. Figure out what Gage means when he asks if we are in a *building*. That's such a curious term. He used it like a noun, not a verb."

Even as Mam sits down at her terminal I can tell she knows exactly where she wants to start. Seeing both Mam and Da so intent on the computer terminals, their eyes flickering across the screen as they open and close documents, well, that makes me proud to be a Keeper.

While Mam and Da input search terms and scan files, I imagine the Governors opening tomorrow's Activity Report. I'd love to see Governor Hawk's face when he sees how many search terms there were over the sleep hours and especially when he starts to read through them. I'm sure his head will explode. I'm almost smiling to myself when the reality of our situation sobers me.

"I'm going to find out how to get *out* of ArHK," I say to nobody in particular.

"What about me?" Sparrow says quietly. She's standing at my elbow. "Everyone has a job but me."

"You're right, Sparrow. There's one job left but it's very important. I don't even know if you are old enough to do it."

Sparrow nods eagerly. "I can do it. I'm old enough."

I take Sparrow to the front of the Archives and tear two small holes in the blinds, right near the floor.

"You can be the watcher. You have to lie here very still and watch to see if anyone wants to come inside."

Sparrow lies down on her tummy and puts her eyes up to the holes.

"I can see lots of feet walking by," she says.

"Is anyone stopping?"

"No."

"Good. Call out if anyone stops."

"Do you want me to let them in?"

"Definitely not. But if anyone stops or wants to come in, you come tell us who it is. Can you do that?" I ask.

"Yes, I can," Sparrow assures me.

"Remember to keep still. Nobody can know you're there."

I watch Sparrow for a moment, long enough to see her lying as still as a carpet on the floor and to hope the job will hold her attention for at least an hour. Then I head to the back of the Archives. On my way past Heath, I stop briefly.

"Are you doing okay?" I ask.

Heath doesn't look up but talks and writes at the same time, like Da. *He does have an aptitude for working in the Archives*, I think to myself.

"Gage says he's been found. His father is there with him. They say the poisonous air ended hundreds of years ago. He wants to know if we have map readers in ArHK."

"What's a map reader?"

"I'm just figuring that out now," Heath says. "But apparently they can help figure out where ArHK is."

When I sit down at the old computer, I think about how the Chosen Ones entered ArHK. The arrival footage showed people climbing down from a huge jet plane, and I wonder if it is still somewhere in ArHK.

"If it's still here," I reason with myself, "it has to be somewhere big, somewhere as big as the sports stadium."

Mam breaks my concentration.

"Look at this!" she says excitedly.

Da and I roll our chairs toward her terminal and see a circular diagram on her screen. It seems familiar, but I can't figure out why. Mam points to the screen.

"I think this is an early diagram of ArHK from the original architects. This must be the Knowledge Level and the concentric circles are the avenues. The smallest circle in the middle, where all the streets meet, is Central Park. And see this red star? If I am reading it right, it would be the Archives or the Great Hall, but I don't know why they marked it and nothing else."

Mam flips to another screen and shows us the blueprints of the lower levels of ArHK.

"This one is the Development Level, then there is Manufacturing, and then Waste Management. Along the outer edges you can see the Growing Sector."

I examine the diagram closely, but it doesn't give me any clues about where to start my search. My head pounds, and I glance at the clock on the wall screen. We have another eight hours before the Governors receive their report and maybe another hour or two before they storm the Archives. Mam and Da return to their searches, and Heath is hunched over, completely focused on his conversation with Gage. Even Sparrow is lying on her tummy, staring intently out at the Avenue. I turn back to my terminal and stare hard at the screen.

"Now is not the time for daydreaming," I scold myself. "Think hard, Rook. What would Grandmam do?"

Then I remember *The Protection of People and Purpose Act* and all the crumbs Grandmam left for me to follow from there. I know one of the links will turn up something useful so I make my way back through the system. Suddenly I'm struck by how obvious it is when I'm looking — the link from the words *jet plane facility*. I take a deep breath and open the file. It's a proposal submitted by a Governor Newt and passed by all Governors to permanently seal the jet plane facility from all citizens of ArHK, even the Head Governor. I wonder if anyone even remembers where it's located anymore. I wonder what other parts of ArHK have been permanently sealed and who is in charge of monitoring the environmental conditions.

The Archives is silent except for the sound of Sparrow tapping the floor with her feet, a sure sign she's starting to get bored. Then my personal messenger beeps and I jump. A split second later, Sparrow comes pounding toward me.

"Ruby's here. She's at the front door!"

I look at my personal messenger. Ruby sent a message.

"I'm outside the Archives but it looks closed. What's going on? Is everything okay?"

GAGE

age studies his father's face in the blue light. He sees the expressions shift across it like clouds across the sky as a storm builds. His father glances around the room more slowly this time. His eyes take in the controls, the dials, the gauges, then the shelves of books.

"You're sure *this* is the Ship of Knowledge? I was expecting something bigger, with more books and artefacts."

"Well, actually, this room isn't the Ship of Knowledge, but this magic square is. It's a computing machine," Gage explains quickly. "On the other end there are people. *They* are in the Ship of Knowledge. Or on it. I'm not sure yet. But they say they've been protecting the knowledge of ancient humans for hundreds of years, since before the Storm Ages."

Gage's father studies him carefully before he steps close and inspects Gage's head.

"Did ya hit your head when you fell?"

"No. I mean, yes. I did hit my head." Gage pulls away from his father. "But I'm fine. I'm not making this up. You watch."

Gage places the palms of his hands on the blank blue square and waits for the rows of letters to appear. He smiles when his father steps back. Then he begins to tap on the letters. As he does, he reads the words aloud to his father.

"Hello. Rook. My father and the other scowts fownd me."

His father reaches the tips of his fingers out to touch the letters.

"That's amazing," his father says. "It's just like your mother's books. You can see the letters, but you can't feel them."

"That's not even the best part. Watch."

Gage nods at the square, then waits impatiently for words to appear. When they finally do, he dances with excitement.

"Look! See that? They wrote, 'Hello Gage's father. It's very nice to meet you. This is Rook's cousin, Heath.'"

Gage's father considers the square before speaking. "You didn't make those words? You're telling me they came from somewhere else?"

Gage's eyes grow wide and he nods emphatically.

"They didn't just come from somewhere else, but from *someone* else. There's a person on the other end writing back."

"Where're these people writing from?"

Gage screws up his mouth and sighs.

"That's the part we hafta figure out."

"They don't know where they are?"

Gage shakes his head.

"Don't they have any map readers?"

Gage shrugs. "I dunno."

While Gage taps a message to Heath, Gage's father examines the room more closely. He runs his fingers over the gauges and dials, taps the small squares, and studies a series of letters etched on a metal plate on the wall.

"Look here, Gage. Do you see this? These numbers and some sorta drawing. It looks like the wheels on the harvest carts from the Middle."

Gage's father wipes the wall until all the symbols are clearly visible. Then he waves the dust away from his face and coughs. Gage brings the flickering torch close. He points to the first row of words.

"This says *Archives of Human Knowledge*. That's where Rook is. And this series of numbers and letters: *82.28 N, 62.30 W.* I'm not sure what they mean or what this circle-like symbol's for. But it's on all the doors down here and on the door up in the cavern that I fell through."

Gage's father is drawn back to the glowing blue square on the wall. He takes the torch from Gage and looks at it from the side and from the bottom. He puts his face up close.

"How's it working? How's it light up? I heard the Scholars talk about how the ancient cities were powered by the forces of nature. By the sun and wind somehow. They could produce light with the flick of a switch. Is this powered by something?"

"Maybe this building is making its own power. Like the heat of the sun. Maybe that's why there aren't any trees growing round. Maybe somehow it's been working all this time."

Gage sits down and starts to tap out a question to Heath, then turns to his father. "We have so much to learn. Think of all the great things humans'll be able to do again!"

Gage's father looks around the room and back at the door. He's clearly trying to work through a problem with his mind.

"We need to tell the others what you found," he says suddenly, as if he has woken up from a trance.

His father goes to the door and pauses, but Gage doesn't turn around. He keeps tapping at the square. Finally, his father clears his throat.

"Gage?" he says.

Gage doesn't take his eyes off the square.

"Gage!" his father says again, more sharply this time.

"What?" Gage asks, without turning around.

"We need to go back to the others. We need to tell Chief Coil. He'll know when the Scholars are due to arrive from the Middle."

"You go ahead. I'll be here."

"I'm not leaving you here alone!" Gage's father says so sternly that Gage finally turns around.

"But I been alone for three days."

"That's not the point. You're coming with me. We need to get you cleaned up and your ankle wrapped. You need a proper meal and a good night's sleep."

Gage feels his chest tighten in panic.

"What if they aren't here when I come back? What if Chief Coil won't let me come back?"

"I'm sure we can reason with Chief Coil. And besides you're a Reader, aren't you? Now c'mon. It's getting late and the walk back to camp will take some time. The others are waiting and probably getting hungry."

Impatience flickers across his father's face. Much like the torch he's holding, his father's patience is starting to wane. Gage realizes he has no choice but to follow him down the corridor and up into the sunshine again.

ROOK

"Crap," I say. "What's Ruby want?"

"Language!" Mam warns without looking away from her computer.

"Sorry, but I don't have time for Ruby right now," I mutter as I glance up at the domed ceiling. The sky is indigo and quickly approaching black. Ruby has probably been to the pod and realized we aren't there.

"Just don't answer her," Sparrow suggests. "Maybe she'll think we went to Central Park or to the public baths."

Da pops his head up from behind his terminal. "We should have turned the lights off an hour ago, like normal."

My messenger beeps again and along with a rush of panic, the perfect lie comes to me. I write back instead of livechatting because my face gives everything away.

"Sorry, Ruby. Sparrow hit her head at school. We're at the clinic now."

"I saw the lights on in the Archives, and the blinds are closed too," Ruby replies.

"We must have forgotten to turn them off in the rush. I'll tell Da to go turn them off when we're done here. Talk later."

Sparrow is dancing on the spot, waiting for me to finish texting Ruby. When I look up she bursts with excitement.

"What did you tell her?"

"I told her we had to take you to the doctor."

"You lied?" she asks, her voice heavy with concern.

I put my finger to my lips. "It was just a little lie. But that's not important right now. Go back and signal when Ruby's out of sight."

Sparrow's eyes widen before she turns and tiptoes through the Archives. She stops partway and sits down, pulls off her shoes, then crawls the last few metres on her hands and knees. She flattens herself in front of the window and peeks through the holes in the blinds before she jumps up and scurries back.

"She's gone now," she says breathlessly. "Do you want me to turn off all the lights?"

"Yes, quickly," I say. "Then go back and watch. See if she comes back or if anyone else comes by."

Sparrow deactivates the lights around the Archives in the same order that Da does every night. She's seen the routine so many times she knows it by heart. Then she returns to her lookout.

"That diagram! Willow, pull up that diagram again!" Da says suddenly. He pushes his chair over to her terminal.

Mam moves through her open files while he drums on the desk with his fingers. "I just thought of something. Hurry!"

"I *am* hurrying. Hold on."

"How many files do you have open?" Da asks.

"It's none of your business," she snaps, then says, "Here it is."

Mam leans back in her chair while Da leans close to the screen. He taps it with his finger.

"I've seen this before. This diagram with the circles and the lines intersecting. It's like the globe in the Great Hall!"

"Globe?" Mam and I say at the same time.

"A globe. Yes. It's round like a ball and it's supposed to represent the planet Earth. It's covered with lines like this. Come on, I'll show you."

Da gets up and steps toward the back of the Archives, toward the heavy metal doors that guard the Great Hall of Human Knowledge. When I don't budge he turns to me.

"Are you coming?"

Mam and I look at each other. Neither of us has ever been in the Great Hall. Mam will never be allowed inside, and there are still several years before I'm given limited, controlled access. As Head Keeper, Da is the only person in ArHK allowed inside, and he can be banished if he allows another person to even step one foot inside.

"Listen, considering all the rules we've broken today, I could already be sent down to the Recycling Sector. So if you don't mind, can you please hurry?"

Mam shoos me away with her hands, and I stumble after Da. My legs tremble as I wait for him to unlock the thick heavy doors to the Great Hall. The doors stretch higher than most doors in ArHK, probably twice as high as the glass doors at the front of the Archives. The door handles are larger too, made of twisted metal shaped like oversized letter Gs. They are so big they look built for a much larger race of humans.

"I sure hope you don't activate an alarm," I stammer as Da presses numbers into the code pad.

Da glances back at me with narrowed eyebrows. I know he wishes I hadn't said that.

When we step through the doors all I can see is blackness until Da activates a series of lights. Da sighs, but my feet freeze in place and my whole body shuts down. For a moment, my lungs forget how to function until my brain screams for oxygen. Da puts his hand on my shoulder to steady me.

"It's something else, isn't it?" he says quietly. "I've been looking forward to showing you since the day I found out Mam was pregnant."

Of course I can't say a thing. All I can do is stare. The Great Hall is enormous, and we're standing above an expanse of artefacts the size of the sports stadium. There's a raised domed ceiling above us and, leading upwards, stacks of railings overlook the main hall. Da closes the doors, then leads me down a short flight of stairs.

"Watch your step," he says gently.

I look down in time to keep myself from tripping and falling all the way to the bottom.

From the floor level, the artefacts are even more impossible to comprehend and many loom high above me. When we pass by a skeleton, I stare slack-jawed at its size.

"It's a dinosaur. T-Rex," Da says without stopping.

"These are real? Not manufactured?" I finally manage to ask.

"I used to think they were manufactured too. Until today, I guess. Now I'm starting to realize everything in here is real, or was real."

"I had no idea it would be so big," I say and let my head drop backwards until I'm staring straight up. "How many floors are there?"

"Ten altogether. There are five up and four down. This is the main floor."

We wind our way among dinosaur skeletons and marble statues, ancient bronze weapons and a variety of flying machines.

"I thought Central Park was big. I thought the stadium was big. But this is the most incredible thing I've ever seen."

"It's a shame, isn't it, that nobody else is allowed to see all this," Da says and sweeps his hands across his chest. "It really changes a person's perspective."

"It's wrong to keep this from people," I say. "I don't understand."

"I don't either exactly, but I'm beginning to."

"What?" I ask.

"I'm beginning to piece together a lot of what Grandmam used to tell me before she got banned. After she left, Governor Hawk told me she was crazy, and I believed him. I discounted all of her ideas and theories. I lost my faith."

Da stops in front of a large stone carving and wipes a tear from his eye.

"I thought she was just a troublemaker, and I couldn't have been more wrong."

Da chokes on his words, and I wrap him in a hug.

"That's okay. We're going to finish this now. For Grandmam and for us and for everyone in ArHK."

"I hope so. I can't bear to think of what will happen if we fail."

"We won't fail," I say as brightly as I can. "Now, where is that globe you were talking about?"

Da leads me farther into the Great Hall. I want to stop and examine every artefact, but of course I can't. The Governors will be onto us soon enough. Finally, we stop in front of a large round object, about a metre in diameter.

"This is it," Da says and rotates the ball slowly. "See these parallel lines running vertically? And these other lines, see? They run around the globe horizontally. If you look really close, each line has a number." Da spins the globe this way and that to illustrate his point. "Now look at the globe from the very top, where all the lines converge." He brings the top of the globe to our eye level. "Doesn't it remind you of the diagram Mam showed us?"

I nod and run my hands over the surface of the globe. I can feel ridges where the numbered lines run. Below the lines are abstract, coloured shapes.

"What does it all mean?"

"When I was a boy, even before I was an apprentice, Grandmam used to tell me about this globe. She swore me to secrecy every time, but then she described it in great detail. She told me when I got to be Head Keeper I should do my rounds quickly so I could spend a minute or two studying it. When she got banned, she told me to be extra careful, not to come in here off schedule because the Governors would be watching me closely. But after so many years, I got bolder."

While Da talks, I spin the globe and examine all the bumps and ridges, the smooth blue patches, and the tiny numbers and words.

"What do the words mean? What's Can-a-da? What's Russ-i-a?"

"Grandmam said those were the ancient countries that made up the planet Earth."

Da rotates the globe and points to a large mass of green and brown. "The United States of America was down here."

"That's where our ancestors came from! That means New York would be somewhere on this globe?"

Da nods.

"And Washington?"

Da nods again.

"But where?"

"I don't know," Da says. "I'm sure there's a book that would help us figure that out, but I haven't read enough to know for sure."

"You aren't supposed to have books in the pod, are you?"

"No. I'm not even supposed to come in here except to do my annual rounds. But sometimes, I sneak in and take a book home. It helps pass the evenings."

"I knew you were breaking a rule," I say proudly.

Da smiles. "It's a big risk. But I can't help myself."

"How did you know about that book on religion you're reading?"

"Luck more than anything. I don't quite under-stand the filing system, but your Grandmam, like you, was very intrigued by ancient religions and natural history, so she showed me where to find those books."

"Did you know that William, the first Head Keeper, catalogued all these books?" I say suddenly. "I read a letter from his wife, and she talked about how he catalogued all the books when he first arrived. I bet there's a way to find what you want without having to look through every book. I bet there's a computer file somewhere."

"That would be helpful," Da says. "Because there are four complete levels of books. Even if we spent the rest of our lives, we'd never get through them all."

I spin the globe until the top is facing us again and study the converging lines.

"Mam said she was showing us a diagram of ArHK. She thought the inner circle was Central Park and the outer circles were the avenues. And there was a star on her diagram, remember?"

Da searches the globe for a star while I run my hands slowly over the coloured surface.

"What's o-ce-an mean?"

"Grandmam said the blue represents water. Oceans were big pools of water. The green and brown parts are the land."

"So the land is divided into countries and the water is divided into oceans?"

"That's how it looks," Da says.

"Then why is some land white, some brown, and some green? And what is the e-qua-tor? The Educators left a lot of stuff about the Outside off the school curriculum.

"Ouch!" I cry when my skin catches on something sharp sticking from the globe.

"What's the matter?"

"I pricked my finger on something," I say and put my finger in my mouth. When I pull it out to look, the tip is bleeding.

"Where was it?"

I point to where I was last touching the globe. "Just over from North Pole. That hurt!"

Da runs his hand over the globe slowly, carefully. Then he stops. "I can feel it too. It feels like a pin. And it's right on top of this word: *Alert*."

"Alert," I laugh. "Is that a sign from Grandmam or what?"

Da puts his eyes as close as he can to the globe. "Look closely. Is it just me or is the font different? It almost looks like the word was added later."

My heart contracts, and all I can think is that we really have discovered another of Grandmam Ivy's crumbs. She didn't leave them only in the computer files but in the Great Hall too.

"Maybe Mam was wrong. Maybe it wasn't a diagram of ArHK but a diagram of ancient Earth!" I suggest.

Pieces of information inside my brain click together.

"Wait a minute. I … think … I get it," I stammer. "Of course. It makes sense now. Earth *is* the Outside. Maybe the pin shows where ArHK is located on Earth!"

My pulse is pounding so loud in my ears, I can't hear what Da says in response. "Pardon?"

"I said, maybe it's both," Da repeats slowly. "Maybe it's a diagram of where ArHK is on Earth *and* a diagram of where the Archives are in ArHK?"

GAGE

When Uncle Winch and Harley pull Gage up through the hole, all the scouts rush forward to greet him. They pat his back and squeeze his shoulders, and every scout, one by one, shakes his hand as he hobbles toward the patch of sunshine at the end of the sloped corridor. Gage reaches for the talisman around his neck and squeezes it gratefully.

"Welcome back, Gage!" Harley says, starting off a series of comments from the other men.

"Our lucky scout. Missing three days and comes out alive."

"That's gotta be a first!"

"Good to see ya, Gage."

Jett is one of the last scouts in the line, and he doesn't say a word. But he grabs Gage's hand with both of his and squeezes hard. Gage can feel the tremble in him.

"I'm okay. Look, I'm fine," Gage says. He knows Jett is thinking it could have been him who fell through.

Jett nods and swallows but still doesn't speak.

As Gage ascends into the full brightness of the day, he covers his eyes and blinks back the sunshine. He didn't remember the world being quite so intense. Suddenly, he's struck by the beauty of the blue sky and the greening trees around him. He takes a deep breath and drinks in the smell of the earth beneath his feet. He looks at the birds flitting about the treetops and smiles when he sees they are chirping and pecking and watching the activity below them. It feels as if he has been down in that room for weeks, and he realizes how easy it is to miss the real world.

Gage's father puts his arm over Gage's shoulder.

"You okay to get back to camp on that ankle?"

Gage nods. "I think so."

His father hands him a walking stick. "Yours is back at camp, but you can use mine for now."

Just then Chief Coil appears and Gage feels heat rise to his cheeks. He looks at the chief and then away, down at the ground again.

"I didn't go exploring on my own," Gage blurts out with his eyes still on the ground. "I opened those metal doors, and when I stepped inside there wasn't any floor."

"You didn't go back outside?" Chief Coil asks.

"I'd never do that! It was just so dark in that room I didn't realize there wasn't any floor 'til it was too late."

Chief Coil listens intently, as if he is judging the truth as much as the words.

"The important thing is we found you." Chief Coil's voice is soft, and Gage dares to raise his eyes. "And I hear you made a big discovery?"

Gage feels his chest fill with air and hope. He feels buoyant.

"There's a computing machine down there that still works. I was writing words to people on the other end. They live in a place called the Archives of Human Knowledge, where they store and protect all the knowledge of ancient humans."

The words tumble from Gage's mouth so quickly he almost runs out of breath.

"Dad says I need to eat and rest and get my ankle taken care of. Then I want to go back and write to them more. They're expecting me back. They need our help."

Chief Coil looks to Gage's father as if to ask, Is he right in the head? Gage's father steps toward Chief Coil and raises his chin so that his deep baritone voice rings out across the forest.

"It's true. What he says. I saw the computing machine myself. And I saw him writing words and receiving words back. There're a great number of artefacts down there too. I believe he's discovered a link to the

Ship of Knowledge," Gage's father says and smiles warmly at him.

Gage feels a flush of pride flow between them.

"You really believe there's a connection to the Ship of Knowledge?" Chief Coil watches Gage's father closely. Gage and his father nod in unison, their eyes locked, as the enormity of what they are saying is shared with the others. They both know their world has changed, that nothing will ever be the same again. The discovery has been worth the decades of searching, suffering, hardship, and loneliness.

"But you say they're lost? Like somewhere on the open waters?"

"It doesn't seem like they're on a boat structure. But somehow they've lost track of where exactly they're located. I know it doesn't make much sense," Gage's father says.

The other scouts have climbed up out of the dim passageway and gathered around Gage, his father, and Chief Coil to hear better. Suddenly, the forest becomes still. Nobody moves their feet in the tree litter. Even the birds have stopped to listen to the news.

"From what I can tell," Gage's father continues, "from what they wrote and from what Gage explained to me, there're thousands of people living someplace where they've stored knowledge about humankind's greatest accomplishments. They say they were sent there five hundred years ago. They call themselves the descendants of the Chosen Ones."

"Five thousand people live there," Gage adds. "The original people got there in five big flying machines. Wherever they are, they can't see the sky. They don't see the stars or the sun. They're worried about the outside air being poisonous."

Again the expression on Chief Coil's face is impossible to read. It almost looks like he doesn't believe what he's hearing.

"How could they not know where they're at?"

"I guess the same way we don't know how to make flying machines or how to make power from the sun and wind. We've lost track of this information. But *they* have it," Gage says.

For the first time since Gage can remember, Chief Coil is at a loss for words, and his authority seems to shrink.

"I don't know what to make of this."

"I'll take you down in the morning," Gage suggests. "It makes more sense when you see it for yourself."

"That's a good idea. Hopefully the Scholars arrive soon. Tomorrow we'll send messengers back to base camp to tell them to start packing up the yurts. We gotta move everyone closer. I think we're gonna be in Washington a long time."

A cheer rises up from the men around them, and before Gage knows what's happening, he's swept off his feet and is moving through the forest on two sets of shoulders. He looks down and sees Uncle Winch and Harley smiling up at him. He's so preoccupied by the activity centred on him, Gage forgets about his ankle until they place him back on the ground at camp. Then he winces.

"I think it's time we take care of that ankle," his father says. "You sit here and I'll go get the medicine bag."

Gage's father makes a poultice by soaking dried mullein and red clover leaves in hot water, then wraps these gently around Gage's swollen ankle. The heat feels good, but when his father takes a long strip of cloth and winds it tightly around Gage's foot and ankle, the relief is immediate.

"Does that feel any better?" his father asks as he re-packs the medicine bag.

Gage nods gratefully. "Much better. Thank you."

• • •

The tone in camp that night is celebratory. Everyone's happy to have Gage back and even more excited about the prospect of what he's found. Harley and Uncle Winch cook up a pot of wild turkey stew to recognize the import-ant night, and Chief Coil opens the bottles of barley wine he stashed among the supplies in case they found some-thing to celebrate. When everyone has a full mug, Chief Coil raises his hand for silence. "To Gage!" he shouts, and the camp erupts in cheers again. Gage feels his cheeks burn from so much attention and the roaring fire.

"It was just an accident," he whispers to his father. "If anyone else fell down that hole, they woulda found the same thing."

"But nobody else fell through that hole. You did," his father says and slaps him on the back.

After everyone is full of stew and feeling relaxed from the wine, Jett and the other young scouts build up the fire until it blazes so hot the men have to sit ten feet back. Then, for the first time since they left base camp, those who play flutes and whistles, drums and shakers, bring them from their packs and begin to play the old-time ballads.

Even with the music and the wine Gage is still the main attraction. The focus makes him feel shy but proud too. He's happy to have his father at his side when the other scouts begin to ask him questions.

"Were you scared?"

"What's the computing machine like?"

"How many books did you say were there?"

"How far do you figure you fell?"

It's almost as if everyone wants a chance to say something to him, no matter how trivial.

"Can I get you another bowl of stew?"

"How's that ankle feeling now?"

"More wine?"

Soon Gage grows tired. All he wants to do is crawl into the lean-to and fall asleep. But there's no chance to sneak away. Finally, Gage yawns and his father gets to his feet. He reaches down and pulls Gage up by the hands.

"C'mon, Gage. It's time to get you to bed. You've had a long few days. And tomorrow's gonna be another big one."

Gage follows his father gratefully and climbs into his bedroll. He's even more grateful when his father lies down next to him. They listen to the scouts filling the night with music.

"Mom and Brindle should be here within the week," Gage says, then yawns again. "We'll be able to sleep in our own cots. With Scruff. I miss that stinky old mutt."

"That's right. Tomorrow Chief Coil is gonna set out boundaries for a new base camp."

"Wait 'til Brindle sees the ruins. Wait 'til everyone sees the Lincoln Memorial."

"They'll be excited, that's for sure."

"You think it'll be safe enough 'round here?" Gage asks.

"I think so. There'll be a lotta rules about where people can go and where they can't, especially at first, but I think it'll work out fine."

"I can't believe we're the first settlers of ancient Washington."

"Just think, by this time next year there'll be hundreds of settlers. I'm afraid our quiet camp life is over," his father says in a way that makes Gage understand he's not afraid at all, but happy. Gage knows his mother will

be happy too. She's wanted to live in a permanent settle-
ment for years.

"Maybe Washington will be the first city to harness
power from nature," Gage says dreamily.

His father murmurs in the darkness of the lean-to.
Beyond their feet they can see the flickering light and
shadows of the men around the fire. Gage tries to imagine life in the centre of an ancient city and what Pepper
will think when she finds out what he's discovered, what
she'll say when she arrives to set up base camp. He rolls
onto his side and hears his father breathing slowly.

"Good night, Dad."

"Sleep tight, son."

Gage pulls the talisman from inside his shirt and
holds it tightly in his fist. Then, as he falls toward sleep,
he thinks about Rook and Heath and how nothing, not
even Chief Coil, can keep him from going back down
into the ground to write to them.

*One day we'll get everyone from ArHK in Washington
too. With their knowledge and our Scholars, we'll build
this city back up again. It'll be the greatest city in the
world*, he thinks sleepily, before he drops abruptly into
a dream.

ROOK

When we step back into the Archives it feels like we've stepped back in time. Somehow, in the short time we were gone, I became a different person. Mam looks up at me from the terminal and searches my face for signs of what I've just seen, and I know she can't imagine what lies beyond the walls of the Archives.

"Did you find anything important?" she asks after a minute when nobody speaks.

I nod but words elude me. Even Da is speechless. It's just too big to explain. Even if we had a month to sort through our thoughts and feelings, we wouldn't be able to make sense of everything.

"Are you two okay?" she asks. "You look like you've seen a ghost."

"There's just. Too much. You can't even imagine," I mumble and shake my head.

Mam looks hurt, left out, but she doesn't complain. She can't. She's been brainwashed to act in certain ways, according to ArHK laws and expectations. We have all been brainwashed. When she recovers, she calls Heath to the back of the Archives.

"Heath learned something interesting while you were gone," she says.

I glance around the room. Sparrow is still at the front by the glass doors, lying on her tummy on the floor, her head resting on her bent arms, her eyes closed. She's fast asleep and Mam has laid a blanket over her small body. The dome above is pitch black, the Avenue is pitch black, and the only light in the Archives comes from the computer monitors. They stain our faces an eerie blue-green colour.

"What have you discovered?" Da asks.

Heath is rubbing his eyes, and when I glance at the clock I see it's the middle of the sleep hours. Normally, we would have been in bed hours ago.

"Gage and his father discovered a series of numbers and letters on one of the control panels. They weren't sure what they meant so I did a search on them."

"What numbers?" I ask.

"Eighty-two point twenty-eight *N* and sixty-two point thirty *W*," Heath says.

"Did you find out what they mean?"

"Apparently they're an ancient system of global location and were used for navigation. This particular set of numbers appears to pinpoint a place near something called the North Pole," Heath explains.

He yawns, then scratches at the back of his neck while we stare at him.

"Did you find a name for this location?"

He nods. "I don't know what it means exactly, but I found a reference to the word *Alert*."

Da and I look at each other and nod.

"What?" Mam asks. "What does it mean? What's *Alert*?"

"We believe it's the location of ArHK on Earth. It's where ArHK is in relation to the Outside," Da says quietly. "I thought I believed in the Outside before, but maybe I didn't. Not really. Now that I know the truth of the Outside, being an actual physical place, I feel like I've been living in a dream."

I'm relieved he's said it. I know Mam would never believe it coming from me.

Heath sinks into a chair, and all of us follow until we are huddled in the middle of the Archives, our heads leaning close together in the dimness.

"What do you mean, exactly?" Mam asks quietly.

"Rook was right. The Outside is all around us. ArHK

is a place within the Outside, on the Earth. Gage and his people, they are at another place on Earth. We are all on this big round ball, the planet called Earth."

"Just like the Creationist legends?" Heath whispers.

"Exactly," I say.

Mam doesn't say a word. I know it's a lot to understand. Nothing makes sense when your idea of existence is turned upside down in a few hours. I can't even keep track of my own thoughts, and I've seen the globe. How could Mam ever hope to understand?

"You have to show them the globe, Da. They need to see the Great Hall."

After so much excitement and after being awake for so many hours exhaustion sets in, and I lay my head on top of my folded arms on the desk.

"Not yet," Da says. "First we have to find a way out of ArHK."

"I can help you search," Heath volunteers. "Gage and his father have gone back to camp for the night so they aren't going to be online for a few more hours."

"That's a good idea," Da says. "Willow, you start searching too. We need to find anything we can about a way in or out of ArHK. Rook said the Chosen Ones came from somewhere and she's right — if they came here, there must be a way to go back."

"Finally someone is listening to me," I say sleepily.

I know I shouldn't close my eyes, but I can't help myself. My tired brain convinces itself that it will be okay if

I rest my eyes for a few minutes. In fact, I tell the others to make sure I don't fall asleep, to wake me in a few minutes if I do. Or, I think I tell the others. I certainly mean to tell the others.

The next thing I know my personal messenger is beeping. In my sleep I think it's Da's or Mam's, and I wish they would answer so the noise would stop and I can keep sleeping.

"Can someone please stop that thing," I mutter.

But the beeping doesn't stop. It goes on and on. Finally, I drag my eyelids open and then it hits me. I'm still in the Archives and I've fallen asleep. I look up at the dome, and the sky is lightening. The wake hours are almost upon us.

I sit up and look around. Heath is head down at a terminal next to me, and Da and Mam are also sleeping. Their heads are upright but, somehow, they've fallen asleep in their chairs. I look to the front of the Archives, and Sparrow is still at the window, her face next to the blinds, her body relaxed and her eyes closed. The blanket is still draped over her shoulders.

"Everyone wake up!" I shout. "We've fallen asleep! Wake up!"

Mam and Da jump up from their chairs, and Heath turns his head slowly but doesn't open his eyes. When the realization dawns on Mam and Da that we've all fallen asleep, their faces register horror.

I pick up my personal messenger. Ruby has sent me fourteen messages in ten minutes. The words *ANSWER ANWER ANSWER* are flashing across the display panel. Without thinking, I hit the answer button. Ruby's face appears on the screen.

"Rook! Where are you?"

"In the Archives," I say before I realize what I've said and wonder if I should trust her. Who knows who's put her up to the messages?

"Quick!" she hisses into her messenger. "You have to hide. All of you. You don't have much time. The Governors are on their way to your pod. They're going to banish you all. Even Sparrow. Governor Hawk was losing it this morning. He came to our pod before the sky even started to lighten. He woke us all up. He was screaming about a breach of policy and security. Screaming something about the Recycling Sector for life."

"What's going on?" I ask. It's all I can think to say.

"He said there was illegal activity happening in the Archives. Something about tracking search terms finally. You have to hide somewhere. Maybe the Growing Sector. Beep Strider. Maybe he can hide you down there. It will take them forever to explore all the fields and gardens."

Ruby's eyes are wide with terror, and the sleepiness falls away from me so quickly even my racing heart can't keep up. Mam and Da are listening closely.

"Go now. Go somewhere. Just go!"

She is screaming at me, and I nod to let her know I have heard and understood. But I don't move.

"They'll be there in no time. When they don't find you at your pod they'll go to the Archives. Move quickly."

Finally, I jump up and run to the front of the Archives. I bundle Sparrow into my arms and run back to Mam and Da.

"What are you doing?" Sparrow asks sleepily. "Why are we still in the Archives? Did we sleep here all night?"

Her voice is angry and her small body stiff with indignation at being woken up so abruptly.

Da takes Sparrow from my arms and leads us to the back of the Archives.

"Follow me," he says. "Heath! Wake up! Come on."

Heath raises his head from the desk. The terror on our faces must hit a nerve in his brain because his eyes widen in fear. If I wasn't so scared myself, I'd probably feel bad for him. It wouldn't be a good way to wake up on the first day of your new job.

"What's wrong?" he mutters.

"We have to get out of here now!" Da says.

"But where?" Mam screams. "If we go out on the Avenue they'll see us for sure. Nobody will be up yet except the vendors."

Sparrow starts to cry when she hears the panic in Mam's voice, and Heath jumps up so quickly in response that he knocks his chair flying. It lands on the floor with a clatter, and I wince.

"What's going on? Are we in trouble? Are we going to be banished?" Sparrow wails into Da's shoulder.

"We're not going to be banished," Da says sharply, although I can tell by the tremble in his voice that even he knows he's lying. "Everyone follow me."

He leads us to the doors of the Great Hall and hands Sparrow to Mam. Sparrow wraps her arms around Mam's neck and her legs around Mam's waist. She buries her head in Mam's shoulder and sobs.

"We aren't allowed in the Great Hall. Nobody's allowed in there but Da. If we go in, we'll be in big trouble."

I want to tell her we're already in the worst imaginable trouble, but I can't say a thing over my pounding heart. It's all I can do to stay standing when my legs want to crumble me into a heap.

Da enters the security code and pushes open the thick heavy doors. Somehow I step through. When Mam stands glued in place, I lean over and tug her arm.

"Let's go."

"I ... dunno. I ... dunno," she stutters over and over.

Heath is also looking reluctant. His face has turned so pale he looks like he might fade into the walls.

"It's too late now for second thoughts," I say quietly.

Then the Archives fills with the sounds of banging and shouting.

"Fern? Fern? Are you in there?"

I could recognize Governor Hawk's rasping voice anywhere, even through ten sets of doors.

"Fern! Open this door now!"

I grab Heath's arm to drag him into the Great Hall, but he pulls free and runs back through the Archives. His feet pound the hard floor. I had no idea he could move so fast.

"Heath! No!" I scream.

He's running toward the front doors. I know the only way he can save himself is to let the Governors in and give us up. He has the perfect excuse and part of me doesn't blame him. We have about two minutes before we're all seized, even Sparrow. I think about closing the doors to the Great Hall, so we won't look as guilty, but I know it's futile. My heart sinks and I start to crumple to the ground. Da steadies me with a hand on my arm. I want to apologize to Mam and Da. To Sparrow and Grandmam Ivy. I failed everyone in ArHK. Worse, I've ruined the lives of the people I love most.

GAGE

G age is the last person to open his eyes the next morning. When he does, the first thing he sees is sunlight sifting through the trees. He props himself on an elbow to look around. His father's bedroll is cold, and camp is in full swing. Gage sits up and rubs his eyes. The buzz of activity is all around, and he wonders why he wasn't woken up earlier.

"Ah, you're awake finally," his father says when he sticks his head inside the lean-to. "How's the ankle?"

"Fine, I guess. You did a good job wrapping it last night," Gage says. "What's going on?"

"We're getting ready to move. The map readers found a secure location for base camp across the river."

"Across the river?"

"Yep, there's a bridge to get back and forth and there's plenty of space."

"We'll have to cross a bridge? Every time?"

"Don't worry. It's solid. They been examining it all morning. It'll be a great place for base camp. There's a big hill so we can build a lookout, and there's not much chance of caverns. It used to be a cemetery."

"Where they buried dead people?" Gage asks skeptically.

"Well, yes, but hundreds of years ago."

"Are they sure it's a good place for base camp?"

"Positive. It's close to where we wanna scout, but there's enough room for a good-sized camp. Plenty of room for when the settlers start arriving. There's even enough room to grow some crops once we clear the land. And there's a fresh supply of water flowing past."

"I'm not fond about the idea of crossing a bridge every day," I mutter.

"You better get up. Chief Coil's ready to see the computing machine."

"He waited for me?"

"Yep, but he's running out of patience."

Gage crawls out of the lean-to and is shocked to see the tents and other lean-tos have been dismantled. Everyone has bundled up their bedrolls and are busy packing up the last of camp.

"We're moving today?" Gage asks.

"Some of us are going back to the Department of Human Safety and Survival while everyone else moves camp. They should be set up by the time we're ready for dinner."

Even though Gage ate a big meal the previous night, he cleans out the porridge pot and devours the last bit of turkey stew his father saved for him. He even eats the last crust of bread, then washes it down with a mug of hot mint tea.

"Are you ready to move out?" Chief Coil asks as he comes up behind Gage.

Gage spins around. "Yes, sir. I just have to roll up my bed things."

"Someone else will get that. We better get moving if we wanna get there and then to the new camp before dark. Are you gonna be able to walk on that ankle?"

Gage takes a few steps and nods to Chief Coil.

"It's almost like new," he says, then looks around for his machete and walking stick. His father appears at the same moment and hands them to him. Harley and Uncle Winch also appear, as if from nowhere.

"All set?"

Uncle Winch's voice booms through the forest, and a small flock of birds takes flight from the tops of the nearby trees. A few of the scouts stop what they're doing to watch the men head out, and before he melts into the forest, Gage sees Jett bundling up a set of tent poles. Jett smiles and Gage waves in return.

The five scouts head through the forest with Uncle Winch in the lead and Chief Coil at the back. Before long they cross what Gage recognizes as an old road, a straight swath where the trees aren't as broad or thick as the ones in the forest surrounding their camp. He takes the hand-drawn map from inside his vest pocket and traces a path with his finger. By his figuring, they've just crossed Independence Avenue. He's tucking the map back in his pocket when Uncle Winch trips and curses. He rolls in the thick undergrowth, rubbing his shin.

"You okay there, Winch?" Harley asks as he looms above him.

"I tripped over something and it was hard."

Harley reaches into the tangle of vines and evergreen shrubs and begins clearing them back. He uncovers a large metal object. Gage also helps pull back the foliage, until he comes face to face with a metal statue.

"It's a person!" he gasps.

Harley peers over and nods. "He looks worried."

Before long the men have completely uncovered the statue.

"He's wearing some sorta helmet and cape," Chief Coil says.

"And carrying a gun," Gage's father adds.

Gage looks around the forest. There are other vine-covered lumps in the undergrowth, and he heads to the nearest one for a closer look.

"This is another one," he shouts to the other scouts. "And it's still standing."

Gage pulls the vines back from the statue's face as if to give it air to breathe. His father comes to inspect it.

"He looks worried too."

Gage shivers.

"We'll have to tell the map readers to investigate as soon as base camp is set up," Chief Coil says. "But for now we have to keep moving."

Gage steps in line behind Harley and glances back at the statue cloaked in thick brown vines and awakening leaves. It feels as if the face is trying to tell him something but he doesn't know what.

Uncle Winch leads them to the entrance in the forest, the *back entrance* they call it. He and Harley stand guard at the opening in the ground that leads down a sloped ramp and into darkness. Only Gage, his father, and Chief Coil continue. Chief Coil lights a torch and descends first. Gage follows second, surprised to feel how quickly the air cools as they descend. At the end of the ramp, they come to the thick metal door with the circular symbol, and beside that is the hole the men chopped through the previous day.

"I'll go down first," Gage's father says and lowers his legs through the hole. He wriggles his hips, then disappears. They hear him land with a thud, and Chief Coil waves the torch through the hole to be sure he made the drop okay.

"Gage, you're next. I'll grab you before you fall on that ankle again."

Gage lowers his legs through the hole and before he drops, Chief Coil takes his hands to slow his descent. He feels his father's arms around his legs as he slides carefully down to the ground.

"You made it," his father says and dusts off his shoulder.

Chief Coil throws the torch down to Gage's feet, then follows quickly, landing like a cat at the bottom.

Now that he's so close to the APE Monitoring Room, so close to Rook and Heath, Gage can barely hold himself back. He picks up the torch.

"C'mon, it's this way," he says and takes off down the dim corridor with his father and Chief Coil behind him.

Gage doesn't stop at the door to watch Chief Coil's expression when he sees all the books and the control panel for the first time. He goes straight to the computing machine and lays his hands against the square. He sighs with relief when it comes to life. He pulls the chair close and sits down. There's a message waiting for him. Even though the words are familiar, it takes him some time to sound them out.

"We have run into some trouble with the Governors and have to retreat to the Great Hall for safety. We will be back soon but for now I am powering down. When you get back, stay Alert. We are going to find a way out of ArHK. I think we are close now. Sincerely, Heath."

Gage reads the message aloud, then turns to see Chief Coil's reaction.

"What's that mean?" Chief Coil asks as he pulls his eyes away from the shelves of books and turns his attention to the blue square on the wall.

"As near as I can figure, the Archives of Human Knowledge is controlled by a group of people called the Governors, and it seems they're unhappy about something. Heath said there was some conflict about the Outside, which I think is how they call the rest of the world. They didn't even believe there were still people living. They believed the poisonous air and the storms killed everyone. I think they're in some sorta building and trying to find a way out."

"How come they don't know how to get out?" Chief Coil asks.

"I dunno," Gage admits.

"When will they write you again?"

"I dunno that either. But I think we should keep someone posted down here from now on. We don't wanna lose contact now."

"We can organize the Readers into shifts. Two at a time. Two shifts a day and one overnight," Chief Coil says.

"Dad and I can stay and take the first shift," Gage suggests hopefully, then turns to tap out a message to Heath and Rook.

ROOK

Heath skids to a stop in front of the Daily Log terminal, then crouches down, and starts typing. At first I'm confused. Then it hits me, and I sigh with both relief and guilt.

"What's he doing?" Da asks.

"I think he's updating Gage. Letting him know we're going to be offline awhile."

The pounding on the front doors increases in intensity. The Governors are banging so loud I'm afraid the glass is going to shatter. It feels like hours that Heath is crouched in front of the Daily Log terminal before he finally stands up and shuts it down. Then he takes one last glance at the front doors and sprints to where we're still perched on the threshold of the Great Hall.

"Good thinking," I say when he joins us again.

"Thanks," he pants. "I didn't want them to see anything we've been writing to Gage."

Heath and I step into the Great Hall at the same time that Da pulls Mam and Sparrow inside. Then Da pushes the doors closed and resets the security system. As before, my breath catches in my throat when he activates the lights, and Heath gasps with surprise. In the silence that follows, Sparrow raises her head from Mam's shoulder. She wipes tears and the strands of hair from her face and scans the view before us.

"Look, Rook! Look, Mam! Look at all this stuff!"

Then she struggles to get down from Mam's arms. She hits the floor with both feet and hurtles herself down the stairs two at a time.

The five of us wander through the main hall. For the first time ever, Heath is speechless. Mam makes little noises in her throat, like the coos and *ohs* Sparrow made when she was a baby. Mam reaches her hand out to touch the thick T-Rex bones, a square stone statue, an ancient round navigating instrument. Then she touches her face, as if she has to remind herself she's not also an exhibit.

A cry from Sparrow, who has wandered deeper into the auditorium than the rest of us, draws our attention.

"Come quick! Everyone, come quick!" Sparrow shouts.

The wonder in her voice pulls me the way the power of gravity pulls untethered objects to the ground. She is silhouetted in the distance, dwarfed by the objects around her. She's pointing up at something in the distance. I'm the first to reach her but she doesn't turn toward me, doesn't move or take her eyes off the object that has captured her attention. I follow the direction of her index finger.

"Is that what I think it is?"

I mean, seeing illustrations or reading descriptions does not prepare someone for seeing the real thing. Knowing something in theory does not mean having an intuitive understanding of that thing, once they see it in real life. Sparrow turns her head slowly, her eyes wide and her bottom jaw lowered.

"An el-e-phant!" she says slowly, stressing each syllable as if the reality of an elephant deserves a new way of pronouncing the word.

In school we learned that elephants were large. We were taught they weighed more than four tons and stood over four metres high. But if someone has never seen an animal before, not a cat or a dog or a mouse, how can they hope to accurately imagine the dimensions of an elephant?

When Mam and Heath arrive they too are amazed.

"Natural history of the Outside was always my least favourite subject," Heath whispers. "But I think I was mistaken."

I turn my head to see we are surrounded by different animals in various poses.

"Look, a polar bear!" Sparrow shouts and sprints away. "And a moose and a raccoon! It's so cute."

"Look at this crocodile!" Heath calls out. "Oh, and an ostrich! Weird."

"I had no idea giraffes had such long necks," Mam says.

"Rook, Sparrow, come over here," Da calls.

We follow his voice through a maze of creatures until we come to a glass case filled with birds. Some of them are posed in flight and suspended in the air; others are huddled in nests or floating on fake water.

"I want to show you your namesakes," Da says gently. "See that little spotted bird over there? The one pecking at the ground?"

"The one with the long tail?" Sparrow asks.

"That's the one. That's a sparrow," Da says triumphantly.

"That's me! That's what I was named after," Sparrow says as she presses her nose up to the glass.

"And this one over here," Da says, pulling me around the corner of the case, "this one is the rook."

The rook is a large black bird with long tail feathers and a thick beak. It's perched on a tree branch, its head tilted toward the sky, up toward the domed ceiling high above the Great Hall.

"That's a rook?" Sparrow asks. "It looks scary. It's not nearly so pretty as the sparrow."

"They're both beautiful," Mam says quietly when she joins us.

When Sparrow starts talking about how pretty the sparrow is compared to the big black rook, I remember Da saying rooks were smart, inquisitive birds that were good at solving problems. I stare hard at the rook, looking for a clue. If Grandmam was going to leave me a crumb, wouldn't it be here, with my namesake?

"This is all very amazing," Mam says finally. "But what are we doing? It's not going to take the Governors long to get into the Archives or to figure out where we are. What then? We need a plan."

"Mam's right," Da says. "We have to figure out what to do next."

Sparrow and Heath continue wandering among the birds and animals and shouting out their discoveries.

"A lemur!"

"There's a kangaroo!"

"Everyone, come see the chimpanzee!"

"Sparrow, honey, come back now," Mam calls out when Sparrow's voice fades in the distance.

I shake my head. "Let her look. If we end up in the Recycling Sector, at least she'll have had a chance to see all this. She can tell her grandchildren about the time she was in the forbidden Great Hall."

"And they'll think she's crazy. Like everyone did with my mam," Da says sadly.

Mam sinks to the floor in front of the glass bird case. I sit down beside her and Da follows.

"What do we do now?" I ask.

"We're safe in here," Da offers. "I'm the only one with the security code, and those doors are too thick to break through."

"But we can't live in here for the rest of our lives! We'll need to eat eventually," Mam reasons.

We sit silently, each lost in our own thoughts, trying to grasp the enormity of what we've done, of where the night has brought us. I can barely comprehend how much has changed in a few short days.

"Let me message Ruby and see what's happening," I say finally.

Da sighs. "And I better let Heath's parents know what's going on. Last I told them he was going to sleep at our pod for the night. But it won't be long before they hear something."

Da turns on his personal messenger and suddenly looks like he might throw up.

"Let me guess. Governor Hawk's been trying to reach you?" I ask.

"Two hundred and thirteen messages in the past four hours."

"He was up early," I say.

"You had your messenger turned off?" Mam asks.

"I thought it would be better not knowing," Da says quietly.

Ruby answers on the first beep as if she's waiting for my call. I can see from the background that she's in her bedroom, and I hope she's alone. I hope I can trust her. It's a big ask to put us ahead of her own family, her position as apprentice Governor, her duty to ArHK.

"Rook!" she hisses. "Where *are* you?"

"That doesn't matter right now," I say and bring the messenger close to my face so she can't see behind me. "What's going on?"

"The Governors called an emergency council session, but no apprentices are allowed. Mam and Da told me to stay in my room and not to leave, no matter what. They said I shouldn't answer if you beep."

"I don't want to get you into trouble," I say. "Maybe I should go."

"Don't be silly. It seems like you need me."

"But can I trust you?"

"Rook! I can't believe you even have to ask. We've been friends since nursery school. Of course you can trust me."

"But you're a Governor."

"I'm an *apprentice* Governor. But I'm your friend first."

"Thanks, Ruby," I say and feel badly for not trusting her in the first place. "So what's happening?"

"They got into the Archives and realized you weren't there. Governor Hawk thinks you've hidden in the Great Hall, but Da convinced him that would be impossible.

Da told him it was more likely you're being sheltered in the Growing Sector by your grandmam's old friends."

"What gave him that idea?"

"Me," Ruby says and smiles. "Now where are you really?"

"You won't believe me if I don't show you," I say. Then I scan my messenger around the Great Hall so she can see where I'm sitting.

"You *are* in the Great Hall!" Ruby hisses into her personal messenger. "Was that an elephant?"

"Yes, and you should see it for real. The thing is enormous. Like, bigger than enormous. It'll blow your mind."

"I didn't think all those animals we learned about were actually real!" Ruby says.

Da clears his throat. I glance up at the dome of the Great Hall and see it turning bright blue. It strikes me suddenly that the Great Hall was once considered a public space, the way the Archives is, the way the stadium and Central Park and the streets and the Avenue are all part of everyone's ArHK.

"Ruby, can you keep a secret?"

Ruby snorts. "Like I'm not keeping one now?"

"True," I say. "But this one is even bigger."

"Nothing can surprise me at this point. Go ahead and spill it."

"Yesterday we were contacted by someone from the Outside. I know you don't think there really is the Outside, but there is. And there are people there. Thousands of people."

"Are you sure?"

"Positive. I promise to tell you everything later, but right now there's not enough time. We have to find the way out of ArHK."

"You're starting to scare me, Rook. Can I talk to your da?"

I hand my personal messenger to Da, and he nods solemnly. Ruby cannot mistake that he's backing my claims.

"Wait!" I shout and pull back the messenger. "All the Governors are in the Council Chamber right now?"

Ruby nods.

"Beep your parents," I say. "Tell them something, anything, to get them home. Then tell them everything I just told you. When you can, let me know their reaction. Got it?"

Ruby nods again.

"It's really important to get them home. Do whatever you have to. Thanks for watching out for us."

When I disconnect I start to tremble. I wish I could slow things down. But I can't. We have to keep moving. We have to find our way out of ArHK as soon as possible or we might not get a second chance.

The next thing I do is beep Strider. He answers with a smile.

"Rook Keeper. What a surprise. How's your apprenticeship going?"

"Hi, Strider," I say as casually as I can manage. I wonder how many seconds of small talk I should make before I get to the point. "Where are you?"

"Just having breakfast before I load my delivery cart."

"Are your parents there?"

"We're all here."

"Can everyone hear me?"

Strider nods and I hear a chorus of hellos in the background.

I decide to dive right in.

"Something strange happened in the Archives yesterday. I don't want to say too much and put you at risk, but it's pretty big."

The expression on Strider's face is hard to read. He's squinting at me, concentrating on what I'm saying, but he's shifting his gaze away every few seconds, like someone in the room is talking to him at the same time.

"Basically, we're in trouble. My whole family. And my cousin, Heath. I think the Governors are planning to banish us. There's a lot more to tell you, but the fact is, we need help. I couldn't think of anyone else to ask. I know Grandmam had a lot of friends down there. I know it was a long time ago but, still, I was hoping …"

The screen on Strider's personal messenger goes blank for a moment, then a new face appears.

"Hi, Rook. It's Strider's father. What sort of help did you have in mind?"

"Um. Well. It turns out the Governors are having an emergency session in the Council Chamber today, and I was hoping you might be able to delay them somehow. We need time to figure a few things out."

I can't believe I'm asking Strider's family to get involved, but even before I can finish my thought, Strider's father speaks up.

"We can manage that."

"I mean, I don't want to get you in trouble but —"

"Don't worry. We'll delay them somehow. Imagine what they'll think if we show up to the Council Chamber and start asking questions? Governor Hawk always complains that citizens don't get involved. Now they can get a taste of their own medicine. Besides, I promised your grandmam I'd watch out for you. She told me you were going to change ArHK. She always said, 'Rook is going to put it all together, Shrike. She's going to cast her eyes upwards and when she does, she's going to need your help.' You tell your family not to worry. We'll be there within the hour and cause some sort of diversion. Something they won't soon forget."

"Maybe you'll even get into the official record," I say.

"Oh, you bet we will."

I don't get a chance to say goodbye or thank you because the screen goes blank. When I turn off my personal messenger and look up, Mam and Da are staring at me, like I've suddenly sprouted an extra set of ears. The Great Hall is deathly quiet. I can no longer hear

Sparrow or Heath discovering new animals or their footsteps echoing through the auditorium.

"At least we have a plan now. Sort of," I say hopefully. But my parents' faces are blank.

In the silence, I think about what Strider's father said about Grandmam. I'm sure it's another crumb, something about casting my eyes upwards.

"Think, Rook. Think!" I tell myself.

I peer into the glass case of birds and study the rook. I look at the way its head is titled up toward the sky, as if it's looking at something. I follow its gaze up, up, up toward the dome of the Great Hall. I can tell from the bright-blue ceiling that it's time for lunch, and I realize my stomach is empty. I know Sparrow and Heath must also be hungry except they're too busy looking at artefacts to care. That's right when, at the very top of the dome, I notice a red star for the first time, visible in the bright sky. A red star! My heart practically leaps out of my chest.

"Da, look!"

I point up at the sky.

"The red star! Like on the diagram Mam found. Like the pin on the globe. That's the way out!"

GAGE

Gage watches the blue square closely for the first hour that he and his father are in the APE Monitoring Room alone. After that, when no messages appear, he grows restless.

"I hope everything's okay with Rook," he says as he paces the perimeter of the small room. "I hope the Governors aren't too upset."

"Why would they be upset?"

"I dunno. But it seems from what Rook and Heath told me, it's very complicated there. There's sectors and apprentices and all sortsa rules and laws. I wonder if our ancient societies were that complicated?"

When the blue square still doesn't change after another hour, Gage wanders back to the shelves of books. His father is examining the numbers and words on the control panel again.

"Hey, Dad. Since we're gonna be down here for a while, do you want to look at some books? I know we aren't supposed to touch the artefacts, but …"

Gage's father smiles broadly. "I thought you'd never ask."

His father approaches the shelves cautiously, like a horse whisperer greeting a wild horse for the first time. He trails his fingers over the spine of the tall hard-covered books and he whistles.

"If only your mother could see all these, she'd be wild with excitement. You hafta remember as many of these as you can and tell her when she gets here."

They examine the spines of the books together until Gage pulls the *World Atlas* off the shelf.

"You'll like this one. It's full of maps. Not just of the United States but from all over the world."

Gage and his father perch together on the bedroll while Gage opens the atlas and lays it carefully on his lap. He starts with a map of North America and searches until he finds Washington, then New York, and finally Columbus. He points each out to his father.

"The world is so big," his father says finally. "I've been from the Middle to Columbus to Washington. It's taken my whole life to travel between them, and I been on the move for almost twenty years."

"Do you know what I been thinking?" Gage says.

His father shakes his head and continues to study the maps.

"If there's people in this place we never even knew existed, then who's to say there isn't people in other places too? Like you say, look how big the world is. Maybe there's other settlements we never heard about. There could be people in some of these other countries. There could be other places like the Archives of Human Knowledge, full of people."

Gage loses himself in thought, wondering again exactly where Rook might be and how long it might take to travel there.

"I suspect you're right. There probably is other people," his father murmurs.

"It's exciting to imagine, isn't it?" Gage says.

For the rest of the afternoon, Gage and his father examine the books, looking up with disappointment when they see the square is still blank.

"I just hope everything's okay," Gage says.

"I wonder what time it is?" his father asks, then stands to stretch. "I wonder how long we've been down here?"

Gage shakes his head but keeps reading. "Who knows? Hard to tell."

Eventually they hear voices and know their shift is up. Gage quickly returns the books they were reading, then goes to the door and calls out.

"Down this way! We're down here."

Soon Uncle Winch appears with two of the other readers — brothers, Skeet and Jig — whom Chief Coil recruited to his scouting camp two years ago. The brothers walk straight into the room, but Uncle Winch hangs at the doorway.

"It's okay to come in if you want," Gage coaxes.

Uncle Winch steps inside tentatively. He stares openly at the control panel and the glowing blue square. Then he steps as close as he dares to the books.

"I've never seen this many books in my whole life, not to mention in one spot. This sure is something," he mutters, then pulls a kerchief out of his pocket and wipes his face. "I swear Pepper's gonna be awful excited to congratulate you on your discovery, Gage. She said it when we left. She said to me straight up, 'You just watch. Gage's gonna find something big. I got a feeling about him.'"

Gage blushes and turns his face away from the other scouts.

"As much as I wanna stay and look some more, I promised to get you two to the new camp before dark, so we best get moving. Harley's waiting up top," Uncle Winch says.

Gage shows Skeet and Jig how to activate the typing pad and how to tap out the letters on the square.

"All you have to do is wait and watch. If any words show up, answer back. Say who you are and explain we're taking shifts. That's about it. Just stay awake and say hello for me. Tell them I'll be back."

With that, Gage follows the others reluctantly.

By the time they get to the bridge and are ready to cross over to the new base camp, the sky is darkening, and Gage can see a fire on the far side of the riverbank.

"Is that it over there?" he asks.

"That's it, all right," Harley says. "Mighty fine camp. I bet you the others are gonna like it too."

"I can see a yurt!" Gage says and points to a white yurt glowing against the dark background.

"Yep, the first three Scholars arrived this afternoon. They came on their fastest horses. They even rode through the nights. They're anxious to meet you and hear all about your discovery," Uncle Winch says.

"Really?" Gage asks. "They wanna meet me?"

"That they do, Gage."

The idea that the Scholars are in camp and waiting to meet him helps Gage cross the bridge. In fact, he barely hesitates before he takes his first step, then stays close on Uncle Winch's heels the whole way down the riverbank to the edge of camp.

As they approach in the dimming light, Gage can tell it's a great location for their camp. The river access is gentle, and there's a flat area not too far from the water's edge, where the Scholars have erected their yurt. Beyond the camp, a forest rises. There aren't any ruins visible, and Gage realizes with relief that Chief

Coil did find the best location, despite its ancient purpose.

Uncle Winch leads Gage directly to the white yurt and nods. "Here you go."

"You think I should go right inside?" Gage whispers, wide-eyed.

"Those were my instructions. To fetch you quick as possible and bring you back to the Scholars."

Gage looks at his father and is encouraged by his nod, but still his feet are rooted to the ground, like the statues they found mired in the undergrowth. When the flap of the yurt flutters open and a tall woman in a flowing white robe appears, Gage swallows hard. He's seen this woman before — Magdalena — when they lived in the Middle, from before they joined Chief Coil's scouting camp. It's the same woman Gage met as a child, the day he wandered accidentally into the Scholars' yurt. His father found him there an hour later and apologized for bothering them and keeping them from their work. But Magdalena had smiled graciously and said, "Teaching a young boy as eager as this one is never a bother."

Now Magdalena is looking at Gage with the same gracious expression on her face.

"You must be Gage?"

Gage nods without speaking.

"We've met before. You were much younger," she says.

Gage nods again. He wishes he could find some words to say, but his mouth is suddenly as dry as a hot summer's day.

Magdalena steps back and opens the flap. "Please come in. My sisters and I have something we want to show you. And of course we want to hear all about the computing machine you discovered. We want to hear all about the people who write from the other end."

Gage steps into the yurt and feels suddenly dirty compared to the clean white surfaces inside. Magdalena leads Gage over to a wide table where a map is laid out and weighted down with smooth round river rocks. It's the largest map Gage has ever seen. There are lines running across and lines running the length of the map. The edges of the map are rounded, like a fat ripe pumpkin ready for harvest.

"Have you ever seen a map like this before?" Magdalena asks.

Gage shakes his head.

"This is a map of the world; every land mass is represented on this one page. The shape is rounded to represent the Earth."

"Astonishing," Gage mutters.

"It's the only one like it we've ever found. Normally we find maps in books that show pieces of the world, one page at a time, but this is the only one that shows the whole world at once."

"There's a map book in the room with the computing machine," Gage offers.

"An atlas?"

"Yep, a *World Atlas*."

"I look forward to seeing it."

Gage stares at the map spread out on the table. He leans as close as he can without touching it, then points at the United States.

"We're here. Somewhere near this open water."

"That's right. You read maps well."

"And these lines are numbered. Do they help map readers find what they're looking for and where they want to go?"

"They do. Exactly. Every location in the world can be found by assigning a set of numbers, first from the lines going up and down and then from the lines going across. Wherever the lines intersect is the location for which you are searching."

Suddenly Gage gasps. "There's a set of numbers by the computing machine. I think it's the numbers to show the location of the Ship of Knowledge. That's where the people were writing me from. Let me see. I think it was eighty-two … twenty-eight … *N* and sixty-two … thirty … *W*. Where'd that be on this map?"

Gage watches Magdalena as she trails her fingers across the surface of the map.

"We need to be at the top of the map to find the northern latitudinal lines that run horizontally, and on the left side of the map to find the western longitudinal lines that run up and down. This line up here is eighty north, then eighty-one north. Ah, here is eighty-two north. And the lines going up and down. Let's see, here is sixty west, and if we go left we should find, yes, there is sixty-two west."

Magdalena points to a place on the map near the very top. Gage looks from there down to where Washington is located. He squints and points to the middle of the United States.

"This is the Middle, around about here, right?"

"Not quite so far west. Just about under those big lakes there."

Magdalena uses her left hand to point at the Middle.

Gage's heart sinks and he looks up at her.

"It's a long way to ArHK then?"

"If your coordinates are correct, then, yes, it's a very long way."

"How'll we ever reach the people living there? How'll they ever reach us?" Gage asks sadly.

"Until last week we never imagined there was a building that could still harvest power from nature. We never imagined we would find a computing machine, and, yet, you have done that very thing. Not only that, you found a computing machine with people on the other end, people who inhabit the Ship of Knowledge. So who knows what next week will bring? Don't despair, Gage. There is much to be hopeful about."

ROOK

"We need to get up near that red star for a closer look," I say to Da. "How do you get to the top level?"

Da looks confused, like he's pulling ideas together at random and trying to make them fit into some sort of order.

"Even from the top floor, the sky is too far to reach," Da says.

"We still need to get up there. There'll be another crumb somewhere along the way. Grandmam wouldn't have left anything to chance."

Da nods. "The stairs. At the far end of the auditorium. They go to the top level."

Da takes the lead through the mammals and birds, the reptiles and invertebrates. Mam calls out for Sparrow and Heath, and they join us as we rush toward the far end of the Great Hall.

"But we're missing some good stuff," Sparrow protests. "I'm not done in here yet!"

"We'll come back later," I say and take Sparrow's hand so she has no choice but keep up.

"I found the rocks and minerals," Heath pants as he trots along beside me, weaving between and around objects. "They're most interesting."

"I saw a whale!" Sparrow shouts.

Da takes the stairs two at a time, and we do our best to keep up. We climb until we get to the top floor. Heath walks directly to the railing and looks over the artefacts in the auditorium five floors below. When I look down, the elephant is suddenly dwarfed but still large in comparison to everything around it.

"Over there is the whale," Sparrow says and points to the far end of the auditorium.

Behind us is another large room and above the arched doorway is a sign that reads *Ancient China*.

"There's more stuff up here?" Sparrow asks excitedly.

"This whole place is full of interesting stuff," Da assures her.

"Can we go in there and look?" she asks.

Da nods. "But stay with Heath."

Sparrow and Heath wander into the hall of artefacts from Ancient China, and I can't help but imagine
ArHK in the early days, when people were allowed to
explore the Great Hall, when children wandered hap-
pily through the enormous rooms with their parents
learning all about the wonders of the Outside.

I locate the red star on the domed ceiling and walk
around the edge of the mezzanine until I'm standing
almost under it. Then I turn, slowly, looking all around
for the next crumb. I can't imagine what I'm looking
for, but I examine every surface knowing Grandmam
will have left something for me to find. Then I see it.
Another star etched on the floor a few metres away. I
go over and stand on that star, then start my search
again. I let my eyes trail over the walls and the floor,
the dome and the railings, beyond Mam and Da, who
are standing beside a long dim hallway, watching me
expectantly.

"What's down there?" I ask Da, pointing beyond his
shoulder down the passageway.

He turns and looks, then shakes his head. "I don't
know that I've ever been down there."

I can't believe there's a corridor Da hasn't explored.
If I had access to the Great Hall, I'd have examined
every square millimetre. I start down the corridor hesi-
tantly, letting my eyes adjust to the low light.

"Can you see anything?" Da asks from where he and
Mam are watching me.

"Just a hallway so far," I call back. "No doors, no stars, no crumbs as far as I can tell."

I'm running my hands along the wall for guidance when I feel a metal ladder. It's solid, attached to the floor and running up the side of the wall.

"There's a ladder here. I'm going up," I call back.

"Be careful, sweetie," Mam calls out.

I grab a metal rung and begin to climb. By now I can see more clearly, unless I look back at the brightness of the Great Hall. Then I'm blinded by the contrast. I climb carefully, steadily, into a narrow opening in the ceiling.

"There's a passageway going through the ceiling," I call back.

"Watch what you're doing," Da says from the bottom of the ladder, below my feet.

"I can't see the end," I say as I continue to climb. "It's not very wide."

"Do you want to come down and let me go first?" Da asks. His voice sounds distant and hollow, and my own voice, when I call back down, echoes through the narrow passageway.

"I think I'm almost there."

At the top of the ladder there's a faintly glowing security pad, the kind Da used to lock and unlock the heavy metal doors to the Great Hall and to get in and out of the Archives.

"Da, your security code is FKXVI? Right?"

"That's right," he yells up at me. "Is there a security pad?"

"I'm going to try your pass code first. I hope it's part of the Archives system."

I press in Da's security code and hear a series of low clicks and hisses directly above my head. When I look up, I see a round red wheel with a star inset touching the edges of the circle. *Another red star*, I think. I reach up and pull on the wheel, but there's no give. Then I turn the wheel, the way I do with the steering wheels on the bumper cars at the Thrill Park. The wheel turns stiffly at first, but after a couple of rotations, it spins easier and easier. Suddenly a round metal door groans open toward me and a rush of cold air hits my face. Above me is another, darker passage. I reach my hand inside and feel another metal ladder. This one is cold though, so cold it hurts my fingers when I grab hold.

"Are you okay?" Da calls up.

"I got the door thing open but there's another passage. I'm going up."

I pull the sleeves of my shirt over my hands so I can hold onto the cold metal and climb through the tight opening into the darkness. When I look down, all I can see is a circle of dim light below me and Da's face looking up. The higher I climb the smaller Da looks and the colder the air becomes. I hope I reach the end soon because the passageway is so narrow I can barely bend my legs.

Finally, I feel another round wheel, and it takes all my strength to turn it. This door doesn't open downwards, however; it hisses and pops up, and the passageway fills suddenly with light and the coldest air I've ever experienced. I pull myself up the last few cold metal rungs, up the last bright metre to the top. When I raise my hand I can feel a thousand sharp prickles on my skin. I drag myself up over the edge of the passageway and onto a flat surface. I raise my head and look around. Everything is white and grey, and the sky above seems to go on forever.

I stand up and feel the sudden force of the wind on my body. My hair whips at my face as I turn in a circle. There are white particles pelting from the sky, the real sky, blowing and gusting around my feet, twining and twisting around my legs and arms. The cold is unbelievable.

"This must the Outside," I yell back down the dark hole, but the wind takes my words and whips them across the grey expanse. As far as I can see is the hard, flat grey surface that I know is ArHK. Below me is everything I have ever experienced, full of the people and places that have filled my life and my ancestors' lives. ArHK stretches so far it blends into the dim grey sky. Above me the limitless sky seems to go on and on, farther than I can possibly see, and yet I can't see anything more than a faint round ball of light obscured by the blowing white particles of what I realize is snow.

This really is the Outside, I think. *This is the top of the world.*

Da is suddenly behind me. The wind is biting his cheeks red, and his hair is flying in all directions.

"I could never have imagined any of this," he says. I can barely make out his words.

"It's so cold!" I laugh and wrap my arms around my body for warmth. I wonder suddenly what happened to the coats the Chosen Ones wore to ArHK. No doubt they ended up in the Recycling Sector to be remade into something new.

Then Sparrow is wrapped around my legs, squealing at the cold and holding her hair in place with one of her hands.

"It's so big up here," she shouts.

Mam and Heath are last to join us in the cold, blowing, snowy Outside. We huddle together and gaze around, trying to reconcile all that we have known with what we are now experiencing.

"They said they missed feeling the wind on their faces," I shout.

"This is snow!" Heath laughs, his bright blue eyes dancing above the redness of his cheeks.

He bends down and scoops up a handful of the snow. Then he puts it to his mouth. "It's just like an ice treat!"

Mam leans close to my ear. I can feel her warm breath on my neck. "I told you the Outside sky was limitless."

Then it happens.

Despite the blowing and cold, despite being so far above ArHK, we hear the piercing sound of the security alarms. They whine and screech and drill into my memory. I've heard them only once before, as a child, before Sparrow was born. The lockdown terrified me, not just because of the noise but because I got separated from Mam and Da. Once it was lifted, once we were all safely together in our pod again and Grandmam had gone to bed, Da took me to my bedroom for a story.

"What's the matter, Da?" I asked when I noticed how tired he looked. "Did the lockdown scare you?"

"I'm fine. There's nothing for you to worry about, little Rook."

"But what happened? Why were those alarms so loud? It hurt my ears. Why did we get locked in the school?"

"Someone tried to breach the security system today."

"Why would someone want to do that?"

I touched his cheek hoping to cheer him up, but it only made him look sadder.

When I look at Da's face now I see the same look of resignation and deep sadness, and I realize it had been Grandmam who set off the alarms all those years ago. Perhaps she was trying to get into the Archives or out of the Records Sector without a pass.

When we hear the security alarms sounding down in the Great Hall, Heath doesn't move, but he looks as scared as I feel. We must all look dreadful, I realize, huddled together in the freezing cold. Nobody speaks of it and Sparrow doesn't dare ask *when*, but we all fear the Governors will find their way into the Great Hall and eventually to us. Governor Hawk is sure to be leading the charge. I wonder what will happen to Strider's father and to Grandmam's other friends from the Growing Sector.

Da grasps my shoulders, and Mam pulls Sparrow into her arms. I take Heath's hand in mine and squeeze tight. It's only been a few minutes, but already I love the limitless sky. I feel it in my soul when I breathe deeply, and I know without a doubt it's what I've been missing all my life. If only Grandmam had been able to see it for herself, even for a brief moment. I glance back at the dark hole leading down into the Great Hall, then turn and look out across the white expanse. I shiver and wonder how far it is to Washington.

ROOK

T he ice-studded wind whips our faces and lashes the skin on our hands and necks. I hold my arms tight around my torso for warmth and see my family doing the same. Mam pulls Sparrow in close.

"We have to go back inside!" Da yells above the noise of the air rushing past my ears. It's such a foreign sensation and sound.

"But we can't. We just got out!" I hold the hair tight against my skull as I lean over to shout into his ear. I would never have imagined the Outside wind could be so loud, so powerful.

"If they lock us out, we'll die," Mam screams and pulls on my arm, tugging me toward the pipe-like structure we emerged from only moments earlier.

Da herds Heath, Mam, and Sparrow back toward the escape hatch.

"We have a better chance of making a difference from the inside," Da yells as I stand rooted in place on top of ArHK and under the limitless sky. I feel desperation splitting me in half. I'm desperate to stay Outside but desperate to stay with my family too, and my panic grows as I watch Sparrow disappear down the ladder, then Heath, then Mam: one by one, rung by rung.

"The Governors will banish us," I protest loudly, although I fear my words have been whipped away by the power of the wind.

Only Da's head and hands are visible now. One more step down and his face will disappear from my sight.

"Come now, Rook. Please! Come with us!"

As his head sinks out of sight, I lunge toward the opening. I'm reaching for the top of the ladder, but I'm too slow, and the hatch closes with a loud finality.

"NO!" I shout.

I try to open the hatch, but it's locked solid. I scratch at the frozen metal with my fingers and pound with my fists until they bleed.

"Open it up. Da, don't leave me out here! Da? DA?" I scream over and over.

But he's gone. My family is gone and I'm trapped again, this time alone on the Outside.

I slouch down next to the hatch, trying to shelter from the ice pellets and wind. Then I fall into a heap and cry. The tears freeze in streams on my face.

That's when I wake up.

I'm sitting straight up in my bunk in our pod when my eyelids flash open. I'm crying, and tears and sweat and snot drip from my face. My hands are clenched, and my heart is hammering in my chest as loud as my fists were pounding against the hatch in my dream. It's been the same dream all week. I wipe my forehead with the sleeve of my pyjamas and take several deep breaths to calm myself. Then I feel the back of my neck, just at the base of my skull. It's still there, a small oblong lump under my flesh: a tracking chip. We all have one now, except Sparrow, and we will at least until our hearing is over.

I lie back in my bunk and try to fall asleep again, but it's no use. Even though it's early, and the wake hours are still two hours away, I get up. I place my feet on the floor. Sparrow is sleeping soundly in her bunk, snoring just slightly, with her arms thrown wide and her blankets twisted around her legs. I sneak to the door, open it, then close it soundlessly. When I stop to listen, I hear someone in the kitchen filling the quick-kettle with water.

Other than a single overhead lamp in the kitchen, Da has left all the lights off in the pod and is standing at the counter in a dim glow. He's staring up at the ceiling.

"Couldn't sleep?" I ask from the doorway, and he spins around.

"No. You either?"

I shake my head and lower myself onto one of the kitchen chairs. "I had that nightmare again."

Da steps over and kisses the top of my head. "We would never have left you alone up there."

"I know," I say. "But it always feels so real." I rest my chin in my hands and stare at the grey flecks in the tabletop.

The quick-kettle beeps, and Da empties a stream of hot water into his mug. "I'm having a cup of cocoa. Would you like one?"

I perk up and nod. Cocoa is a rare treat.

Da places a steaming cup in front of me, then sits down across the table. We sip our cocoa in silence. The taste makes my brain think there's something to celebrate, when in reality nothing could be further from the truth.

"Are you nervous about the hearing this afternoon?" I ask, after too much silence has built up between us. There's no way either of us can be thinking about anything else.

Da turns his mug in half-circles and stares at his hands. His thumbs tap the table. "I think it would be foolish not to be nervous. But I'm not afraid."

I look up at him, surprised.

"You're not afraid?"

"Not really. I'm glad we're going to have a chance to tell the Governors what we discovered. I have no idea what it means for the future of ArHK, or for *our* future. But there's no turning back. And even if there was, I wouldn't want to."

I'm surprised by my father's confession but relieved too. It would be easy to blame me. In fact, *I* blame me. But he has a point, and there's nothing we can do about our circumstances now. There's no reversing time.

"But what are the chances they'll believe anything we tell them? What's to keep them from denouncing our account and banishing us to the Recycling Sector?"

Da tilts his head and looks up at me at the same time. It makes him look a little bit like the rook in the Great Hall staring up at the sky.

"Ruby? Strider? The other folks in the Growing Sector? We have truth on our side. And good people."

I look across the living room and out the front window. The sky is brightening above the pods across the street. Somehow, Da and I sat through ninety minutes of silence and both our mugs are empty. It won't be long before Mam and Sparrow are up, before Mam starts to cook breakfast and Sparrow starts asking a million questions about the hearing.

Da rinses both of our mugs and tucks them into the washing drawer.

"I guess it's time to start getting ready for the Archives," he says and turns to leave the kitchen.

His comment is so routine, so familiar, I'm struck by the absurdity and laugh out loud. How — on the day of

our hearing, on the most important day of our lives —
are we still going to the Archives to carry on as if nothing has changed? Da glances at the clock on the corner
of the wall screen.

"Governor Hawk will be here to escort us in thirty
minutes."

I'm just heading down the hall to the bathroom
when I hear the doorbell sound. I sneak back and listen
as Da opens the door.

"Oh! Our grain shares have arrived. Perfect timing.
We ran out of flour yesterday. Thank you so much."

I peek around the corner to see one of the delivery
boys — Rain — hand Da an overflowing basket.

"Let me put these in the kitchen. I'll be right back."

I slip into the kitchen and help Da unload the basket.
We quickly peer into every bag and jar as we place them
on the counter.

"Here," he hisses at me and points to a small square
of plexpaper hidden in the bag of cornmeal. "Now
quick, take the basket back to Rain."

When I return to the kitchen, Da hands me the note.
It's short, but it brings me a measure of comfort, and by
the look of satisfaction on Da's face I can tell he feels the
same way.

The resistance is growing. The Growers
have formed a counter-government with the
Manufacturing Level. The images Rook captured

*on her personal messenger have convinced many
that the Outside is real, although some are claim-
ing a hoax and that the Entertainers are in on the
conspiracy. We have a strong delegation and will
demand access to the hearing. You are not alone.
Stay strong.* Veritas vos liberabit.

Da smiles to himself, tucks the note under the edge
of his sleeve, and disappears down the hall.

Like clockwork, Governor Hawk arrives at eight. I
don't even glance at his narrow, smug face when I slip
past him on my way out the door. Then I stare at the
ground as we walk to the Archives with the sound of his
hard-soled shoes chasing me along the Avenue. People
stop and whisper as we pass, but still I don't look up.
My ears burn with anger. If only they knew the truth,
I think.

Governor Hawk perches on a chair at the front of
the Archives where he can watch both Da and I work.
We shuffle quietly to our seats: Da at his normal workstation near the front and me on the Daily Log terminal — the system Governor Hawk thinks is used to monitor the environmental conditions in the Great Hall.

I'm only allowed a few minutes per day, so I try not
to look impatient as I shield the screen with my body by
sitting as close as possible.

"Gage?" I type.

A reply comes quickly.

"It is Magdalena. Gage is at base camp welcoming the rest of the scouting families to their new home. It is a day of celebration."

I've been communicating with Magdalena and the other Scholars all week, as well as with Gage, so while I miss Gage on the other end of the computer today, I'm also happy he's being reunited with his mother and sister.

"We have our hearing with the judges today. The Governors are charging us with Rebellious Treason with Intent to Harm Purpose and Society. But there's a revolution underway. They're going to demand justice and that all of ArHK learn the truth. If all goes well, we'll be free soon."

Magdalena's response is rapid.

"This is good news. We are working on logistics on our end as well and acquiring a great deal of knowledge from the journals we found in this room."

I glance back to see Governor Hawk staring in my direction. Then I turn back to the screen and input words faster than I ever thought possible.

"I must go but please check for updates tomorrow. And please pass on a message to Gage. It's important. Tell him I PROMISE that we will get out of ArHK. Me and my family and everyone else. All 5028 of us. And somehow, someday, we will find our way to Washington."

Governor Hawk stands up, and I hear the soles of his shoes beat a track toward me. I glance down and quickly read the last message from Magdalena.

"Godspeed, Rook. Your message will be delivered and we will be here every day for updates."

I close the Daily Log and the screen goes blank. I take a deep breath to compose myself, then stand up with as much calm as I can muster. I smooth down my hair, straighten my vest, and will my feet to walk me to my regular workstation at the front of the Archives, by Da.

"All steady in the Great Hall," I call out to Da as I pass by Governor Hawk. "Humidity, temperature, barometric pressure all good. At first I thought there was a slight change in the active radiation, but I checked the turbidity calculations and realized I was reading the airflow scales wrong. Sorry it took so long."

Da glances over as I sit down and I shrug, ever so slightly. We both know I'm talking nonsense, but Governor Hawk has no idea. There are advantages to being the only Keepers. I pull up a report that is waiting in the queue for formatting and make an effort to look busy and efficient, even though I'm distracted.

Governor Hawk switches from walking behind our chairs and breathing loudly through his pinched nose to pacing along the windows at the front of the Archives, where people have started to gather and wait for our hearing to begin. I stare at the screen and fantasize about luring Governor Hawk through the Great Hall, up the passage, and onto the top of ArHK, then locking him Outside. Forever. A proper banishment.

Somehow the morning passes, and Mam arrives with Heath and Sparrow. My insides clench when I see the commotion their arrival makes. They're flanked on either side by Governors Gorse and Thorn, who are looking decidedly uncomfortable, and are trailed by Heath's parents, distraught and leaning on one another for support.

When they make their way through the crowd and inside the Archives, Da and I turn off our computer screens, remove and hang our vests on the back of our chairs, then join Mam at the front doors. If I had to describe her expression, I'd say she looks stoic. But I can see her nerves erupting along her jawline as she clenches and unclenches her teeth. Sparrow is uncharacteristically subdued, staring with wide, round eyes at all the people on the Avenue. Heath appears to be the most afraid, and he avoids looking at his parents, who are wiping their eyes with brightly coloured squares of cloth.

We haven't planned it, but Da and I each take one of Mam's hands in unison. Sparrow shuffles close to my side and tucks her little hand into mine. I squeeze and she squeezes back. Then I look over at Heath.

"Shouldn't you be up here with the rest of us Keepers?" I ask.

Despite the gravity of the moment, he smiles faintly, then steps forward and slots himself between me and Mam. The five of us stand so close our shoulders are touching and form an impenetrable human wall.

Before we step forward, we look one another in the eyes — Da, Mam, Heath, Sparrow, and me — and a zap of determination flows through us. We straighten our backs and focus our eyes forward, and when Governor Hawk opens the door and leads us out onto the Avenue toward the Court Chambers, we hold our heads high.

ACKNOWLEDGEMENTS

It takes many people to make a writer and many more to publish a book — too many to mention here. But I would like to say a special thank you to all the amazing writers, mentors, teachers, and classmates who helped me develop my passion, dedication, and skills along the way. I would also like to thank Callie Norwich, Bella Goudie, and Leo Goudie for their enthusiasm when ArHK was first taking shape in my mind and on the page. I might never have persevered without your encouragement. Thanks to Monica Pacheco and Rachel Letofsky for being early readers and providing invaluable input to help me move this story forward at critical junctures, and to my agent, Stacey Kondla, for always having my back. I would also like to thank Kathryn Lane and the entire Dundurn Press team for getting this book past the finish line. And finally, a huge shout-out to Robyn So for her exceptional editing skills and for helping Rook, Gage, and all the other characters in this book sparkle.

ABOUT THE AUTHOR

Christina Kilbourne writes fiction for all ages, including adults, young adults, and the middle grades. She has been the recipient of various awards, including a Snow Willow Award, a Red Cedar Award, and a Manitoba Young Readers Choice Award for her book *Dear Jo*. After graduating from university, Christina travelled through Africa and Latin America and spent two years in New Zealand. She still loves to travel, especially to warm destinations during cold months. When she isn't reading or writing, Christina is outdoors hiking, paddling, skiing, cycling, and plotting her next novel. She lives in Bracebridge, Ontario, with her family and one furry friend.